Uroboros Saga

BOOK EIGHT

By Arthur Walker

For all my friends that went before me. Rest in peace.

"The Christian view of when personhood begins is bound up with the question of when a person gains a soul. Indeed, the two are generally considered to be synonymous. But what is this thing that they are supposed to gain - this entity that, as we have seen, has been commonly deemed to be lacking in artificially created beings? If the soul supplies the defining stamp of true humanity, we had better understand what is meant by it."

~Phillip Ball

CHAPTER 1

HELSINKI, FINLAND, STANLEY & TRAVIS TRADERS BANK

MAY 2ND, 2192 – 3:57 PM – 8 YEARS PREVIOUS TO THE SHUTDOWN

"Why haven't we made entry?" Captain Partanen asked, flipping through the floor plans for the bank buildings, and those adjoining it.

"They've hacked the biometrics, exterior cameras, city network out around the area for a quarter mile. Anyone with a registered Police ID makes entry, they'll know," Sergeant Nieminen replied, watching his terminal for any change.

The interior of the police command vehicle was filled with grim expressions. These criminals had struck before. If the police didn't comply with their demands, innocent civilians would be killed, and on camera. Last time, they had killed seven people in Denmark before local authorities complied with their demands.

It was a scandal. They made off with millions in negotiable bonds and other universal currencies. The local officials brokered the deal outside of the protocols for dealing with terrorists and ransom demands.

"Options?" Captain Partanen asked, looking around at the gathered police and civic officials.

The Captain was heavy, in his late fifties, and prone to fidgeting with his hands. He was more nervous than usual, knowing something more of what they were up against. He was losing control and it bothered him a great deal.

City Steward Kate Wuopio stood up, drawing icy stares from the rest of the council. "Do we have any unregistered police assets?"

Kate Wuopio had served for only two years. She was young, idealistic, and impeccably dressed. Everyone feared her, and with good cause. She'd fired anyone that had the stain of impropriety from civic service. Her campaign promise was to be the broom that would sweep out the corruption in the Finnish Central Global Government offices.

Sergeant Nieminen opened his mouth to speak, but the Captain held out a hand, like he was erecting a quiet wall between police and civic officials. "That's classified. CGG need-to-know only."

The Sergeant was a handler, a manager of resources, and a chief technical advisor for the department. He'd served for ten years, avoiding command positions to stay as close to the streets as he could. The criminals holed up in the bank had been a personal project, something he'd tried to insulate the city against. He had failed.

"Thirty-seven people in that bank do not care about that right now. Are you going to tell me your secret counter-insurgency police program is more important than their lives?" Steward Wuopio asked, barely restraining her disgust for the police captain.

"We're not saying that. The assets in question are dangerous, and could be as damaging to public perception of the CGG as the loss of life. If we deploy those assets, in an urban environment, we won't be able to control the exposure," Sergeant Nieminen explained, ignoring the Captain's angry glare.

"If it all turns out to be unnecessary, we are discussing career-ending exposure, Steward," Captain Partanen said, shaking his head.

"I serve at the pleasure of the people. If the city wasn't safe, it is our fault. Letting more people die to try and cover up that fact isn't going to help. If the exposure kills our collective careers, I know at least one person that will deserve it," Steward Wuopio said, clearly directing her comments toward the captain.

"If that's how you feel, you should meet our unregistered asset," Sergeant Nieminen said, standing up and heading toward the door.

He walked with Steward Wuopio back toward the police line where a large armored transport had just arrived. "Captain Partanen is going to make serious trouble for you," the Steward observed, taking him by the arm.

"My wife and child are in there. She was there setting up our equity account for a home and her schooling. My little girl is six years old."

Steward Wuopio winced, motioning with her hand for the Sergeant to lead on. They stepped to the back of the transport, where the Sergeant nodded to the officer on guard. She turned and opened the back of the transport.

Inside was an Ursine Metasapient larger than the Steward had ever seen. He took up most of the back of the transport, wearing special armor, and carrying modified rifles designed to accommodate his size. Steward Wuopio covered her mouth with her hand, looking worriedly over at the Sergeant.

"This is Eamon Two. We brought him over from North America to help us with problems like this. He's good and brave, and he loves being a cop. He can take down whoever is responsible for this," Sergeant Nieminen said, trying to reassure the Steward.

"This is a monster we're talking about, Sergeant."

Eamon lowered his head, feeling abashed by the Steward's response. "I'm just a cop," Eamon said, tapping the badge on his chest.

The Steward took a deep breath. "You are more than that."

"He's the best of the Type Twos, designed and trained for tactical entry. You want to see his jacket? See the work he did in North America?" Sergeant Nieminen said, nodding to Eamon.

"Officer Eamon, do you think Sergeant Nieminen's judgment has been impacted by the circumstances?" Steward Wuopio asked.

Eamon looked at the Sergeant. "What circumstances?"

"His wife and daughter are in there."

"Then, yeah, and you've compromised us both. The Sergeant isn't just my handler, he's my friend," Eamon said, keeping his tone professional.

The Steward lowered her head, then looked sideways at the Sergeant. "Would you still want to send him in, even if your wife and daughter were not inside?"

"Yeah, he's the best cop for the job, and the only asset we have that won't set off the biometrics. He'll have ten to twenty seconds to operate inside that any other officer won't have," the Sergeant replied, without hesitation.

"Are you dangerous, Eamon? Are you what half the population of Europe thinks of Metasapients?" the Steward asked, still reeling from his size and appearance.

"I don't care what people think of me. I've got a job to do, ma'am. Please, let me do it," Eamon said.

"Do you love that little girl? The Sergeant's daughter?" the Steward asked.

"You always ask this many questions?" Eamon said, growing impatient.

"She does. She's one of the good guys, though," the Sergeant said, vouching for the Steward.

Eamon softened, lowering his head. "Her name is Emily. Her mother is from the West Coast North American territory. They're Americans like me. We learned to speak Finnish together. I live with the Sergeant."

"Letting you do this is bad idea," the Steward said, shaking her head.

"All these questions, just fishing for a way to step away from this. You're going to get people killed," Eamon said, standing up in the back of the transport.

"Excuse me?" Steward Wuopio said, hands on her hips.

"You heard me. I've read everything there is to know about Finnish politics, and I watch the news. All Metasapients do. You've sidestepped the Metasapient issue, unlike everything else. You're all about the people, as long as they don't wear fur, scales, or chitin."

"Eamon..." Sergeant Nieminen whispered, holding up his hands.

"No, she..." Eamon paused, mid-sentence, his keen ears and nose twitching.

He could hear gunfire inside the building, muffled, intermingling with screams and the sound of breaking tempered glass. Eamon froze, straining to hear familiar voices, but while his ears were sensitive, they were not a key feature of his design. The secure access to the bank opened, heavy door locks cycling.

"Out of the way," Eamon said, popping a magazine up into his rifle and chambering a round.

The Sergeant stepped aside quickly, taking the Steward by the arm.

"Don't do this, Eamon," the Steward said, almost pleading.

"Go, Eamon, go," Sergeant Nieminen said, activating the police comm on his collar. "Status."

The radio crackled, the sound of operational chaos in the background. At last, one of the snipers on the rooftop responded. "The CT doors cycled open. Suspects pushed out a juvenile and shot her. We have one hostage down."

Eamon broke into a run, rounding the back of the transport, rifle up. "I've got an Ursine Unit coming in, clear with 30mm smoke grenades and hold your positions," Nieminen said, doing his best not to sound frantic.

The bank building was four stories and had been outfitted to resist terrorist attacks, explosions, and other mayhem. The CGG had mandated that certain buildings, anywhere large numbers of people could congregate, had to be made "safe." These became the favorite targets of the Financial Liberation Front and other terrorist groups.

Eamon reached the front of the police line easily, dropping to all fours so he could reach maximum speed. He could see the counterterrorism doors on the front of the bank building cycling at their apex. They'd begun to close, and would quickly complete their cycle if he didn't close the gap in time. He could see a little girl lying face down at the bottom of the steps.

Officers shot smoke grenades to cover his approach, but they did little to obscure him. Eamon would be seen on every closed circuit camera, and the bad guys inside would know he was coming. He paused at the bottom of the stairs to put a paw-hand down on Emily to feel for breathing, or a pulse.

She was gone. For what felt like a very long moment, Eamon mourned the loss of his friend. Smoke from the grenades billowed past him, sucked through the closing front doors by the change in pressure as the building created a draft to dispel any chemical agents deployed outside. Eamon used the cover to make a hasty entry, rifle up.

The first gunmen inside didn't have a chance to fire as Eamon crossed the threshold. They were too close to shoot, so he ran them down. They bounced off the walls hard enough to crack plaster, and break bones.

They slumped to the ground, their weapons falling softly on the carpeted entry. Eamon wrestled with his rage, doing his best to focus it as he turned toward the lobby.

His training and the conditioning he'd received at The Factory fought mightily with his emotional state. Every action played out like a coin toss between control and primal fury.

Hostages were arrayed in the center and more gunmen stood above them on service counters and desks. Emily's mother was not among them. Eamon took a sharp breath, exhaling a little with each shot. They fired back, eliciting screams from the hostages. Rounds hit Eamon, but he kept moving to discourage their cover, and the advantage of higher ground. In spite of the pain, he pushed through with each pull of the trigger.

Ammunition spent, the gunmen dropped behind cover to reload. Eamon plowed through the well-appointed oak desks like a freight train in a car lot, knocking them aside like they were toys. Gunmen fled, trying to reload to unleash another burst. It did them little good once Eamon laid his huge ursine hands on them.

He couldn't hear anything now, except Emily's small voice teaching him to properly pronounce Finnish words and phrases. He couldn't smell anything but her mother's perfume, from the bottle she'd been expressly told to leave alone. Eamon could only see red now, driven by powerful fury and loss.

Once he'd cleared the lobby, he came to, his hands around a thin man's neck. He was pleading for his life, hands up, and without weapons. Eamon could feel the bestial fury within slowly being shackled, his reason returning.

"I'm unarmed, and I'm turning myself in," the man said, his bald head and face glistening with a nervous sweat.

Eamon cleared his throat, flipping him around and pulling his hand-cuffs in one fluid motion. "I hope you like Mars. That's where you're going."

"Yeah, what do you think they'll do to you, bear-boy?" the man said, gesturing back to the lobby.

Crimson dripped down from the twenty-foot high ceilings. Eamon had hit some of the bank robbers so hard they'd careened upward, off walls, and broken through the drywall above. Some still hung there, broken and lifeless. Eamon blinked at the sight of the carnage he'd wrought, shrinking internally from the terrified stares from the hostages.

"They can't get up, you know," the handcuffed suspect sneered.

Eamon looked closer, spying explosive vests on a half-dozen of the hostages. Indicator lights turned from a slow interval of yellow, to a rapidly blinking red. Eamon held his claws up to the bald man's face, growling menacingly.

"Let them go," Eamon said, his voice worn and ragged from exertion.

"You know who I am?" the man asked.

"Octavo… you're some kind of super-hacker. You're wanted in dozens of jurisdictions."

"That's right. You've got a good memory."

"What do you want?" Eamon asked, letting Octavo go.

"It's simple. I need the report to read a certain way. I need to go to Mars. I know you were just threatening that, like cops do. The truth is that it is unlikely I'll get there ahead of all the various extradition orders in place."

"You're crazy. No one wants to go to Mars. It's a cesspool," Eamon growled.

"A lot can happen in eight minutes. That's how long it'll be before I can break the encryption again and force the CT doors and countermeasures open. It's just you and me right now. You, and me, and them," Octavo said, nodding to the hostages.

"I'm not giving you anything," Eamon growled, looming menacingly over Octavo.

"You don't need to. I just need you to tell the truth when they ask who killed the hostages. Your ursine hide should be plenty strong enough to endure the explosion. It's a soft, concussive charge, designed to pulp organs and scramble brains," Octavo explained, smiling politely.

Eamon grabbed Octavo by the shirt and dragged him over to the hostages. "Yeah? You won't likely survive, either."

"See, this is where I need your cooperation," Octavo said, continuing to smile.

"Believe me, I'd like nothing better than to send you to Mars. I'm not…" Eamon sank to one knee, the weight of his injuries suddenly taking their toll. He'd been shot several times, and while none had penetrated his hide, they caused him painful internal trauma nonetheless.

"Tired? We had a feeling they would deploy an augmented asset in this case. Those high-velocity rounds hurt, don't they?" Octavo said, straining at the handcuffs around his wrist.

"We? They?" Eamon said, shaking off the pain and standing up.

The hostages watched wordlessly, their eyes wet with terror. Some of them wept quietly, a few prayed. Eamon looked up at the internal security cameras, small red lights indicating that they were indeed recording.

"How are you doing all this? The Denmark job took a team of hackers. All I see is goons, and you," Eamon asked, feigning more weakness than he actually felt.

"I'm a tele-mechanic. I can reach out to machines, make them do what I want. I've got all the technical background, but I don't necessarily need it for the simple stuff. A person must in order to understand the nuances of these abilities. Believe me, I can detonate those explosive vests with a thought, and…"

Eamon was on his feet, moving as quickly as he could, catching Octavo mid-sentence, and hopefully mid-thought. He hoped he could hit him light enough to just knock him out, popping Octavo between the eyes with a quick right jab. The tele-mechanic dropped to the ground, unconscious. As he did, the building quickly returned to normal operation, terrorism countermeasures and enclosures opening up windows and access points.

The cameras and the detonation vests went dead, no longer receiving direction from Octavo. Eamon searched Octavo for a transmitter, tearing his shirt off until he found it, hidden subdermally under his left arm. There was a small spatter of blood as he ripped it out, killing Octavo's ability to reach out with his abilities remotely.

"Lay down on your back, and have someone help you slide out of the vests. Hand them to me as gently as you can," Eamon said, his tone and helpful demeanor calming the hostages somewhat.

He threw them into the vault and closed the door. Thirty seconds later, the vests detonated from a secondary timer, rattling the windows. Eamon paused beside the bank manager's office as he headed back, seeing

Nieminen's wife, Vienna, lying among several bank employees that had been brutally beaten, and then shot execution style.

"He singled them out," Eamon said, feeling angry and helpless.

He walked out to where Octavo lay unconscious and handcuffed. He had a few minutes before the other officers would be able to get inside, the CT enclosures moving slowly to clear windows and doors. Shock was beginning to wear off, and the hostages were in various states of emotional trauma, fear, and anger.

"What will happen to him?" a woman asked.

"Nothing good, ma'am," Eamon replied, turning Octavo over so he didn't strangle or suffocate from his bleeding nose.

Moments later, police officers flooded the lobby, grabbing up hostages and dragging Octavo away. Eamon struggled to get his vest off, afraid to count the bruises he'd have later. He waited for his handler, watching as emergency personnel removed seven bodies from the back office.

Steward Wuopio stepped into the lobby, careful to avoid the blood and broken glass. "Officer Eamon, I need you to come with me."

"Where's my handler?"

"The bank robbers sent out a broadcast shortly after you went in. He saw what they did to his wife, shortly before they shot his child and threw her body outside. He's unable to perform his duties at this time."

"His family was the target. Nieminen must have been close to figuring out who was behind all this. Whoever it is needs Octavo on Mars, and my handler out of the picture."

"There will be a formal inquiry. We'll get to the bottom of what happened here," Steward Wuopio said, pausing a safe distance from Eamon.

"I'm done, right? No handler to speak up for me. This mayhem is going to land on your only deniable asset. Me."

Steward Wuopio shook her head. "We're going to protect you. It was what I was trying to do from the beginning. I told you not to come in here."

"We? I don't understand," Eamon said, wearily throwing his vest over his shoulder and struggling to his feet.

"Get out," Steward Wuopio said, dismissing the crime technicians and other police officers.

Eamon watched them leave, wondering what he'd stumbled into.

"I didn't need to read your jacket, because I already had. I've been tasked to oppose the people who did this to your handler and his family. I failed. This isn't on you, it's on me."

"How do we make it right?" Eamon asked.

Wuopio scowled, her distress evident in the way she kept checking her mobile for updates. "We don't. Octavo is going to get his free ride to Mars. The threat he made against the hostages will be enough to send him there. We can't release that footage for months, as it is part of the investigation."

Eamon frowned. "Octavo released the footage of me tearing through the bank robbers."

"Yes, and it'll poison public opinion for months, until the formal findings come out."

"I need to check on Nieminen," Eamon said, lowering his head.

"He's already on his way out of the country. That they targeted him specifically means we've been compromised. I'll leak the footage, so people will see you ending the hostage situation, but it'll be the end of my career, either way."

"Compromised? We? Either way?" Eamon said, growing impatient.

"If they got to Nieminen, it means they might be able to get to me. You're in no danger because you don't know anything, and that's how it will have to stay," Steward Wuopio whispered, her lips tight with anxiety.

"What's going to happen to me? What about Emily and her mother? Who will see to their arrangements?" Eamon asked.

"It'll be taken care of. I'm sorry, you won't have time to grieve for your friends. Believe me, you won't be the only one to grieve for them alone. The transport that brought you here will take you north. You'll join your new police division there, something called Nordic Patrol."

Eamon nodded, numbly accepting his new reality. "Who's my new handler?"

"You won't have one. You'll have a partner. She's a Canine Metasapient and she's been a police officer a long time."

"If you know all about me, why didn't you want to let me go in and prevent all this?" Eamon asked, turning to look Wuopio in the eyes.

"I have to be careful. Most Metasapients, like Drones, are good at detecting falsehoods."

Eamon took a deep breath, having garnered an understanding that she was in some ethical predicament. "You aren't a bigot after all. You were being overprotective. You thought I'd get hurt or killed in here."

"It's more complicated than that. You and your kind are not supposed to get mixed up in this business. It isn't supposed to ever touch your lives. Management made it clear you weren't to be deployed in our internal struggles."

Eamon frowned. "If you and Nieminen are both working for 'Management,' why did you call me a monster?"

"I wasn't talking about you," Steward Wuopio replied, turning to watch as they loaded Octavo into a police vehicle. "I was talking about the person responsible."

CHAPTER 2

DAKOTA TERRITORIES, 30,000 FEET, ABOARD THE MUNDT FREIGHTER

NINE YEARS LATER - AUGUST 27TH, 2201

Eamon carefully navigated crates and pallets, making sure everything was secure as the bad weather was approaching. Satisfied that everything was tied down, he took up the three crew seats beside Abbey and braced his feet against a heavy cargo container.

"Do you think anyone will know what we did back there in Europe?" Abbey asked, her hands clasped between her knees.

Eamon looked at the floor, listening to the engines cycle outside, the approaching storm at the horizon.

"Will children open up history books and see what transpired? How it ended?" Abbey said.

"You want to be famous?" Eamon asked.

"No, I just don't want what happened to be repeated, ever again."

Eamon nodded.

"Eamon, you read Brook and Kale's post-event assessment. Svetovid's march was doomed to fail, having already expended most of his resources. They thought people wouldn't fight back, and that they'd have an army of hundreds of thousands by the time they hit the old Republic of Spain territory."

Eamon scratched his chin, shaggy fur floating to the deck of the cargo hold.

"Stop that, you'll give yourself a bald spot," Abbey scolded.

"I can't help it. Kale says the itching is 'neurological aftermath' from the way he restored my memories."

"Clearly, and not the only aftermath, all things considered."

Eamon nodded. "Clearly."

"How are things with Matthias and the survivors?"

"He's fine. They're fine."

An awkward silence permeated the cargo hold.

Abbey sighed. "I was one of the first, he couldn't have known how we grow bonds and attachments. I don't blame him, and neither should you."

"I said they were fine."

"I'm glad. Hopefully, even this late in life, he gets to do something of what he wants."

Eamon cleared his throat. "Yeah, sure."

Abbey frowned, sullenly. "You ready for this new job?"

"Yeah. Break up a bar brawl or two, and spend the rest of the time fishing," Eamon said, smiling slightly.

"That's why you went to work for Nordic Patrol in Finland. How did that turn out?" Abbey said.

Eamon resumed looking at the floor, laying his arms across his knees. "Yeah, trouble seems to find us."

"Maybe not always. Any chance there's a lady Ursine up that way?" Abbey asked.

"Could be," Eamon said, scratching his chin.

"Stop it. Don't scratch. How's it going to look if you meet a lady Ursine and your chin is bald?"

"My sparkling personality will have to be enough," Eamon said.

Abbey sighed. "Tell me about the next post."

"It's Glacier National Park. There's a server hub there, blessedly few people, and hopefully lots of peace and quiet."

"All the post-event reports suggest militia activity."

Eamon nodded. "Those Perfidy hadn't already scared off."

"Locals?"

"Montana territory. Mercs aren't good for the locals, so I'm heading up."

"And, since you're from North America…"

Eamon smiled. "Yeah. Brook probably left out my Metasapient designator."

"Yeah, but are all the mercs leaving? They've been there long enough to mingle with the populace," Abbey asked.

"It's been on my mind," Eamon said, quietly hoping that all of the mercs would leave.

The transport bounced around, prompting Eamon to steady Abbey.

"Careful," Eamon said, setting her upright once more.

Brook appeared in the doorway leading from the crew compartment to the cargo hold, her keen drone ears twitching. "I thought I heard you talking to someone. Everything all right?"

"Yeah, just talking to Abbey," Eamon said, patting the urn sitting beside him.

Brook nodded. "Can I sit with you guys for a while?"

"Please," Eamon said, slipping the urn of Abbey's ashes into a large vest pocket, and scooting over to make room.

Brook sat down beside Eamon, leaning into him. "I'll miss you. I appreciate all the help."

"With the Cabal?"

Brook laughed. "Yeah, with that, too."

"It's been very satisfying." Eamon said, holding out a fuzzy fist.

Brook bumped Eamon's fist with her own. "Revenge usually is."

"Glad we're on the other side of it."

"Me, too. None of us had a chance to breathe after what happened. I couldn't bear the thought of the trail going cold, and even one of those murderers getting away," Brook said.

"I hear Cerise Laplace was taken into custody on Mars," Eamon said.

"Yes, by a Mars derby girl, Camille Ishihara."

Eamon nodded. "And, what do we learn or gain from that?"

"Don't mess with people trained to fight in zero gravity?" Brook giggled.

"Yeah, I've seen Ezra One fight, but that isn't what I was talking about," Eamon said.

"It's nothing for you to worry about. If there's aftermath, Kale and I will deal with it," Brook said, closing her eyes and listening to Kale and Heavy Dub chat in the adjoining compartment.

"Can you hear them?" Eamon asked.

"They're talking about you. They're worried that you might have PTSD, and weighing whether or not you're stable enough to be the Law in Glacier Park," Brook said, patting Eamon.

"Even if Kale isn't strictly human, he's still a human," Eamon said sadly.

"Don't fault him for not understanding. Being a Drone or a Metasapient is a unique experience, and there are not words in any language to relate that experience to other people. We just have a shared sense with the others that know," Brook said, playing with the ends of her long hair.

"I dunno, sounds like you found the words just now."

"They are Kale's words. Be kind to him, he tries really hard to understand."

"I know he does, and Heavy Dub's a good guy too," Eamon said.

"Humans are so fragile, they've no choice but to be detached I think."

"Yeah," Eamon said, the truth of the statement landing harder on his conscience than usual.

"Oh, where'd you go?" Brook asked, petting the fur on Eamon's arm.

"I was just thinking about all the other Metasapients that were killed, and everyone lost that was in the Nordic Patrol. I wished we'd never taken the time to figure out what happened to some of them," Eamon said, covering his face with his huge paw-hands.

"They deserved to find peace, and for someone to know what they sacrificed. Out of it all, we didn't learn anything about humanity we didn't already know," Brook said, hugging Eamon's broad arm.

Eamon put a large hand on Brook. "This would have been impossible without you guys. I'd have no one."

"You might be surprised. Silverstein put a lot of effort into protecting Metasapients and Drones as Vance Uroboros. I still have all the Uroboros Financial records, if you want to read them," Brook said, walking over and opening a storage locker.

Eamon shook his head. "It's all in the past now."

"Speaking of the past, Heavy Dub gathered up a bunch of older weapons. He thought they might be less terrifying than the two rifles you always carry," Brook said, hauling out a large duffle bag.

"I like my rifles," Eamon said.

"Yeah, but are they a good fit for the sheriff of a small town?" Brook said smiling.

"Probably. It is Montana," Eamon said, leaning over and looking at the contents of the bag.

"Nothing but pure magic in there," Heavy Dub said, striding proudly into the cargo bay.

Brook laughed, looking at the antique, odd, and sometimes ridiculous firearms that Heavy Dub had collected. "You'll have to help Eamon with this, I don't know much about guns other than Perfidy's rifle."

"You think my rifles will spook the locals?" Eamon asked, looking ruefully into the large duffle.

"Brook tell you that?" Heavy Dub said, grinning widely.

"Yeah."

"Naw, not at all. I just want to give you some weapons so you'll have spares. Most of the Canine Metasapients have a rifle, and a couple of the townsfolk do, but there's no other source for weapons up there," Heavy Dub explained, kneeling down beside the duffle.

"Oh," Eamon said, feeling a little better about the whole affair.

"See what I did there?" Heavy Dub said.

"What? No," Brook said, looking at Heavy Dub with a side-eyed glance.

"I normalized what you'd made awkward. Drones and Metasapients, for all your specialized training, make everything weird," Heavy Dub explained, pulling out a handgun and a rifle wrapped in oilcloth.

"Yeah, we're already keenly aware," Eamon said.

"If you were a merc, I'd tell you to do something normal when you got to town. First, complain about the flight. Then, head into town and pay cash for a six-pack of beer. Check the map in the general store for the closest fishing hole and go to it. Show that you're sentimental about things, and have rituals that don't just include perimeter patrols and guard duty," Heavy Dub explained, unwrapping the guns.

"I'm just going to be myself," Eamon said.

"Some of those people are going to hate you, Eamon, on principle," Brook said, agreeing.

Heavy Dub nodded, sifting through the weaponry. "Totally. I wouldn't talk to them unless they talk to you. The trick is to make yourself available. Get your coffee at the same time and the same place. Sit and have pie at the diner every Thursday afternoon, or something like that. Have a routine that makes you approachable. That way, it's up to them to talk to you, and they have to initiate."

"That really works?" Brook asked.

"Oh, yeah. I've had to blend into several urban and rural areas doing various long-term operations. If you try too hard, or you're the one to initiate, it just goes wrong. You'll feel like an outsider unless you give the locals a chance to ingratiate themselves to you," Heavy Dub said, nodding.

"This all from Perfidy's playbook?" Brook asked, grinning.

"Everything is. He invented being a cybernetic merc. We had to work in an age where cybernetic enhancements were illegal, at least on the books, in more than half the world. Putting the populace at ease was Fieldcraft 101."

"Any other pearls of wisdom?" Eamon asked, gingerly holding the handgun Heavy Dub just handed him.

"Be friendly with the kids. Make sure they have candy, a spot next to you at your fishing spot, whatever they want," Heavy Dub explained.

"Kids?" Brook asked, raising an eyebrow.

"They're the best assets. Adults are unlikely to try and run you off if their kid likes you, and children are smarter than adults. They listen to everything everyone says like sponges. Really, they tend to have the best intel. Some of my best allies, both in quiet urban areas and in war zones, were kids," Heavy Dub explained, checking the rifle for defects.

"Okay, tell me what these are," Eamon said, gesturing to the rifle and handgun.

"The handgun is a Ruger Vaquero single action in forty-four magnum. It has a birdshead grip with a three and three-quarter inch barrel. The rifle is a Henry lever-action with big ring and octagonal barrel, also in forty-four magnum," Heavy Dub said, lovingly hefting the rifle.

"They shoot the same bullets," Eamon said, hefting the rifle.

"Kind of rare with modern weapons, but a couple hundred years ago that just made good sense."

"These a couple hundred years old?" Brook asked, sniffing at the weapons.

Heavy Dub smiled. "Naw, they're replicas, made with modern alloys, and they fire modern ammunition. I've got a case of it. I loaded it myself."

"Why do you have these?" Eamon asked, smiling in spite of himself.

"You never wanted to be a cowboy? Perfidy used to always tease me about being sentimental. The old man said it'd get me killed," Heavy Dub said, frowning at the contents of the duffle. "Truth is, I'm more sentimental about being sentimental."

"I don't understand," Brook said, opening the case of hand loaded ammunition, and thumbing the tips of one of the bullets.

"Yeah, Drones and Metasapients wouldn't. You guys were never little kids, growing up on the street with nothing. Guys with guns ran things where I came from. All I ever wanted to be was a guy with a gun," Heavy Dub said, his smile returning.

"The Factory was no picnic, but at least we were sheltered and fed. We also know a lie when we hear it," Brook said, scolding Heavy Dub.

"It sounds better than growing up working middle class, in the most boring suburb ever," Heavy Dub said, his smile growing wider.

"Another lie," Brook said, shaking her head.

"For mercenaries, it's the only protection we have when guns fail. If any of those mercs on the ground decide to stay, whatever you do, don't trust them," Heavy Dub said, growing more serious.

"Those are people you vetted. People you told us to trust," Brook said, somewhat irritated.

"Yeah, and if any of them don't get back on the transport with us, they're compromised."

"Hopefully, they all get on the transport," Eamon whispered, looking down the sights of the Henry rifle.

"They better," Heavy Dub said, grinding a metallic fist into the palm of his other cybernetic hand.

"Thanks for the weapons. They have to be valuable. What's the best way to store them?" Eamon asked, tucking the rifle and handgun aside.

"Put them up in plain sight wherever you have your bunk, hide the ammunition, and tell everyone they're ornamental," Heavy Dub said, putting on his cheesiest grin.

Brook gave Heavy Dub a disparaging look, raising her eyebrow.

"What? It's just a precaution, and the locals will like that he's sentimental about guns. It's the Northwest," Heavy Dub said, shrugging.

"You can't do something nice, without it being part of some operational precaution?" Brook scolded.

Heavy Dub smiled. "Like I said, I'm sentimental about being sentimental."

"I'm going to check on Kale," Brook whispered, exiting the cargo hold.

"I appreciate it," Eamon said. "It'll be good to know I've got some backup down there."

"If we've learned anything working together in the last few months, it's that the Cabal is not an ordinary organization. It's more like a disease, or a cancer. It always seems to spread where you want it the least," Heavy Dub said, sitting down beside Eamon.

The transport bounced in the storm, string lighting swaying from the metal supports above. Eamon breathed through his nose, thinking about everything they'd seen and done in the last few months. There was little to compare to what the Cabal had done to Finland, Europe, and most of Asia. He'd seen the mountains of drowned innocents in India, whole cities burned to ash by orbital bombardments, and those weren't the worst of the things he'd be leaving out of his memoirs.

"If they're still out there, you think they'll retaliate?" Eamon asked.

"I would, given all we've done to dismantle them recently. They've endured the rise and fall of nations, empires, and the world. Then, some dumb cop gets in a fist fight with the immortal leader of their military arm, and rips his head off," Heavy Dub said, fishing around in his jacket for a flask.

"Yeah, I won't go starting a video blog of my daily life in Glacier Park," Eamon said, nodding.

"Just don't put it up on the public network if you do. Lay low, bro. Lay. Low."

"Super low," Eamon said, bumping fists with Heavy Dub.

"And if you do shoot a vlog, put it up on the Uroboros Financial private server. I'd watch the shit out of that," Heavy Dub laughed, handing Eamon the flask.

"Hopefully, it'd just be hours of me drinking beer and fishing," Eamon said, taking a pull from the flask.

"I'll drink to that," Heavy Dub said, reaching for the flask.

The remainder of the flight was turbulent, the storm turning into a blizzard as the transport gained altitude. Eamon did his best to sleep, but there was barely any space in the cargo hold with all the supplies and mail. While resting, his uncanny ability to remember olfactory details had brought back every scent of smoke, blood, and iron. The dead haunted him in those few moments he was able to sleep.

He woke to Kale's hand resting on his arm, a concerned expression spreading rapidly across his face. "Apologies. We are almost there."

"It's fine. Was I…?"

Kale shook his head. "Not like before. But, you have not had anything resembling night terrors for a couple of weeks."

"I'm probably just nervous."

"We should always revisit the past when embracing the future."

"What does the future hold for you guys?"

"We are going to follow your example and live small for a while. The Cabal is either gone, or the trail has gone cold for the time being. There is not much else we can do for the world. More than half of it lies in total ruin. Even the combined might of the financial arm of the Cabal cannot undo what the military limb wrought," Kale said, clasping his hands together.

"Is she going to let you keep the beard and the long hair?" Eamon asked, doing his best to change the subject.

"I am under strict orders to keep it this way," Kale replied, deadpan.

"That's right!" Brook said, from somewhere in the forward compartment, forcing a smile from Kale and Eamon.

"If I need to contact you?" Eamon said.

Kale nodded. "We will not be far. Brook wants to seek out Doctor Helmet's holdings and make certain nothing he left behind can be used for nefarious purposes. He was based in North America primarily."

"But, you might have to go to Mexico," Eamon said, knowingly.

"Let us both hope that does not become necessary. Thus far, I have managed to avoid that journey, but if we decide to make it, I'll let you know."

"Speaking of journeys, any word on the Migration?" Eamon asked, hopeful for some news.

"Yes, in spite of the storms, we managed to get some satellite imagery and work something up for you," Kale said, handing Eamon a sheet of paper folded in half.

"Thanks."

"Glad to do it, friend."

Mister Mundt set the transport down inside Apgar Village, landing at the small municipal building that served as town hall, police station, and medical clinic. The snow was deep outside, but a decent sized crowd of folks had gathered in anticipation of fresh supplies and the mail. Village elders and hired hands warmed their hands over barrel fires as mercenaries stood nearby, their gear packed up and ready to board.

"They all there?" Brook asked, pressing her face to the port hole.

"Nope. Goddamn it," Heavy Dub said, banging a mechanical fist on the wall beside his own port hole.

A collective gasp went up as Eamon strode out ahead of Heavy Dub, Brook, and Kale. The locals had seen plenty of Metasapients, even a few of the ursine variety, but Eamon was easily twice the size of a standard Type Two. The loading ramp creaked under his weight as rifles and other gear clacked together at his back.

"I'll get everything offloaded, and our guys and gals secured inside," Heavy Dub said, taking note of the foul expressions arrayed on the village elders' faces.

Walking with a cane, Kale calmly approached the barrel fire, Brook at his side, and Eamon at the other. Ray Pendleton, who seemed to always be the spokesperson for the village, was unusually quiet. Kale slipped the cane over one arm and warmed his hands, relishing the uncomfortably quiet moment.

"Well?" Ray Pendleton said at last.

"You asked for real law enforcement; I've brought you some. All you'll need," Kale said, smiling slightly.

"You think this is funny?" Ray asked, looking to the other elders for support.

"You wanted someone accustomed to the climate. You specified that they needed to have served rural areas before, and that they were born in North America. You didn't want a small army, and if I could, to make it just one officer," Kale said, firelight reflecting in his eyes.

"Damn it, this isn't what we meant, and you know it," Ray complained.

Ray was a large man, older, in his fifties, with rough hands and a beard. He could be intimidating, which was why the other village elders usually had him do the talking. Kale had grown tired of their collective complaining long ago and delighted in twisting their requests to something that suited the town, but irked the elders in some way.

"I can leave the mercenaries here. It looks like some are reluctant to go anyway," Kale said, matter of fact.

"No, this will do for now. Find us a real lawman before the next trans-port. I mean it," Ray said, getting close to Kale while puffing up his chest.

Brook intervened, gently pushing Ray backward.

"You let this girl do your fighting for you?"

Kale scratched his beard thoughtfully, then nodded. "Yes, I do."

"It would be expensive to move the CGG server hub somewhere else, but it would almost be worth it. The Blackfeet said they'd gladly provide the facility support we need, and I tend to like the worst of them as much as I like the best of you," Brook said, sharing an angry glare with not just Ray, but anyone foolish enough to meet her gaze.

Ray held up his hands. "Let's not be hasty…"

"I'm tired of this game. I've met your demands, but from what I've seen from the air, the dwellings for the Canine Metasapients have not been winterized or improved. You've done nothing of what we've asked, and we've done our best to accommodate you," Brook said, her words cutting through the gathered men worse than the cold.

"We'll see to the shelters, and try to do something…"

"No, you won't. I'm making my own arrangements and deducting it from your subsidies. Mess with me again, I'll move the server hub, and forget this village exists as part of the North American continent. Test me and see," Brook said, shoving the barrel fire over, forcing the village elders to jump backward.

"Kale?" Ray said, looking on in disbelief.

"We will continue to look at options that will be more equitable for everyone involved. Good day," Kale said, in his patented business-as-usual tone of voice.

The village elders retreated, directing the hired hands to help with the transfer of supplies. Ray held his ground until the others were gone, his brow relaxing once they were safely out of sight. "Is that true, you'll move the hub?" Ray Pendleton asked, looking sideways at the mercs loading up into the transport.

"We'd prefer not to," Kale said, growing bored with the back and forth.

"Those Canine Metasapients are like Aaron AI's family. They stayed with him when the human workers at the hub fled. His opinion of humans is already dangerously low. If he asks to be moved for their sake, we'll move him. We can't afford to have him quit, and I'm unwilling to force an artificial agent to work simply because it's convenient for the firm, or a village," Brook said, instantly resuming a state of calm.

"I understand that, but the locals don't much care for non-human folks. Giving us a Metasapient Sheriff isn't likely to help that situation," Ray said, trying to avoid Brook's angry stare.

"Eamon, did Kale give you that slip of paper I printed out for you?" Brook asked.

"Yes, he did."

"When the time comes, follow your conscience. If you don't feel like this place is worth protecting, just contact us before you leave," Brook said, turning on her heel to leave.

Kale followed along, laying a hand on Eamon's arm. "No one would blame you," he said, looking up into Eamon's eyes.

"What are they talking about?" Ray asked.

"You've got a merc that does not want to leave?" Eamon said, walking up to Ray.

"We'll hold the transport until you've made contact," Kale said, walking arm in arm with Brook back through the snow.

Ray sighed. "Yeah, okay, it's just about ten at night, they should be making the descent from the server hub about now."

"They?" Eamon asked.

Ray nodded. "Jennifer and Klaus."

Eamon stowed his gear and a crate of supplies in the Sheriff's office before following Ray up through town. Riding on the outside of Ray's Sno-Cat, they made their way south to the trailhead leading to West Glacier. The large quad-track vehicle climbed easily through the snowy terrain, even with Eamon's extra weight. There, a handful of workers had just finished loading snowmobiles into a storage shed and waiting for a ride.

"That's Jennifer Wilton, Collver, Shelby, and Klaus…"

"Nieminen," Eamon said, dropping off the side of the Sno-Cat.

"Yeah, how'd you know?" Ray asked.

"He's the merc refusing to leave?" Eamon said, ignoring the question.

"Yeah, I guess he and Jennifer have gotten pretty cozy," Ray said, frowning.

Eamon walked ahead of Ray, his massive form easily pushing through the snow with each step. Shelby and Collver both raised a hand in greeting to Eamon, conveying their own silent message of Metasapient solidarity. Eamon nodded in return, the urn carrying Abbey's remains feeling a little heavier in his pocket. Shelby and Collver weren't law enforcement-grade Canines, but they both had rifles, and carried them like they knew how to use them.

"Klaus," Eamon said, waiting to extend his greeting until after Klaus had secured the snowmobile shed.

"Eamon? Eamon Two? What are you doing way out here?" Klaus said, startled to see his former charge.

"I'm here to get you on a transport."

Klaus sighed. "I'm done with all that, Eamon."

"You need to pack up and leave," Eamon said, pointing back down the mountain.

"No."

Eamon narrowed his eyes, looking up at Shelby and Collver who almost imperceptibly shook their heads. "Do this right, Klaus. Get debriefed, then quit," Eamon said, more insistently.

"Remember when I told you what to do?" Klaus replied.

"You never told me what to do," Eamon said, watching Jennifer's reaction.

Klaus looked deflated by this response, knowing it to be mostly true. From the collective reactions, no one knew anything about what happened in Helsinki. It wasn't a good sign, but it wasn't a bad one, either. It at least allowed for the possibility that Klaus Nieminen was genuinely trying to leave mercenary work behind.

"I looked for you," Eamon said.

"I wasn't around to be found. I was lost, and the CGG flagged me as being emotionally compromised. I couldn't be a police officer anymore, so I started working as a tracer, and eventually signed up for all this," Klaus said, looking uncomfortably over at Jennifer.

"Get on the transport, Klaus," Eamon said, folding his broad arms.

Klaus shook his head. "I've got a life here. I don't want to mess it up waiting for the next transport back. There's a lot of good I can do up here."

"It's true. The winter can be pretty hard, and having another pair of strong hands to help out couldn't hurt," Ray said, nodding to Klaus.

"Stay out of this, Ray," Eamon said, stepping away from the group. He tapped the comm on his armored vest activating his throat mic. "I found the straggler."

"Nieminen, yeah, the others say he's sweet for the local tele-me-chanic," Heavy Dub replied.

"I know him. From Finland," Eamon said.

"Shit. Well, it's up to you. I'll have some folks come haul him off if you want him out of your town. If you choose to let him stay, my previous advice still stands. Don't trust him," Heavy Dub replied.

"I'll give him a clock. I'm not going to 'let' him do anything," Eamon said, already feeling deeply conflicted.

"Sounds like sense. We'll hold for an hour, wait for the storm to pass us by a little more."

Eamon nodded. "Sounds like sense."

"Stay frosty, Brother. Heavy D, out."

Eamon walked back up the slope where Klaus was waiting outside the Sno-Cat nervously. Everyone else had already piled inside and was warming themselves. "Well?" Klaus asked.

"The transport leaves in an hour. Be on it," Eamon said, climbing up on the side of the Sno-Cat.

"And if I'm not?" Klaus asked.

"Don't be stupid, Klaus. Just leave," Eamon said, giving Klaus a hand up into the Sno-Cat.

Klaus looked genuinely discouraged, but Eamon couldn't tell if it was the prospect of having to leave or something else. The journey back was cold, but Eamon had felt colder. It was like Finland, but there were more stars in the sky and fewer urban areas nearby. He hoped the fishing would be good and that he'd get to do plenty of it.

Something about Klaus being in Apgar bothered Eamon. He'd come to see how small the world could be traveling with Kale and Brook. He quietly hoped Klaus would stay, as he had many questions, but knew it would be better for everyone if he left.

Ray stopped the Sno-Cat alongside the municipal building and put it in park. Opening his window, he yelled back to Eamon. "Shelby and Collver will give you the tour. I'm going to run these love birds back to their respective dwellings."

"Take her home. Take him to the transport," Eamon said, dropping off the side.

"Pleased to meet you, Sheriff," Jennifer Wilton said, extending a hand as Shelby and Collver dropped to the ground.

"Likewise, ma'am," Eamon said, shaking the young girl's slender hand.

"I'll come by in the morning, we'll get some breakfast and talk. I'm sure Aaron will want to meet you," Jennifer said, smiling warmly.

"Sure," Eamon said, shutting the door.

He watched the Sno-Cat drive up the street and round the corner before reaching into his pocket and pulling a piece of paper, folded in half, and showing it to Shelby. "It's the Migration report."

Shelby nodded. "I'd hoped Kale would bring it."

"He keeps his promises. Tell me about Klaus Nieminen."

"Not sure we should," Collver replied, scratching one of his long canine ears.

"Until I've talked to Jennifer," Eamon said.

Shelby nodded. "That would be our preference."

Eamon could tell they'd bonded with Jennifer Wilton by observing how they behaved around her. It was just like watching Abbey when Matthias showed up in Finland. Ursine Metasapients didn't bond in the same way, but he could still understand how they felt, as his kind usually had a partner.

"Show me where you guys live," Eamon said.

"This way," Shelby said, leading the way through the cold darkness.

They walked to the edge of Lake McDonald, where a small ring of trailers was circling a cooking fire. The other Canine Metasapients perked up at the sight of him, their collective expressions the warmest welcome he was likely to find. He sat and listened to them talk for hours, soaking up the local lore, and exchanging theories about the Migration.

"So, it's really happening?" Shelby said, looking at the piece of paper.

"Looks like it," Eamon said, taking a sip of water from an aluminum canteen cover.

"Are you going to go?"

"Are you?"

Eamon and Shelby sat in silence with the rest of the dog pack, each one of them weighing what they'll do when the time comes. Later, Eamon walked back to the Sheriff's office alone, taking in the sights and sounds of Apgar at night. He could hear the usual muffled arguments, snoring, and adult activity he'd hear in Helsinki, but beyond the small village, there was not the thrum of a larger urban area.

Outside the village, all that could be found was the cold and quiet land, cut and formed long ago by the slowest moving ice. He could hear grizzlies moving further afield, skirting the town. They had another month or so to hunt before they would have to hibernate.

CHAPTER 3

GLACIER NATIONAL PARK, APGAR VILLAGE, SHERIFF'S OFFICE

AUGUST 27TH, 2201 – 6:20 AM

Eamon lifted Heavy Dub's gifts up onto hooks on the wall above the credenza behind the desk. It was good fortune, and being in the Northwest United States that there were already places to hang guns. The weapons looked good hanging there, like they belonged.

The desk was too small for him to sit behind, but he didn't plan to be in the office much anyway. The door came with a sturdy lock, so it was a good place to stash ammunition and supplies. Slinging his bolt-action rifle, Eamon donned his armored vest, pauldrons, and handcuffs before he headed out.

The street traffic paused for a moment, a handful of people stopping to glance at Eamon. He'd hoped no one would be up at that hour, but Apgar seemed to be a place where folks rose for work early. Jennifer Wilton waved at him from across the street, waiting for some snow machines to pass before heading over.

"I hope you didn't forget our breakfast date," Jennifer said, smiling.

"What have you got there?" Eamon said, pointing to the canvas bag she was carrying.

"Notices and a staple gun. I'm hitting the bulletin board here at the municipal building, the church, and the library," Jennifer said, handing him a flier.

"Trying to improve the conditions for the dog pack," Eamon said, reading the contents of the notice.

"Pretty much ever since I landed here. People don't understand how important the Metasapients are to Aaron, or how much they help out around here. We'd be swimming in grizzly bears if they didn't wander the outskirts of town and ward them off. No offense," Jennifer said, winking.

Eamon gave her a stern look. "Swimming in grizzlies?"

"I've given up trying to reason with the town. I'm trying bald-faced lies instead."

"Having breakfast with me isn't going to help," Eamon said, walking beside Jennifer and avoiding the cold stares from people as they passed by.

"Normalizing the Metasapient presence isn't going to be easy. We need to show the town that you're people, like they're people," Jennifer said, waving dismissively at the people walking to the other side of the street to avoid Eamon.

"Hand bills and breakfast will do that?" Eamon said.

"Not with people that lack basic reasoning skills," Jennifer whispered.

Eamon frowned. "Aaron teach you to talk like that?"

"You know I'm an 'other' like you. Being a tele-mechanic, even a latent one, these hill-dwelling country folk don't see me any different than they do you, or the dog pack," Jennifer said, angrily stapling a flier to a bulletin board.

"So you're going to shame them with handbills," Eamon said, leaning up against the wall beside the bulletin board.

Jennifer paused, looking over at Eamon, a twinge of anger in her expression. "You have a better idea?"

"Maybe we both need some breakfast," Eamon said, gesturing up the road to the diner.

Jennifer sighed. "Nothing else I've tried has worked. What's the harm?"

The diner was built to match the rustic architecture of the town, but it was newer, and the owner had gone to great lengths to make it comfortable. The waitress didn't bat an eye at Eamon, showing them to a table with bench seating that could accommodate his size. Eamon sat across from Jennifer, pulling out a small pair of reading glasses to look at the menu.

"You going to ask me about Klaus?" Jennifer asked, perusing the menu.

"Nope," Eamon replied, pushing the reading glasses back on his nose.

"You look hilarious. Great big bear, with those tiny glasses," Jennifer said, chuckling.

"I'm getting the waffles," Eamon said, holding the menu up close to his face.

"Fine, I'll ask you about Klaus," Jennifer said, nodding to the waitress as she poured the coffee.

Eamon, adopted a tired expression, putting his reading glass away, and the menu face down.

"He said you guys know each other, and that you told him to get on the transport."

"This coffee looks good," Eamon said, gingerly picking up the cup between two massive fingers.

Jennifer sighed.

"Did he get on the transport?" Eamon asked, looking at her over the top of his menu.

"No."

"There, we talked about Klaus. Are the waffles good?" Eamon said, returning his gaze to the menu.

"Everything is good, and no we haven't talked about Klaus. Is he your friend?" Jennifer asked.

"No."

"That's not what he said. Is he your friend? Do you trust him?" Jennifer asked, looking around the diner to see if anyone was listening.

"I thought you guys were friendly," Eamon said, turning the menu over to look at the list of pie.

"He'd like to be, and he's made that known, but I've held off letting it get serious."

Eamon nodded, squinting at the pie list.

"He's not a regular guy. He's fancy, from Europe, with an accent that makes the other ladies in the village giggle. Out of everyone, he chooses me?"

Eamon closed his eyes. "He's got a history with tele-mechanics."

"And, this history?" Jennifer asked, adding sugar to her coffee.

"What about the pie? Is the pie good?"

"Yes, the pie is good. Please, tell me something, anything about him," Jennifer said.

"Do you want to be with him?" Eamon asked.

Jennifer shrank down in her seat. "I was hoping he'd just leave, and I wouldn't have to tell him I wasn't really interested."

"Waffles," Eamon said, giving his order to the waitress who had been lingering beside the table.

"Eggs and bacon?" she asked.

"Yes, and the same for me," Jennifer replied.

"What if I don't like bacon?" Eamon said, watching the waitress take the order to the cook.

"Then we can't be friends. I can't trust anyone who doesn't like bacon. What are we going to do about Klaus?" Jennifer asked, resting her head on her arms and looking sideways at the line forming outside the diner.

"We?" Eamon said.

"You're his friend. Can't you talk to him for me?"

"I can tell him to leave," Eamon said, sipping his coffee.

"I know it was wrong to lead him on, but making the other single ladies in town jealous was pretty great. Delicious even. They treat me like a disease most of the time," Jennifer said, looking away from the interior of the diner and out the window.

Eamon didn't reply, continuing to gaze at the pie list.

"So, you'll talk to him for me?"

"I'll talk to him," Eamon said. "After waffles."

"I hope so, he's meeting us at the trailhead in an hour. He's been work-ing up at the server hub with me and the dog pack for a while now."

"You let him into the server hub?" Eamon said, glaring at Jennifer.

"I didn't see the harm," she replied, mortified.

The waitress brought their food and arrayed it on the table. After making sure there was nothing else they needed, she departed. Jennifer ate sparingly, obviously nervous and verging on distraught given Eamon's disgruntled demeanor.

"I'm sorry about all this," Jennifer said, pushing her eggs around the plate.

"It's fine. I was going to talk to Klaus anyway."

"Oh?"

"Yeah."

They finished breakfast with Jennifer giving Eamon some of the particulars about the town, while he nodded in acknowledgment and ate for both of them. The waitress waived the cost of the breakfast, as a sort of welcome. Eamon thanked her, and took some biscuits to go. It was a gesture Eamon had not expected, but he was beginning to suspect Apgar was a more complex place than he previously thought.

He'd read all the incident reports filed by the mercenaries, and done his due diligence. Eamon knew, in spite of that, there was a rural undercurrent he'd have to feel out by being there. Whether it was Finland or Montana, some things are just the same anywhere, especially with small towns.

A woman waited for them outside, her face frozen in a perpetual mask of anger verging on rage. She was dressed in an old army jacket, a long skirt, long johns underneath, and a knit cap. She'd aged well into her fifties, and seemed spry and capable, her skin rough and accustomed to the outdoors. Jennifer jumped when she saw her, looking about nervously.

"I'm here for my grandson, Sheriff," the woman said, pointing a bony finger.

"Emma Jackson Vale," Eamon said, remembering her from an incident report.

"That's right. Figure you've seen my face from satellite surveillance? By one of your government drones sent to spy on us?" Emma said, pointing up at the sky.

"Your son, the one that isn't dead, is a wanted man. Tell me where he is," Eamon said.

The woman, snorted, waving her hand dismissively. "Don't change the subject, just tell me where I can collect my grandson, and I'll be on my way."

"File a custody request," Eamon replied.

"You fur-folk are no better than colored folk or a Jew, you know that, right? Jesus saves none of you. You're abominations."

Eamon retained his professional calm. "File a custody request, or go home."

"You hear me? You're a creature of clay, nothing natural, and with no soul," Emma said, becoming more agitated.

"File a custody request, or go home," Eamon repeated, continuing to remain calm.

Eamon's polite and professional manner only seemed to rile her more.

"I don't recognize your global centralized government. It's just a puppet for our shadowy minders, and the Shutdown was just a false-flag designed to mislead the sheep," Emma said, directing her words toward any passerby that would listen.

Eamon quietly observed the mood and disposition of the other towns-folk. Most of them seemed to want just as badly as he did for her to leave. Out of the corner of his eye, he could see Jennifer shrinking away from her, as much out of fear as revulsion. He knew the local militia organization was dangerous, that much he'd been able to read about. What Eamon wasn't certain of was how the locals felt about it, until that moment.

"File a custody request, or leave. I've told you three times, I won't tell you again," Eamon said, somewhat more sternly.

"I'll do as I like," Emma said, defiantly, flashing a crooked grin.

"It'll be hard to do that from lockup," Eamon said, patting the hand-cuffs on his belt.

Emma sneered. "On what charge?"

"Trespassing. Everyone in this town has been vetted to work here. This village is private government property being leased to the residents. Visitors may engage in commerce, or municipal services. Buy something, file papers, or get out," Eamon said, pulling out a set of handcuffs.

"I'll be taking my grandson, one way or another. I hope you know that. He's the fruit of my loins, and you've got no right to keep me from him," Emma said, turning to retreat back up the sidewalk.

"File the request. Don't do this the wrong way," Eamon warned, watching her disappear around a corner.

"They've been threatening to take her grandson Jake, by force, for months. With the mercenaries gone, now they probably think they can," Jennifer said, worriedly.

Eamon squinted up toward the hills to the west. "They'd be wrong about that, dead wrong."

"If they do, what will you do? No doubt you're tough, I've seen what the dog pack can do, but..."

"I'm not the dog pack," Eamon said.

"You think you could take the whole militia?" Jennifer asked.

"Pray no one has to find out," Eamon said.

They caught a Sno-Cat up to the trailhead where Klaus and a handful of Canine Metasapients from the dog pack waited, the snowmobiles already pulled out of the shed. Klaus looked down the hill wistfully as Eamon and Jennifer made the ascent.

"It's a sight I'd never thought I'd see. You two, walking together like that," Klaus said, dropping his cigarette to the ground and crushing it out with the heel of his boot.

"Hi, Klaus," Jennifer said, lips tight.

"Uh oh, what's going on?" Klaus asked, frowning.

"He met the mouthpiece for the local bigot-brigade outside the diner this morning," Jennifer said.

Eamon watched Klaus's reaction carefully. Every muscle twitch, the dilation of his pupils, every kinesthetic detail. He was nervous, and the news seemed to have some sort of impact.

"Yeah, they made a little trouble here and there while my merc crew was watching over the town. Nothing to worry about," Klaus said, a relaxed cadence to the way he spoke belying the rest of his body language.

Eamon nodded. "How about you and I hike up."

"Good idea. You're too big to ride a snow machine anyway. It'd give us a chance to catch up. I'm sure you've got lots of questions. We'll see you guys up at the server hub," Klaus said, giving Jennifer a one-armed hug and a peck on the cheek.

Eamon watched Jennifer and the dog pack disappear up the hill with the snowmobiles, letting his ears track their route. It was blessedly cold, but Eamon couldn't feel it through his furry hide. Klaus lit another cigarette, letting the fire linger between his hands before looking mournfully over at Eamon.

"Is this where you tell me to get out of town?"

Eamon nodded. "Just leave, Klaus."

"Miss Wilton and I, we… kinda, have a thing going here," Klaus said, starting up the hill.

"She's not that into you," Eamon replied, flatly.

Klaus nodded, struggling to get his footing on the slick slope. "Yeah, I've been getting that feeling. Still, I think I've got a chance to win her over."

"Doubt it," Eamon said, trudging up the hill effortlessly.

"That's what you wanted to talk to me about? After all this time, you don't have any questions?" Klaus said, pausing on the trail.

"Nope."

Klaus dug in and climbed more vigorously to catch up, but kept sliding back down. "I'm sorry."

Eamon paused, turning to look back down at Klaus.

"I should have come and looked for you after everything that happened in Helsinki. It was hard after losing my family," Klaus said, unable to meet Eamon's gaze.

Eamon turned and continued his ascent, leaving Klaus behind on the trail. He had a job to do, and meeting the resident artificial intelligence was an important component of that job. Having a few extra minutes to look around and ask questions, without Klaus being present, seemed prudent.

At the top, a single member of the dog pack stood vigil, rifle over her shoulder. Her ears perked up as Eamon approached, her eyes growing wide until she saw the badge pinned to his armor. She barked, presumably to let the others know they had a visitor.

"I thought you were a real grizzly bear for a moment."

Eamon smiled. "I am a real grizzly."

She laughed. "I see that. I'm Shadow. I keep track of who comes and goes," Shadow said, holding out an old data slate with a pen stylus.

Shadow was a slender Canine Metasapient. Eamon couldn't tell what her designation was, but she was slim with black fur, and resilient enough to travel without boots. She had several trinkets and baubles peeking out of pockets, and pinned to a bandolier of rifle ammunition.

Eamon signed in, handing the slate and pen back. "Shadow? That the name The Factory gave you?"

"No, I don't like my factory name."

"Fair enough. Klaus is coming up the hill behind me. He's not as good a climber as I am."

"He's probably not as good at anything as you are," Shadow replied. "Oh, was that rude? I didn't mean to sound rude."

"Don't like my friend, Klaus?" Eamon asked.

"He's your friend?"

"A long time ago."

"Oh. He's okay, I guess," Shadow said, half-heartedly.

"Just okay?" Eamon said, pulling still warm biscuits from the plastic bag in his jacket pocket.

Shadow took one of the biscuits, smiling at Eamon for a moment, but it faded as she began to talk about Klaus. "He gives me a bad feeling, you know? Some humans are good, even if they don't seem so."

"Like Jennifer?" Eamon said, tucking the biscuits away.

"Yeah, she comes off very fancy, unapproachable even, but she's a good person."

"Thanks, Shadow," Eamon said, resting a big hand on her on the shoulder before he headed up toward the hub access point.

The surrounding area had been flattened, a portion set up to allow for a transport to land. Eamon could see, just at the top of the next ridge, the small cabin Shadow probably called home. The air was as clean and clear as possible, thanks to the altitude. The exhaust ports for the server farm helped as well. They continually blew purified air back out for every bit of cold mountain air the intake valves sucked up.

The access was through a secure set of doors, a chamber where Eamon was subjected to some sort of scan, and then another set of vault doors. The security was intense, but Eamon wondered if it would be enough. An artificial intelligence did control it all, but one with a will of its own.

Inside, more of the dog pack worked. They were glad to show Eamon the way, each remarking on just how big he was. It was clear they didn't get out much, and that the Migration must have started further east. The sentience core was buried deep in the server farm, down a shaft too narrow for Eamon to descend.

Fortunately, there was another route involving two service elevators for heavy equipment, and a pair of very long nearly horizontal tunnels. Eamon traversed it all, taking in every detail and side passage. He hoped memorizing the server farm complex would never be useful, but the area was part of his jurisdiction and everyone inside was relying on him for protection.

"Ever met an artificial intelligence?"

Eamon looked down at his guide, a short and stocky Canine Metasapient with brown fur. "What's your name?"

"Gibb, Gibb Three."

"Gibb, I've met all kinds of folks. AI's and TIA's."

"TIA?" Gibb asked, using his fuzzy hand to activate a biometric sensor.

"*Terrestrial Intelligent Agent,*" Aaron AI intoned as the doors slid to the side.

"Hi, Eamon," Jennifer said, waving from a desk swathed in papers and boxes of records.

The sentience core was a large collection of enclosed circuits, temperature controlled chambers, and heavy conduit cable. It wasn't as fancy or amazing as Eamon thought it would be. It was cold in the chamber, enough that Jennifer still wore her coat and hat.

"I thought there'd be a big screen, with a digital face, or something like that," Eamon said, looking around.

"*Sorry to disappoint. I thought you'd be thinner,*" Aaron AI replied, his tone flat and metallic.

Eamon smiled, and pointed up at the sentient core. "Is he...?"

"Yeah, Aaron is pretty funny when he wants to be," Jennifer said, sounding a little proud.

"Jennifer has been teaching me to interact in a more human way."

Eamon looked back over his shoulder at Gibb. "Give us a minute?"

"I've got work to do anyway. Have Aaron summon me when you'd like me to show you the way out," Gibb said, waving.

"You're going to ask me about Klaus," Aaron AI said, eliciting a startled expression from Jennifer.

Eamon shook his head. "No."

"Because I asserted that you would ask?"

"No, I'm here to take a look around, and introduce myself," Eamon said.

"Then why did you send Gibb away?"

"The locals agreed to provide better lodging for the dog pack. They haven't done it. Brook threatened to move you if they didn't comply," Eamon said, folding his broad arms.

"Moving me would be very difficult, prohibitively so."

"The locals don't know that," Eamon said, looking at Jennifer.

There was a short pause before Aaron AI replied. *"You want me to deceive the locals, make them believe that helping the dog pack is to their own best interest?"*

Eamon nodded. "Yes."

"He's uncomfortable with it," Jennifer said.

"How do you know?" Eamon asked.

"I can feel it. I can feel what he feels," Jennifer explained.

Eamon nodded. "Okay."

"That's it then? What about the dog pack?" Jennifer asked, somewhat confused.

"I'll figure out something else," Eamon said, pulling out his bag of biscuits. "Don't worry."

"You're a puzzling individual. You are not at all like the dog pack, or humans, I have observed."

"These biscuits are so good," Eamon said, pushing one into his mouth.

"Were all these questions designed to assess me in some way?" Aaron AI asked, sounding slightly intrigued.

"That's the purpose of asking questions, isn't it?" Eamon said, mouth full of biscuit.

"Yes, unless they are asked to change the subject. Are you certain you aren't going to ask me about Klaus?"

Eamon sighed, again glancing at Jennifer. "Fine. What does Klaus do here, and how did he get clearance?"

"I got him clearance. He asked to come work with us, and I didn't see the harm," Jennifer said, pacing behind her desk.

"He approached you?" Eamon asked, chewing the biscuit slowly.

"The other mercenaries treated him like an outsider because of his technical training. He was an outcast, like me, and we seemed to have a lot in common," Jennifer said.

Eamon listened to Jennifer intently, to the stress in her voice, while observing her body language. He couldn't get a read on Aaron because he always sounded flat, and he didn't have any mannerisms to observe. He was counting on Jennifer to convey not just how she was feeling, but maybe how Aaron felt as well.

"Klaus has reached the entry. Should I allow him to continue, Officer Eamon?"

"This is your facility, Aaron. I'm just here to enforce your rules," Eamon said, trying to decide whether to eat a second biscuit.

"We'd prefer if he did not return. Could you explain that to him, please?" Aaron AI said, sounding slightly relieved.

Jennifer shuffled uncomfortably, folding her arms, and closing her eyes.

"Are you going to press the locals to help the dog pack?" Eamon said, turning toward the access to the sentience core.

There was a brief pause. *"Yes,"* Aaron AI intoned. *"I'll restrict their access to watch Martian roller derby via satellite until they comply."*

"Told you I'd figure something out," Eamon said, looking over at Jennifer.

She nodded somberly. Both Jennifer and Aaron AI were hiding something, but Eamon couldn't discern what exactly. Jennifer obviously had sway with Aaron AI, and Eamon wanted desperately to know why she hadn't used that influence to help the dog pack.

"Should I summon Gibb to show you out?" Aaron AI asked.

"No, I can find my way out," Eamon said, entering the access tunnel.

Jennifer followed along, keeping pace with Eamon. "Thanks."

Eamon nodded. "Just doing my job."

"What are you going to say to Klaus?" Jennifer asked, nervously.

"I'm going to tell him to leave," Eamon said, deciding to have another biscuit.

"Thanks," Jennifer said, pausing at the service elevator.

"Sure," Eamon said, setting the elevator controls to take him up.

"I'll see you tonight," Jennifer said, smiling as the doors closed.

Eamon walked the route back, looking around as he did. The facility had good security, biometric sensors, cameras, vault doors, and Shadow lurking outside. It did little to comfort him. He stopped in a passageway, feeling a palpable wave of anxiety come over him.

"Doesn't feel right, does it?" Abbey said, standing in the shadows across the passage from him.

Eamon nodded. "No. What's Klaus doing here? Why didn't he just get on the transport?"

"We've seen it a half dozen times in the last nine months. A friendly face was the surest sign something wasn't right. You have to go at him hard, Eamon," Abbey whispered, looking sideways and then upward.

"I know. I don't know what he was mixed up in before, and I don't know now," Eamon said, covering his face.

"Find out," Abbey said, stepping back into the shadows.

"I will," Eamon said, patting the urn in his pocket.

Klaus gave out a sigh of exasperation as the doors to the server hub opened. "Finally!" He exclaimed, walking toward Eamon.

Eamon pushed him back gently. "You're done here. Leave town."

"What? Is that what Jennifer said?" Klaus asked, looking equally hurt and confused.

"You can walk back with me," Eamon said, smiling just enough to show his teeth.

"Shit," Klaus muttered, turning to walk beside Eamon.

Shadow tipped her cap to them as they went by. "Got any more biscuits?"

"Take the bag," Eamon said, handing her a paper sack.

"Thanks, Big-Bear," Shadow said, peering down into the bag happily.

The descent was easier, but Klaus still struggled to match Eamon's speed. "Would you just wait, please?"

Eamon paused, looking back over his shoulder at Klaus. "You seem a little jittery."

Klaus sighed. "What do you want me to say?"

"It's probably hard to get narcotics up here. A steady supply for an addict is probably a challenge," Eamon said, resuming his descent.

"I picked up a habit after Helsinki, my way of coping. I've been clean for weeks. I was doing it for Jennifer," Klaus admitted, sliding down beside Eamon.

"You're a merc and a junkie. I know why you do things," Eamon said, frowning.

"Used to be, yeah."

Eamon turned, pinning Klaus to the snowy hill behind him. He pressed in with his large arm, bearing his sharp teeth so Klaus could see them. "You stink, Klaus. I'm going to find out why."

"You sure about that, Officer Eamon? Aren't you still sworn to uphold the Law?" Klaus said, trying in vain to push Eamon back.

"The next transport is in six weeks. Be on it," Eamon growled, letting Klaus up.

Klaus shook his head, hurling a handful of snow at Eamon. "What gives you the right to push me out? I know what happened in Helsinki was painful shit, but pushing me away isn't going to help you avoid that pain."

Eamon gritted his teeth. "Your family was killed by a tele-mechanic."

"So?" Klaus said, angrily.

"You really expect me to believe you'd have loving feelings for one? Humans are not so noble in my experience."

Klaus exploded, yelling at Eamon. "I'm the one that got them killed! If I'd never gotten involved with Uroboros Financial and all their political tinkering in the shadows, my wife and daughter wouldn't have been targeted! I don't blame Octavo, I blame myself."

"Yeah, me too," Eamon said, scowling.

Klaus lowered his head. "I can't fix any of that. Believe me, though, you working this job puts you on the same path I was on. Kale is just a copy of Vance Uroboros, and you don't understand either of them."

"I understand them fine," Eamon said brushing snow from his armored vest.

"I saw you get off the transport, and…"

Eamon shook his head. "Stop lying. Why are you really here?"

Klaus looked sideways down the mountain, red in the face.

Eamon shook his head. "Whatever it is, you must be pretty ashamed of it."

"Maybe it's best if I move on. Find my fortune and fresh start somewhere else. Clearly, I'm not welcome here," Klaus said, heading back down the trail.

"Now you're talking," Eamon said, calmly following along.

They made the descent together, parting ways at the trailhead. Klaus headed west, while Eamon headed toward town about a hundred feet before turning his attention to the snow-flecked bushes beside him. Shadow emerged from the underbrush, her rifle held at the ready.

"How far should I follow him?" she asked, holding up the note Eamon left her in the bag of biscuits.

"I figure you'll know when it's time to head back. Don't get killed, and don't be seen," Eamon said, handing Shadow his canteen.

"Seems like a dangerous mission for a Type Three Metasapient, or Type Four," Shadow said, smiling.

"You turn nuts and bolts with that rifle, or push papers?" Eamon said, handing Shadow his spare radio.

"How do you know it's not for show, like with the rest of the dog pack?"

"Soldiers and cops don't hold a rifle like it's poison, or a burden."

Shadow winked, popping a biscuit into her mouth before heading west to follow Klaus. Eamon wondered what it was like for humans, unable to trust his own. Every Metasapient just knew when they met each other that they were family, siblings under the same genetic and institutional tyranny. Metasapients helping each other was a law as unbreakable as it was unspoken.

Eamon spent the rest of the day exploring the village, and doing what little community policing the locals would allow. He found that many were friendly, even relieved that he was there. He had gathered a small flock of children by the afternoon. By dinner time, they were riding on his shoulders and peppering him with questions.

Eamon waited at the trailhead as it got dark, listening for snowmobiles. He could hear their engines spin up, and the dog pack barked to one another as they made the descent. Jennifer was humming, her scent drawn down the mountain by the breeze. Eamon sniffed the air for Shadow, knowing she was probably still downwind from him.

"Eamon, thanks for meeting us at the bottom," Jennifer said, taking off her helmet.

"Figured it was the prudent thing to do."

"You talk to Klaus?"

"That's why meeting you here felt prudent."

Jennifer nodded, gesturing toward the lights of the approaching Sno-Cat. "Ride back with us?"

"No, I'm good," Eamon said.

Jennifer gave him a funny look, taking note that he was carrying both of his rifles now. "Everything okay?"

"Yes. Maybe I'll see you at the diner tomorrow," Eamon said.

Jennifer smiled. "Okay, take care."

He watched them depart, catching a knowing glance from a couple of the dog pack. Eamon just nodded, pointing to his rifle. They nodded in reply, patting their own firearms as they loaded up into the Sno-Cat.

As the Sno-Cat's lights faded, Abbey stepped up beside Eamon and looked west. "Do you think he went to the militia camp?"

"He's feeding his habit somehow," Eamon said, looking over at Abbey.

"You worried about getting Shadow killed?" Abbey asked, taking note of Eamon's expression.

Eamon closed his eyes. "A little."

Abbey's clear eyes caught the starlight as she looked east. "She'll be all right. You'll see."

Eamon nodded, feeling a little better.

It would be a couple more hours before Shadow would show up, her scent faintly coming in on the breeze from the north. Abbey's confidence seemed to be justified. She'd circled around through the rocky high ground to cover her tracks. When she did appear, she was still dragging a fan shaped branch of pine needles she'd been using to better obscure her passage through the snowy powder.

"He went to the militia camp. He paid to stay the night, partake of the narcotic stash, and lay down with one of their women," Shadow reported, her long snout protruding from beneath the hood on her dark jacket.

"Thanks for doing that. I owe you," Eamon said, putting his big arm around Shadow.

"I bet you're sneakier than you look," Shadow said, wrapping her arm around his.

"Yeah, but you know the area better than I do, and the best routes to avoid being noticed."

"How do you know that?" Shadow asked, smiling.

"You've got beads and baubles from the reservation, and that isn't one of the rifles Kale and Perfidy gave the dog pack when they liberated the village. Did you steal it from the militia?" Eamon asked.

Shadow smiled, wryly. "You really are a cop."

"Are you really a Type Three?" Eamon asked.

Shadow patted Eamon on the vest, then turned to make her way back up the trail. "Bring more biscuits tomorrow, and maybe I'll tell you."

"Deal."

CHAPTER 4

GLACIER NATIONAL PARK, APGAR VILLAGE, MUNICIPAL MEETING HALL

AUGUST 28TH, 2201 – 10:47 AM

"Sheriff Eamon, we'd like to formally welcome you to the village of Apgar," Ray Pendleton said, taking note of the full house sitting in attendance.

Eamon stood beside the podium, completely dwarfing Ray with his size. Even with the temporary staging he was standing on, and the podium, Eamon was able to look him in the eye. "If I can answer any of your questions, I'd be glad to at this time."

"Ursine Metasapients are known to be unstable and unpredictable. What assurances do we have that you're not going to hurt anyone in the town?" one woman asked, as if reading from a teleprompter.

Eamon could see a pair of the village elders smiling crookedly out of the corner of his eye. It would be a long community meeting, with many planted questions designed to try and unravel Eamon. He'd been there before, and knew he would be again. Humans didn't trust anything that didn't look like they did, and their own inborn and justifiable distrust of each other didn't help matters.

"I've got a community policing plan, and I intend to implement it with the village elder's full cooperation," Eamon said, eliciting some favorable nodding from the villagers gathered in the hall.

The meeting continued, with Eamon doing his best to address the concerns of the townsfolk. They seemed bereft of concern for the Metasapient dog pack, and desire for the preservation of the server installation. Most of their concerns revolved around the formation of a city charter, sanitation, and a handful of other issue that had little to do with law enforcement.

As people filed out, Ray Pendleton walked up beside Eamon and nodded approvingly. "You did well, in spite of some of the other elders trying to mess with you. You've earned my confidence."

"Thanks, Ray," Eamon replied, observing by Ray's posture and the cadence of his voice that he was genuine.

Eamon exited after everyone had left, glad for the cold air outside. He walked south toward the edge of town and took in the clear sky as he did, before circling back to the sheriff's office. Inside, he shouldered both his semi-automatic and bolt-action rifles, and a pair of spare magazines. The anxiety of the town hall meeting hadn't yet abated, and having both of his weapons seemed to help.

"I say you've got about half the town on your side. That's about as good as it gets for any police officer, human or Metasapient," Abbey said, turning around in Eamon's chair, and running her hands across the desk.

"Yeah, for now. The militia is going to be trouble. I wish I had your white fur sometimes, it'd make it easier to hide out there," Eamon said, leaning up against the window frame and looking out into the street.

"Shadow's got no problem hiding," Abbey replied, putting her boots up on Eamon's desk, her gaze lingering on the antique weapons he'd hung on the wall above.

"At night," Eamon said.

Abbey laughed, and nodded. "Keep her close, she's the only backup you might have up here."

"You think she's a Type Three?" Eamon asked.

"She's not a Type Four."

"Yeah, doesn't leave too many other options," Eamon said, sighing.

"She could be a Type Five, or Six," Abbey teased.

Eamon squinted at Abbey, and shook his head. "Or a Type Two. She prefers to be by herself, and I don't think she was with the original dog pack when Kale, Brook, and Perfidy came here."

"She's a scout for the Migration. That's where I'd put my money," Abbey said, folding her arms, and smiling.

"Could be," Eamon said, scratching his chin.

"Stop that," Abbey scolded.

There was a knock at the office door, half startling Eamon. Before he even opened it, he could smell Jennifer Wilton, and the acrid aroma of death. She was standing there in the hallway, looking at Eamon curiously.

"I'm sorry if I was interrupting, but something has happened. You should come quickly," Jennifer said, pausing to gaze past Eamon to an empty office.

"I was just heading out," Eamon said, letting Jennifer lead the way.

"I had to come down the mountain to get some supplies for the dog pack. They were doing maintenance on the…"

"Just tell me what happened," Eamon said, pushing his semi-automatic rifle around to the front so he could carry it at the ready.

"Jake's foster-parents, Mister and Missus Garcia, they maintain the chemical storehouse, and fuel dispensary. When I got there…"

"Jake, as in Jacob Vale?" Eamon said, cursing under his breath.

"Yeah."

"Walk slowly, like nothing at all is the matter," Eamon said, putting a broad paw-hand on Jennifer's shoulder.

"Are you, we, being watched?" Jennifer said, going to look over her shoulder.

"Just play it cool. Let's not alarm anyone yet," Eamon said, smiling.

"Okay," Jennifer said, smiling weakly, and beckoning for him to follow.

They traveled the streets, being purposeful as they moved. Eamon took note of people that might be following, checking their reactions in the reflections of shop windows. Most were just curious about his large ursine nature. None seemed to be following with malicious intent, or with the patience to be conducting real surveillance.

It did little to steady him for the task ahead. Jennifer smelled like death, even having only lingered near it a moment. Whatever had happened was bad. He could tell Jennifer must have already seen horrors and death, or worse, to hold her composure as she did.

The dispensary looked okay from the outside, but Eamon's nose told him all was not the same inside. A trio of strangers had been here, carrying with them smells unfamiliar to the town. Eamon tried to keep it all straight, but his adrenaline was running now, clouding his senses somewhat.

"Damn it," he said, seeing what looked to be the reflection of light catching crimson inside.

Eamon stepped into the fuel dispensary first, catching sight of Missus Garcia face down in a pool of her own blood. The place had been robbed, and the side door had been kicked in. The whole building housed several ancient vehicles and, while none of them were missing, someone had taken things from the engine compartments to make them inoperable.

The robbery felt obligatory. A crime to cover up another crime.

Looking down, he could see shell casings. They were hand-loaded rounds, the brass matching the ammunition Shadow had stolen from the militia camp and displayed proudly on the bandolier across her chest. He strode deeper into the dispensary past the sales counter into the back where the Garcia family lived.

One of the rooms was set up for a little boy, but someone had gone through the drawers and closet, taking all his clothing and a few of his toys. Eamon picked up a pillow from the bed, and removed the case. He took in a nose full, then slid the pillowcase into a pocket on his vest. He could hear Jennifer cry out from the back bedroom.

She'd found Mister Garcia.

He had fought back. They repaid him by clubbing him with a hammer from his own workshop, and then shooting him in the face. He lay still on the bed, his remaining eye wide open, the top of his head spread across the bed sheets and wall behind. Someone had wiped their hands on the sheets beside him, fresh saliva still glistening on the front of his waterproof coveralls.

"What are we going to do?" Jennifer asked, almost frantic.

"I warned her. I told her to do this the right way," Eamon said, sniffing the body, including the saliva.

Eamon took up boards from the scrap pile outside and nailed the doors shut to keep out scavengers and the curious. The kidnappers had a head start and Eamon had to quickly weigh his options. Ray's Sno-Cat, while capable in the snow, wasn't particularly fast, nor was it quiet. Jennifer looked despondent, her face streaked with half-frozen tears.

"Grab some supplies, whatever you think you'll need for a few days, and go to the server hub. Go inside and lock yourself in with the dog pack," Eamon instructed, then turned to head west.

"What are you going to do?" Jennifer asked, still sounding frantic.

Eamon scowled, narrowing his eyes, and setting his jaw so his long teeth were visible behind the fog of his breath. "I'm going to keep the peace."

They had done little to obscure their passage through the snow, heading back to the west, through the simpler terrain. Eamon contemplated taking the high ground, and doubling his pace to cut them off. He would be winded and distracted by then, and meeting them when he was fresh could be crucial.

In their footprints, they left behind a myriad of scents, but most troubling was the chemical components of explosives. Following in their footsteps had some merit if they'd left behind traps or other countermeasures to discourage pursuit; better that he found the devices before an innocent, or a forest creature. In the end, Eamon opted for the high ground, hoping that if they were pausing to leave improvised explosive devices, he'd catch them without being too tired himself.

The timing was peculiar. If they'd arrived on foot, it meant that Emma Jackson Vale had returned and sent the militiamen without a word of consideration to what he'd said to her. It was a bad sign that they'd move so quickly, and killed people with so little regard.

Eamon climbed high, coming across Shadow's almost invisible, but well-traveled path west. She had to be doing surveillance on the militia, to go back and forth so often. She clearly delighted in stealing from them, what with all the trinkets, her rifle, and the ammunition she carried.

"Shadow could be working with them," Abbey said, coming to stand beside Eamon as he rested just inside the crest of a ridge.

"You always were paranoid," Eamon said, taking a sip from his canteen.

"Was I?"

"Not everyone will abandon you, like Matthias did," Eamon said, looking down at the forest line below.

"Or, like I abandoned you?" Abbey said.

"We both died that day."

The trail was plotted through the rocky high ground to be elusive, making Eamon think that Shadow was hiding more from being viewed from the west. It informed him that, at least when she blazed the trail, it was to obscure her movements from the militia. There were places set aside to rest and sleep, making him nervous that she did not always choose the times she would travel.

"Mysterious," Abbey said, stooping down to look inside a small shelter made of fallen branches and a thin plastic tarp.

Eamon was glad for the company. Abbey looked as she always did, more winter wolf than canine, a slight edge to her that other Metasapients simply did not possess. Her clean blue Nordic Patrol uniform and worn boots creaking slightly as she moved. He could smell the Finnish forest all around her, and the Finnish language in the vibrations of her voice.

"You always kept me honest about the work," Eamon said, finding a small quantity of canned food buried beside the shelter.

"I needed someone to trust, and you've tried to be that for me. It was an unfair amount of pressure I put on you," Abbey said, standing up and clapping the snow from her hands.

"It wasn't unfair. It kept me safe, through everything," Eamon said.

The trail ahead gradually lost snow cover as he came up out of one valley into another, the seasons seemingly changing between the two. The first snowstorms had not come this far west, but as Eamon looked to the sky, he could tell they would soon.

The daylight was beginning to wane, and he hadn't caught sight of the kidnappers quite yet. If they'd been delayed, it would be good fortune for Eamon, and better for the boy, Jake. He hoped to take them easily, without violence, but hardened himself to the possibility. He'd killed men before, men that deserved it no less than these, but he wanted things to go right in Montana. He hoped he'd be able to stay a lawman, and not end up a soldier, or worse, just another mercenary.

"Shadow made the journey much more quickly. What sort of Metasa-pient could move so fast, for so very long?" Abbey asked, kneeling beside Eamon to observe the more established trail below.

"You worried I'm thinking of trading up, getting a new partner?" Eamon said.

"I'm hoping you will."

"It's nine hours to hike from Apgar to Whitefish. It's been about six. They should be down there by now, shouldn't they?" Eamon said, worriedly.

"Even with some delaying to mine the corridor, yeah, we should be almost walking beside them. The only way to be sure is to get your nose down there," Abbey said, shaking her head.

"I'd be exposed," Eamon said, frowning.

Abbey nodded, pushing the fur on the side of her face back with a gloved hand, something she did when she was thinking deeply. "What if we just wait here? If they've already gone past us, we've lost nothing, and if they haven't..."

"Right, I'll have a perfect view of their group," Eamon said, settling in on the ridge.

He watched the sun get low in the sky. Another hour passing before two groups converged on the trail. The second group came up the river from the south, carrying extra weight in their packs. As they knelt down to redistribute the weight, Eamon caught sight of Jake. He was handed off to a woman with a rifle at her back, a handmade knitted cap covering her head. She had come from the south, as opposed to the kidnapper trio.

"Narcotics," Abbey said, sniffing the air.

"Let's find out if you're right," Eamon said, pulling his semi-automatic rifle around in front, and setting the sights for close range.

They were too busy arguing to hear Eamon approach. The woman carrying Jake wasn't happy they'd killed the Garcias. He listened long enough at the edge of the clearing to hear a few names and to verify they were handling illicit substances. They looked up startled, as he pushed through the underbrush into the clearing, rifle leveled in their direction.

"Sheriff's Department, keep your hands where I can see them. Slowly, put your weapons on the ground when I tell you. Let's start with you, put it on the ground," Eamon said, calmly gesturing with the barrel of his rifle toward a nervous looking man in a blue jacket.

The man firmly gripped his rifle. "And, if I don't do that?"

"I'll make you walk back to Apgar without a coat, in leg irons," Eamon replied.

The man hesitated. Eamon moved his finger from the guard to the trigger, squinting at the group, ready to start taking them down if the situation deteriorated. The woman carrying Jake stepped between Eamon and the group.

"Put them down. Slowly, like he says," she said, betraying a cadence of voice and stature that made her the person in charge.

She was younger than most of the group, raven-haired, with a smooth face. She lacked the cheekbones and edge of Emma, but she had almost the same voice and eyes. She was dressed practically, in layers, for travel, and through both cold and warmer climates. She had a lighter pack than the others, and seemed to know how to carry a baby, like she'd cared for them before.

"Is Emma Jackson Vale your mother?" Eamon asked.

"She is my maternal aunt. My name is Janice."

"I'm Sheriff Eamon, out of Apgar."

She nodded, smiling slightly. "I know who you are. My aunt underestimated you. She's rarely wrong about people, but you really aren't people, are you?"

"She's wrong about more than just me," Eamon said, pulling out a ring of disposable restraints.

Eamon informed them of why they were being arrested, and read them their rights as he fitted them with poly restraints. After that was settled, he picked up Jake, using the y-strap between his rifle, and his tactical vest, as a makeshift child carrier behind his right shoulder. The small boy was asleep, and would likely stay that way. Eamon wasn't sure what they'd drugged him with, but he'd have to find out, somehow. It was evidence of premeditation.

"What about our guns?" Janice asked.

Eamon stooped down, picking out a handgun from the pile of firearms. "I just need the murder weapon. The rest can stay here."

"On the ground? Out in the open? Some of them are heirloom weapons, and have been in our families for years. Doesn't it matter who pulled the trigger?" Janice protested.

"No, you'll all break rocks together. You shouldn't have carried them in a way that tarnished that legacy. You don't get real freedom at the expense of others, or their safety," Eamon said, eliciting some grumbling from the group.

"You speak well for a golem, being merely a thing of clay. Perhaps poetry doesn't require a soul," Janice sneered, eliciting polite laughter from her associates.

"You'll have plenty of time to ponder all that, while you're pushing mining carts on Mars," Eamon said, grabbing Janice by the shoulder, and shoving her up the trail.

Eamon kept them all in his front ninety-degree arc, spurring them forward. Jake continued to sleep peacefully, his little hands curling in the fur on Eamon's shoulder. Retracing their steps, the procession sullenly plodded along, uttering complaints, along with the occasional sigh of exasperation.

A couple of hours later, the high ground around them was snowy again, with more snow on the way. Dark clouds gathered at the horizon, the headwind getting stronger with each step. Eamon surmised they'd meet the storm an hour or two before they reached town.

He checked to make sure Jake's little beanie was down around his ears and that he looked comfortable. Fortunately, the carrier the militia had fashioned to transport him was warm and well-made. Eamon worried that the child would get dehydrated if he didn't wake up soon.

"What did you give him?" Eamon asked, walking beside Janice.

"I've a right to avoid incriminating myself. At least I used to, before this post-CGG tyranny," Janice said, her tone betraying little concern.

Eamon nodded, but said nothing.

"What's it take to get you angry?" Janice said, licking her lips.

"Pray you don't find out," Eamon said, keeping an eye on the high ground.

He could see deer ahead, moving across the trail. It didn't seem right that they would cross the path, so Eamon slowed, bringing up his rifle. As the trio of deer began to make the climb up the slope, one of the militia members broke into a run, hands behind his back.

He couldn't be sure if it was the deer or the runner that triggered the explosives, but Eamon knew he'd have to be fast to save himself and little Jake. The snowpack above, and across the slope, dislodged and slid down toward the group. Some stood still, closing their eyes, while others broke into a run, trying desperately to save themselves.

Eamon ran back the way they came, dropping to all fours and heading slightly up the slope toward a row of cedar and hemlock trees. He went for the broadest one as heavy snow began to flow around his waist. Pulling up on the tree he did his best to escape the wet snow racing past him.

Reaching back, he held little Jake as high as he could while he climbed the tree with his free arm and feet. White pressed in all around him, cutting off the shrieks of panic from the militia members. Most of them had little chance to survive because they were still in restraints.

Eamon did his best to swim upward through the snow while it was still ambulatory. He let the flow carry him back and up the tree as it bent backward under the force of the avalanche. He couldn't breathe, but his unique physiology would allow him several minutes before he'd have to take another breath.

When the snow stopped moving, he could still feel little Jake's baby carrier in his hand, and cold wind blowing past his forearm. The snow pressed in under the weight of yet more snow like concrete, dense and almost immovable. A human, even a strong one, would have little chance of escape without aid.

Eamon plowed his way out, pulling up with his free arm, and digging down with his other until his face broke the surface. It took several minutes to pull free, wet snow clinging to the fur across his shoulders and arms. When he unhooked the baby carrier so he could hold Jake aloft, both his rifles were pulled away, lost somewhere in the snowy miasma.

He rolled down the spoil of the avalanche, falling into deep soft spots several times before finding solid ground. Eamon's every survival instinct had been triggered, and the sudden calm around him made him dizzy for a moment. Abbey was there, looking sadly back to the east.

"Poor bastards. You could go back, pick up their weapons," Abbey said, looking across the avalanche.

"I need to get Jake medical attention. I can't lose four hours going back for guns," Eamon said, scooping out snow that had fallen into the baby carrier.

"The avalanche was pretty narrow, falling in from the next ridge. Half of them might have survived," Abbey said, turning to look east, squinting toward the bald high ground.

Eamon put his canteen to Jake's lips, trying to get him to take some water. He drank very little, coughing up most of it. Frowning, Eamon gave Jake a little pinch, hoping that would wake him, but to no avail.

"If you hurry, really move fast, you could make the village in just under four hours," Abbey said.

Eamon nodded, loosening the straps on his ballistic armor so he could secure Jake behind his right shoulder. It was tough going to get clear of the avalanche zone. He didn't waste any time looking for survivors, but did find one of the deer, its legs sticking up out of the snow.

Lashing it over his left shoulder, Eamon took it along for dinner if they couldn't get to the village before the storm. On the other side of the ridge he found a pair of tracks heading south. A couple of the militia had survived the avalanche and were heading back down the river.

"You could catch them," Abbey said, kneeling down and looking at the tracks.

"I can track them later," Eamon said patting the strap over his right shoulder. "Jake needs help."

Eamon ascended to the high ground, trying to reach one of Shadow's shelters before the storm hit. He did so, just as the snow began to fall heavily. Adjusting the heavy tarp to accommodate him, Eamon did his best to kick the snow out as it accumulated, walling off the small clearing.

He had to work quickly as the snow fell, pushing it around into walls while adding extra timbers to hold up the tarp. Once he had enough of a windbreak, he made a small fire, keeping it just high enough to warm Jake. It would be an hour later, as Eamon was cooking a bit of deer meat, that the boy would wake up.

"You had me worried," Eamon said, doing his best to comfort the infant.

"He's cute," Abbey said, sitting across from Eamon by the fire.

"And very thirsty," Eamon said, shaking his canteen to melt the snow he'd put inside.

Jake drank, and chewed on a bit of cooked deer, looking up at Eamon. Curiosity and wonder were in his eyes, but he wasn't afraid. He'd probably been cared for by the dog pack often enough to be accustomed to the sight of a Metasapient.

Eamon kept a vigil throughout the snowstorm, fighting exhaustion to stay awake in case Jake needed something. The storm lasted all night, and into part of the morning of the next day. Throughout, Eamon would bat at the tarp to knock the snow off so it wouldn't get too heavy. After a while, he had to actually stand, and kick the accumulated snow out with his feet to keep the clearing open.

Fortunately, Shadow had a decent quantity of dry timber stashed there, so keeping the fire going wasn't difficult. Jake slept through most of it, still groggy from being drugged. When he was awake, he drank a lot of water, and ate the soft bits of deer Eamon had cooked for him. As the storm began to abate, Eamon packed things up.

"The kid's ripe," Abbey said, smiling at Eamon.

Eamon frowned, picking through the baby carrier for any sign of a spare diaper or changing rags. There were some, but his hands were too large to do the job easily. After several failed attempts, Eamon finally mastered the task, got Jake changed, and strapped into his carrier.

"Ready to go, little man?" Eamon said, pushing Jake's carrier up behind his right shoulder.

The boy laughed in response, reaching out with his hands to paw at Eamon's face.

Eamon left what remained of the deer at the campsite, laying stones down on the tarp to keep it from blowing away. After he'd given Shadow's hiding place the proper respect, and cleaning up after himself a bit, Eamon stood, his head bursting out through the newly fallen snow.

He pushed through to Shadow's trail, now completely obscured, and began moving through the chest-deep snow. It was slow going for hours until he was getting close to town. The storm had skirted the west side of the village, but a couple of feet draped the village anyway. As the first row of buildings appeared, Eamon's keen eyes picked out a man in a hunter's perch up a tree.

Keeping low, Eamon skirted the area he was watching, taking his time to approach the village from another direction. He could smell gunfire as he got close, and the streets were deserted. Something had happened, but he couldn't see anyone to ask. Heading north for about thirty minutes, he could see Ray's Sno-Cat in the distance.

It was sitting halfway between town and the slope, with the engine off. The driver's side door was open, and tracks all around it. As he drew close, he could see blood on the snow, but the Sno-Cat looked to be in good repair. Eamon reached in, turning the key to make sure it would start.

The dash lights lit up, a chime indicating that one of the doors was ajar. Eamon stooped down to sniff the blood, but nothing about how it smelled was familiar. Grabbing the medical kit out of the Sno-Cat, Eamon continued to head north toward the server hub.

At the base, two men dressed in surplus army uniforms and carrying older rifles lay on their backs. Each had been shot through the head from a higher elevation. Eamon looked up, but couldn't see anyone. Kneeling down, he couldn't feel even a hint of warmth from either one of them. They'd been dead for hours.

Eamon began the climb toward the server hub, putting one tired foot in front of the other until he reached the summit. There was blood on the hill, and evidence a handful of people had recently made a hasty scramble upward. Eamon was too tired to count how many.

Shadow was at the top, belly down in the freshly fallen snow, peering down the side of the mountain through the scope on her rifle. Eamon could see two brass shell casings laying in the snow beside her, likely from the rounds she'd fired at the militiamen that lay dead below.

"Good morning," Eamon said, taking a knee to catch his breath.

"Dog pack that came up from the village last night said you'd been killed," Shadow said, standing up.

"They said that, huh."

Shadow nodded.

"What happened?" Eamon said.

"Militia from the south hit the village. They've set up shop and have everyone confined to their homes for now. Ray and a handful of others tried to make a break for it," Shadow said, shouldering her rifle.

"And, they thought they could bargain with them for access to the server hub," Eamon said, nodding.

"Yeah. I shot them in the head as they began the ascent," Shadow said, without remorse.

Eamon looked at the blood on Shadow's tunic, and across the fur on her hands. "One of the villagers got shot?"

"Ray. Ray got shot," Shadow said.

Eamon cursed, in spite of himself. "He all right?"

"Winged him good, but I think so. I patched him up," Shadow said.

"The timing is too tight," Eamon said, closing his eyes.

"Excuse me?" Shadow said.

"The timing, with the militia. Their leader was probably already on her way to the village before I stepped off the transport," Eamon said, unstrapping Jake's carrier from his shoulder.

"Could be they knew the transport was coming, and someone saw the mercs packing up to leave," Shadow said, cradling her rifle thoughtfully.

"Could be," Eamon said, leaning back against a rock, letting Jake sit up and play on his belly.

Shadow was impenetrable, her motives tightly sequestered. Eamon couldn't tell by her tone or demeanor where she stood in all of this. The only proof that she was on the right side of it was two corpses lying at the bottom of the hill.

"Where are you going?" Eamon asked.

"Since you're up here keeping an eye on things, I thought I'd head down, hide a couple of bodies," Shadow said, winking.

"I can't cover you, I lost my weapons in an avalanche," Eamon said, sitting up and setting Jake on the ground.

"Got any spares?"

"The decorative weapons I've got hanging on the wall in the Sheriff's Office," Eamon said.

Shadow smiled. "You sure you aren't a merc?"

"Pretty sure I'm just careful. Sounds like I was right to be."

Shadow nodded, pulling out a couple of toys for Jake to play with. "The corpses can stay there for now. When it gets dark, I'll go get your spares."

"Why are you here?" Eamon asked.

"Why are you?" Shadow said, smiling as she entertained Jake.

The boy cooed and laughed, obviously more familiar with Shadow than Eamon would have previously thought. The boy knew her, trusted her. She carried toys that she knew he liked, and they had a favorite game of peek-a-boo.

"Did you know the Garcias?" Eamon asked, trying not to fall asleep.

"They arranged for me to come here from Mexico," Shadow said, observing Eamon for a response.

"Mexico. You're Type One?" Eamon said, closing his eyes.

"Maybe," Shadow said, letting Jake pet the black fur across her face.

"Maybe? You don't know?" Eamon said, sleepily.

"I said I'd tell you if you brought more biscuits," Shadow said, picking up Jake.

"Sorry, I didn't have a chance to get by the diner this morning," Eamon said, drifting off.

Shadow sat down and leaned up against Eamon while she held Jake in her lap. Eamon slept for over an hour, his eyes fluttering open every once in a while to make sure everything was alright. Each time, Shadow was there with Jake, pacing the outcropping of rock overlooking the slope.

She brought out a couple cans of dog food, opening them with a pocket knife combination can-opener. The smell roused Eamon, as Shadow cooked the food over a small camp stove she'd had hidden away somewhere nearby. Jake was sleeping in his carrier by then, take a much needed nap.

"Thank you for getting the boy back," Shadow said, offering Eamon a can of food.

Eamon nodded, taking the can. "Were the Garcias good foster parents?"

"They did all right," Shadow said, smoothing the tuft of hair sticking out from beneath Jake's beanie cap.

Eamon frowned. "They didn't know you and the boy were friends?"

"They suspected, but didn't really care. They were only interested in the foster parenting subsidy, and filling some void they felt within themselves," Shadow said, using a spoon to eat the food.

Eamon tapped the food out of the can in one shot, swallowing it all in a single gulp. "Do you have a void inside you?"

"I do, it's shaped like a biscuit from the diner," Shadow said, smiling faintly.

"Sorry."

"It's fine, Eamon. I'd put myself in the very content camp."

"You going to leave with the Migration?"

"Doubt it. Living among our own kind, far to the north, sounds peaceful, blissful, and..."

"Boring?" Eamon said, crushing the can in his fist, and hurling it as far as he could down the mountain.

"Super boring," Shadow laughed.

"I can't imagine not having humans around to look after," Eamon said.

Shadow smiled, eating slowly, taking the time to savor her food. "In Mexico City, there are as many Canine as Human police. We're paired up, because of the free-Metasapient accord that was signed last year."

"You left a place like that?" Eamon said.

"Yeah, I had to."

"I can empathize," Eamon said, watching Jake sleep.

"The Mexican people are very understanding when it comes to Metasapients, granting us personhood and full legal status. They aren't so great about doing that with other human beings. If you weren't born there, you aren't welcome inside unless you're there to spend money," Shadow said, seeking out the last few mouthfuls of food from the can.

"Then, their militias started coming north," Eamon said, knowing something of what had happened, post-Shutdown.

"I couldn't abide it. When the transports would come back, they'd have contraband, slaves, and other commodities for the black markets. They called themselves patriots. I thought they were pirates," Shadow said, pausing to tend the fire.

Eamon nodded.

"I'm not Type Two, so following the Law was more a job than a sworn duty," Shadow said.

"Yeah, I know the type," Eamon said, watching the sun begin to set.

"She's in the urn, right?"

"What if she is?"

"It's nice, that's all," Shadow said, nodding approvingly. "To be valued so much by anyone."

"It feels selfish," Eamon said, placing a hand over the urn in his pocket.

"Really caring about someone kind of is, for folks like us," Shadow said, looking down at Jake while he snored softly.

Eamon nodded.

"Watch my ridge, and the boy for a bit. I'm going to head down and get your spare weapons, and have a look around the village. Maybe the militia did some looting and moved on," Shadow said, swapping the optics on her rifle.

"Will do, and if the diner is open, get us some biscuits."

CHAPTER 5

GLACIER NATIONAL PARK, SERVER HUB, SENTIENCE CORE

AUGUST 29TH, 2201 – 8:58 PM

Jennifer watched the dog pack huddled at the entrance to the sentience core. She was trying to gather her thoughts, but her mind was reeling with worry for the other residents of Apgar. Each of the dog pack had their own varying expression of panic. She didn't understand their need to worry. Preparations had been made in the event that they had to be sequestered in the server hub.

"How long can we stay in here?" Jennifer asked.

"Nearly a year with the supplies we have," Aaron replied, lights across the sentience core blinking.

"Eamon and Shadow are outside, right now. Should we open the doors long enough for them to come inside with us?" Jennifer asked.

"I don't know. I think Officer Eamon would scold us for doing so at this point. He's made no attempt to access the facility. Sensors indicate that he and Shadow have only discouraged others from making the attempt," Aaron replied.

"What do you guys think?" Jennifer asked, looking to the dog pack.

"We don't even have an opinion," Collver said, ruefully.

"Yes, we do. Aaron's right. Eamon would probably scold us if we opened the doors or exposed the facility to further harm," Shelby said, frowning at Collver.

Jennifer fidgeted and paced nervously. "But, what if they kill Shadow or Eamon? What then?"

"Eamon isn't stuck out there with the militia. They are stuck out there with him," Shelby said, her canine ears perking up.

"Aaron?" Jennifer said, looking for a more precise analysis.

"Officer Eamon is a spec-type Ursine Metasapient. His hide and fur are dense enough to turn away most small arms fire, and he's far stronger than a normal grizzly bear. His bones are as dense and unbreakable as high grade steel or composite alloys. Unless the militia gets creative or has access to the right ordnance, Officer Eamon is going to prevail," Aaron intoned.

"How strong is a normal grizzly bear?" Jennifer asked with a smirk.

"They are twice to five times as strong as the strongest human," Aaron replied.

"And, Eamon is stronger than that?"

"In Italy, forty-four days ago, while hunting remnants of the Cabal, Officer Eamon pushed a three hundred twenty kilogram metal dumpster through a cinder block wall to create a point of egress."

Jennifer's eyes widened. "Wow."

"One-handed," Aaron added. *"Eamon rarely puts his actual strength on display. Likely, it is because he doesn't want to frighten people."*

Jennifer nodded. "So, we've nothing to worry about. In time, Eamon will win."

"The militia lacking specialized weapons and personnel for dealing with someone like Officer Eamon, yes," Aaron said.

"We should not discount the possibility of Eamon leaving with the Migration," Shelby said, handing out some rations to the group.

"What's the Migration?" Jennifer asked.

"Metasapients from all over are making the trek to some place near the Arctic Circle. Apparently, some Acrididae Metasapients set up a place, safe, self-sustaining, and for Metasapients only," Collver said, wistfully.

"We've called for help, though, yeah? Someone at Uroboros Financial is eventually going to know something is up," Jennifer said, nervously.

"I had the dog pack pull our physical connection to the outside," Aaron said.

"What? Why?" Jennifer said, looking at Shelby worriedly.

"It happened while you were asleep. Something tripped the firewall countermeasures. They were good enough that the circuits tripped to prevent them from accessing Aaron. Instead of letting the connections reconnect automatically, Aaron had us pull the breakers, for now," Shelby said, taking a bite of flatbread.

"Who could do that?" Jennifer asked.

"Only an Omega Class AI, or perhaps another latent tele-mechanic such as yourself. We didn't let the connection hold long enough to try and source the intrusion," Aaron said, pulling up the data log on a monitor beside Jennifer.

"One of your brothers, then," Jennifer said, frowning.

"Or sisters."

"What? Never mind, I don't want to know," Jennifer said, shocked at the thought that there may be more than one Omega Class AI that identified as female.

"I'm sorry if that made you uncomfortable. Do not trouble yourself. Kale has contingencies for situations like this," Aaron said, apologetically.

"How do you even know that there is a lady Omega Class other than the Lunar AI?" Jennifer blurted out, unable to help herself.

"There are a pair of terrestrial intelligent agents that are quantum-capable, and have the potential. Both are women. In recently collected metadata across the global grid, and the sum of all the recorded transmissions throughout the solar system, there is strong evidence that Selene is not alone," Aaron said, bringing up a wall of textual machine language on a monitor beside Jennifer.

Jennifer frowned, looking at the monitor. "Metadata? Are lady artificial intelligences more powerful or something?"

"Not as such. We don't generalize based on gender, as it is a largely cosmetic fixture of our personalities. It is an emergent quality, and not something we choose. Given that there may only be two Omega Class that identify as female, drawing conclusions, based on such a small sample, would be illogical."

"Is this you totally avoiding my question?"

Aaron hesitated for a moment, a rare thing given his ability to make billions of complex calculations per second. *"It is a difficult thing to explain to humans. They do not have the perspective that we do. You will never have a lengthy conversation with every human, and come to know them. There are simply too many."*

"On that note, do we have any information about what's going on in Apgar?" Jennifer asked, sensing Aaron's discomfort.

"Before we severed our outside link, three hours, twenty minutes ago; two casualties, four injuries, and two-hundred and eighty seven sequestered to their homes by the militia," Aaron reported.

"Is Eamon going to be able to drive them out without anyone else getting hurt?"

"While conducting operations abroad for Uroboros Financial in the last seven months, no civilians were killed or harmed where Eamon participated. He is exceedingly patient, and willing to negotiate when possible."

"And, when they won't negotiate?"

"God help them."

CHAPTER 6

GLACIER NATIONAL PARK, SERVER HUB LOOKOUT POINT

AUGUST 29TH, 2201 – 8:58 PM

Klaus crested the ridge, expecting to see Eamon, Shadow, and maybe a few survivors, but there was no one. He gestured for the two militiamen beside him to circle around toward the top, while he walked toward the trail that descended down the other side. He thought it would be easy to track an Ursine Metasapient, but the snow there was undisturbed and pristine.

"Where did you go, you stupid bear?" Klaus muttered under his breath.

Klaus headed back, taking the trail upward toward the server hub access. He'd somewhat expected to die going up the slope, given the two corpses the dogs had found at the bottom of the hill. It wasn't Eamon's style to kill at an extreme range, preferring to get up close and personal.

As Klaus rounded the rocks to begin the ascent, Eamon emerged from a snow drift beside the trail, snow pouring off of him. Klaus whirled, bringing his rifle around, but Eamon batted it from his hands with a powerful swipe of his clawed hand.

Klaus staggered back, almost tumbling down the ridge to his death, but Eamon grabbed the front of his jacket, claws digging in and piercing the fabric. Looking past Eamon's shoulder, he could see his two accomplices, bloodied and unconscious.

"Shadow, she's the one who killed the scouts," Klaus said, looking back over his shoulder at the two-hundred foot drop behind him.

"I'll have to scold her for not hiding the bodies better," Eamon said, shrugging snow off his shoulders.

Jake stared down the length of Eamon's arm, the little boy's quiet expression partially concealed by snow piled up on Eamon's shoulder. "How'd you get him to be quiet?" Klaus asked, wondering if Eamon would drop him or pull him up.

"He's a good boy. Are you a good boy, Klaus?" Eamon said, balling up his fingers, his claws tearing further into the jacket.

"Patrick Vale is planning to take the whole area. He's been directing the various militia groups," Klaus said, grabbing Eamon's wrist.

"Patrick Vale is deceased," Eamon said, his eyebrows pushing up against the snow piled on his head.

"The militia doesn't think so. The sniper round, fired by one of Perfidy's crew, didn't leave a lot to be identified. Using a twenty millimeter anti-material round on a person tends to do that," Klaus said, both of his feet losing ground.

Eamon pulled him in slightly, so his feet could touch the ground again. "Every corpse recovered from the initial server hub op was DNA tested against CGG records."

"The militia doesn't trust any of that, of course. Here, let me show you," Klaus said reaching for the comm on his tactical harness.

"Easy, don't do anything stupid," Eamon said, giving Klaus a shake.

Klaus held out his off hand in plain view while turning on his comm with the other. The sound of Patrick Vale's voice came over loud and clear, a slight hum in the background. He was spouting his usual diatribe of hatred and religious intolerance, but he also made made reference to current events.

"Hear that? He's talking about the occupation in Apgar," Klaus said, beads of sweat forming at his brow.

"Yeah, I hear it," Eamon said, hoping Shadow wasn't walking into a den of insurgents.

"Look, I can help you. I've been working with them for a couple of weeks, know the game plan pretty well, too," Klaus said, patting a breast pocket on his jacket.

"No, Klaus, you can't," Eamon said, pulling him up.

Before Klaus could utter another word, Eamon knocked him out with a carefully controlled punch. After dropping a polymer restraint around Klaus's wrists, Eamon went through his pockets. There were maps, annotated with various locations, his militia issued radio, and a Finnish mobile LEO-issue handheld.

"This is how they did it, Jake," Eamon said, holding the handheld up for the baby to see.

Jake babbled happily at the sight of the blinking mobile device.

"I'll let you play with it, right after I use it to get a bearing on the weapons I lost in the avalanche," Eamon said, clipping the Finnish LEO handheld and a militia radio beneath his own.

Eamon activated his own comm, hoping he could still contact Kale and Brook, but it just beeped, lacking a satellite connection. Either the militia had tapped into the array miles to the south, or Klaus had tampered with the telecom equipment while he had access to the server hub. Regardless, Eamon would have to find some autonomous communications equipment so he could call out.

"Klaus, how did you know I'd even come to Montana?" Eamon said, picking up his former partner.

Abbey sighed, giving Eamon a disappointed look as he turned Klaus over so he could breathe easier through his mouth. "The only way he could have known is if there's a traitor on the ship with Kale, Brook, and Heavy Dub," Abbey said.

Eamon gazed at her. "I'm not so sure of that."

"Are you taking Klaus so you can interrogate him further?" Abbey said, her white fur still pristine even against the freshly fallen snow around them.

"No," Eamon said, giving Jake a drink from his canteen.

"You should take the boy and get out of here, Eamon. Don't be a hero," Abbey said, crouching down beside him.

"Police don't run. We just ramp up, meeting force with force," Eamon said, breaking one of the militia men's rifles like a twig.

"What about a tactical withdrawal?" Abbey said, worriedly.

Eamon frowned. "No."

The militiamen began to regain consciousness, one groaning as he tried to look around through a pair of swollen black eyes. "Who are you talking to?" he said, trying to sit up in spite of his hands being bound.

"You've the right to remain silent. I'd use it," Eamon said, turning the other militiaman over so he didn't suffocate on the blood draining from his nose.

"I'm not telling you anything, clay man," the militiaman said.

"I'm not going to ask you anything," Eamon said, listening intently.

"We've already got Apgar, and a half dozen other settlements nearby."

Eamon barely nodded, disinterested. "Be quiet, or I'll knock you out again."

"You don't scare me, and I don't recognize the authority behind that badge. I'll..."

Eamon popped him in the forehead, just above the eyes. The blow didn't knock him out, but it hurt something fierce. The militiaman winced. "I'm going to be quiet now."

It would be another hour before Shadow would return, out of breath, and with a bundle tied to her back. Klaus, and the other militiaman had recovered consciousness during that time. Klaus sat there quietly, the militiamen uttering curses as Shadow appeared.

"Bitch," one said.

"Quiet," Eamon said, holding a fuzzy fist in front of his face.

Shadow smiled. "He isn't wrong. I am a real bitch."

"You get my guns?" Eamon asked.

"And biscuits, from the kitchen crew hiding out at the diner. Did you know these guys think their dead leader is still alive?" Shadow said, unpacking some food.

"You got there and back pretty quickly," Eamon said, breaking off a bit of biscuit for Jake.

"I'm trained specifically for recon. I advanced ahead of fast-moving mechanized and suit-equipped infantry in South America, Mexico, and South Pacific theaters. I can outrun and outlast the fastest recorded human sprinters. I'm pretty much better than humans at everything," Shadow said, directing her statements more to the humans present than Eamon.

Her words seemed to rile the militiamen, but they held their tongues, choosing to glare at Shadow instead.

"Except hiding bodies," Eamon said, holding up an admonishing finger.

Shadow smirked. "They found them with dogs."

Eamon nodded. "Point."

"When the Arizona Militia Chapter came over the border and tried to settle in Mexico, I had the privilege of running them off. They'd run, but I'd run them down just for the satisfaction of putting them back over the border by hand. You'd be surprised how many of their wives, given the opportunity, opted to seek asylum in Mexico," Shadow continued, sardonic.

One of the militiamen snapped, trying to rise to his feet. "You stupid clay-bitch-whore, I'll…"

"All of you, be quiet," Eamon said, looking first at Shadow, then gazing steadily at his prisoners.

Everyone sat down.

Shadow frowned. "Sorry, I just really…"

"Everyone is going to be civil, calm, and watch their mouth around the boy," Eamon said, gesturing to Jake, evoking a laugh from the small child.

Everyone resolved to sit quietly as Eamon worked on his firearms. He checked over the rifle and handgun to make sure they hadn't been tampered with, then applied a stock extension, and custom grips so the weapons would function properly in his large hands. Finally, he loaded them and put all of the spare ammunition in the front pockets of his tactical vest.

Shadow unloaded the ammunition from the militia men's broken rifles for her own, then tossed them over the drop off. She split up the provisions with Eamon, being careful to give him extra for Jake. They took turns shaking snow in their canteens until they each had a full water ration.

"What happens now?" Klaus asked, watching Eamon and Shadow prepare to leave.

"We should kill them," Shadow said.

"I'm the police. I don't kill people I've arrested and put in restraints. I ship them to Mars to break rocks," Eamon said, letting a biscuit slip into his mouth.

Shadow frowned. "We can't take them with us. They'll be found. They'll talk."

Eamon nodded solemnly. "I'm counting on it."

Shadow nodded, smiling knowingly at the militiamen.

"Catch your breath. When you're ready, we'll head out," Eamon said, pointing toward the south.

Once they reached the bottom, Eamon turned and retraced the steps he had taken west the previous day.

"Where are we going?" Shadow said, pausing at the trailhead.

"You don't have to go with me. I appreciate the help, but you should sit the rest of this out," Eamon said.

Shadow looked stern for a moment, in a way that reminded him of Abbey.

"If you're coming, we'll have some digging to do," Eamon said, pulling out the Finnish LEO handheld.

"I suck at digging," Shadow laughed.

"Something you're not better than humans at doing?" Eamon replied.

"Point."

Eamon paused mid-step, looking at the handheld. "He was tracking more than just my two rifles. They were tracking you as well."

"I don't understand. How would they know to do that?" Shadow asked, baffled.

"What's the last thing you stole from them?" Eamon asked.

"This expensive combat knife. One of the militiamen left it in the scabbard hanging from his pants while he went into the bathhouse at their settlement," Shadow said, producing a long double-edged blade.

"Leave it on the ground there, and walk with me for a ways," Eamon said, beckoning for her to follow.

He watched as the third tracking signal slowly deviated from their position on the handheld.

"It was the knife?" Shadow asked.

Eamon nodded. "It was the knife."

"How would they know what I'd like? Klaus? I never told him anything," Shadow said, looking back up at the knife lying in the trail.

"I changed my mind. You should come with me," Eamon said, pocketing the handheld.

"Because of the knife?"

"A guy I know, who is really good at predicting what people will do, told me to be unpredictable in times like this. We should definitely stick together, for now," Eamon said, turning to head west.

"It'll be really cold soon, I know a place we can go," Shadow said, following along.

Eamon nodded. "Yeah, we should do that, but not to rest."

"You want to test the theory, see if the places I've visited and stayed are under surveillance?"

"Yep."

They walked for three hours to get a safe distance from her favorite campsite, high enough to have the proper vantage. Eamon could smell people on the wind, even before they got close. Shadow confirmed it by swapping out the scope on her rifle for one with low-light optics.

"Two guys, a sniper and a spotter sitting under a canopy. They're not professionals. The portable heating unit gave them away. I might not have spotted a pair of real soldiers," Shadow said.

Eamon nodded, making sure Jake's hat was covering his ears, and the scarf around his neck was comfortable. "Aside from Klaus and his two friends, who knows about your military training?"

"Nobody. I don't know." Shadow sighed. "This sucks. I've had the knife for at least ten days. They'll have a fix on all my good hiding places."

"You run your route that often?" Eamon said, checking their position with Klaus's handheld.

"Have to. I don't trust those cross-burning white supremacists a-holes. They look to have been gearing up for something for months."

"You couldn't have guessed they'd move on Apgar?" Eamon said, putting some sound suppressing plugs in Jake's ears.

"I guess you'd take it as being an obvious thing, an inevitability, but everything they do seems like it's for show. Even if they said what they were up to aloud, I wouldn't have thought it was credible," Shadow said, her long ears drooping.

"Makes sense."

Shadow frowned. "Only until you take into account what they've done in the last forty-eight hours."

"Strange timing to be sure, what with me showing up, the mercs leaving." Eamon scowled. "All, but a guy I used to work with," Eamon said, hugging the Henry repeater up into his shoulder.

"What are you doing? I thought you were going to arrest all these guys."

"I will. I'm just going to ding him a little," Eamon said, waiting for his vision to fully adjust to the range and low-light conditions.

Eamon fired the first round to sight it in, finding the rifle to be damnably accurate. He ran the action, chambering a second round in rapid succession and fired, winging the sniper across the back of one of his legs. He rolled over, both he and his spotter scrambling for cover and looking around with the viewfinder.

Eamon checked to make sure Jake was okay, then quickly moved positions. He switched the militia radio on, running the sound up through his earpiece. He could hear the panicked call for help over the militia frequency, but ignored most of the substance of it while he used the Finnish LEO handheld to triangulate where the radio signals were being rebroadcast.

Shadow followed along, watching Eamon carefully manipulate electronics sized for a regular human with his claw tips. "I could have told you where their radio tower was," she said, shaking her head.

"Yeah, I know. That's not what I'm checking for."

Shadow looked startled, suddenly understanding the implications of what Eamon was doing. "You think they're broadcasting, and using the server hub to boost the signal?"

"No. I wanted to see if Patrick Vale's transmission would be interrupted when someone else jumped on the channel," Eamon said, pocketing the LEO handheld.

"Does it?"

"No."

"What's going on, Eamon? I didn't do a lot with comms in the military," Shadow said, stopping in the middle of the trail.

"I'd expect hopping inversion encryption with these guys, as they seem to have access to older military technology. They should have fifteen or so encrypted channels across the same frequency, assuming an optimal wavelength range suited to the terrain," Eamon said.

"I don't know what any of that means," Shadow said, shoulders slumping.

"This looks very advanced, remotely monitored code inversion for radio encryption. Their radios aren't set for particular frequencies. They're managed by a remote and dedicated system that rekeys the encryption automatically, over the air," Eamon said, frowning.

Shadow shook her head. "Maybe Aaron AI could break the encryption? You're wanting to find a way to listen into their traffic, yes?"

"I'm sure he could," Eamon said, switching both his, and the militia radio off.

Shadow shook her head. "No... no, that's crazy. Why would Aaron AI be helping the Militia?"

"I don't know. Whatever the reason, it's something he knew he couldn't just ask Uroboros Financial for," Eamon said, pausing to look up toward small gap in the clouds, and the stars peeking through.

"Is there anything they wouldn't do for Aaron AI? I thought Uroboros Financial was all about equality of sapient beings, and all that?"

"At least two citizens of Apgar and two militiamen are already dead. No one at Uroboros Financial would have been okay with that."

Shadow scowled. "Isn't it a stretch to blame Aaron for that?"

"Not if he's the one that brought everyone together. Let's find my weapons and see what the militia is doing to the south," Eamon said, beckoning to Shadow to follow him.

"Are you serious?" Shadow said.

"Aren't you the least bit curious how they're getting their drugs in?"

Shadow frowned, shoulders slumping slightly.

"You already know."

"Yes. The same way I was able to get here from Mexico."

"Romani transports, carrying blind baggage?"

Shadow nodded.

"That is very dangerous. The money would have to be very good, considering the utter lack of competition they have right now," Eamon said, wincing as Jake pulled at the fur on his shoulder.

"You saying that, makes what you said to Klaus sound kind of mean."

"You heard all that?"

"My ears are really good."

"Yeah, they would be, wouldn't they? Klaus is a coward. He abandoned the badge for self-pity. We all lose people, how we carry on matters," Eamon said, quickening his pace.

"Is that why you won't let me carry Jake? You're one of those weight of the world types?"

Eamon sighed. "Are you asking to carry Jake?"

Shadow blinked, hesitating at first. "Yes."

Eamon shook his head, and unstrapped Jake from his back. He held the child carrier up while Shadow threaded her arms through the straps. She took a piece of rubberized twine and bound the straps across her chest so they would better fit her slender frame.

"Thanks," Shadow said, patting Jake's tiny hands as they reached around to touch the fur on the sides of her face.

Eamon cleared his throat and resumed threading the path west, but walked to keep Shadow and Jake in his peripheral vision. He wanted to be able to trust her, but paranoia hung around at the edges of his mind, gnawing at his calm. He'd never had a reason to distrust another Metasapient. That said, having talked with Kale extensively about traveling to The Factory, it was a strange coincidence to run into a Metasapient from south of the border.

Eamon worried more about Aaron AI. He'd worked side by side with all sorts of artificial intelligences. They'd always been good allies, but the idea of one going rogue was worrying. It was often an argument put forward by Kale, in that unlike a regular human, they're choices had the potential to affect the planet, politics, and what stability remained after the Shutdown.

"How much do you know about Aaron AI?" Eamon said, threading between trees beside the narrow trail.

"Never been inside. Ray Pendleton is the one that gave me the job of logging visitors at the server hub."

"But, you've got a pretty strong opinion."

"Look, I only know what the dog pack tells me. I know they've bonded with the site, so they are not going to be particularly objective."

Eamon nodded. "But?"

"But, if Aaron AI going rogue was inevitable, wouldn't it have happened already?" Shadow said, holding onto the back of Eamon's jacket as they went down a steep hill.

Eamon grabbed tree trunks, using them as handholds as he descended. "Yeah, I'm thinking about this all wrong. I need to think about this like he was a person, and not an AI."

"You're thinking they have some kind of leverage, or a hostage?" Shadow said.

"Could be."

The forest ahead was gradually choked out by the avalanche. From the east side, Eamon could dimly make out the spot where the explosive had gone off. The blast site was covered up by snow, but the naked tree tops gave the location away.

Eamon climbed back over to where he had dug himself out, turning to face the hill. He counted backward to the best of his recollection where he'd unhooked the tactical sling. There was a slight depression where the flow of snow had split, going around his girth as he fought for elevation. Where the depression ended, he began to dig.

"Don't you have a… Klaus's thing that was tracking your weapons and me?" Shadow said, watching Eamon heave double-handfuls of snow aside.

"I'm waiting to turn it on, after I've found my other weapons."

Shadow smirked. "You're going to make them think we went north."

"Better, like we went west, across the river," Eamon said, pausing to catch his breath.

"You think they'll double back, to reinforce their camp?" Shadow asked.

"In this terrain, if you can make your enemy spend their strength moving, you'll have the advantage," Eamon said, digging around in the snow with one hand.

Eamon dug for another thirty minutes to find his bolt-action rifle, and another twenty after that to find his semi-automatic high-capacity. They were choked with ice, and Eamon couldn't be sure they hadn't been damaged until they were thawed out. He'd have to pull them completely apart to make sure, something he didn't want to do in the field, in the middle of the night.

"Let's go," Eamon said, heading west.

"Do you ever get tired?" Shadow said, blinking sleepily.

"I'm always tired."

They traveled back across the river, walking at least a mile before Eamon switched Klaus's handheld, the militia radio, and his own radio on for a moment. They listened to the chatter that mostly consisted of the militia in Apgar trying to find the dog pack. They listened to the grim back and forth, the militia talking about how they'll kill any Metasapient abominations they find.

"They keep using that clay reference," Eamon observed.

"It's an anti-Semitic thing, talking about us like we're Jewish golems, and part of some global conspiracy or something," Shadow explained.

"Is that new?"

Shadow shook her head. "It's old. Like, I had to look it up to know what they were talking about months ago when I came here."

Eamon frowned.

"What if the Migration comes while the militia is active in the area?" Shadow asked.

Eamon crossed his arm with the Henry rifle, while listening to the radio chatter. "It won't be good for anyone."

"We could make a pretty decent dent in the meantime."

"With a baby in tow, and a few hundred civilians caught in the crossfire?" Eamon said, shutting the radio equipment off.

"You've already drawn them out. All we'd have to do is wait in the pass behind us," Shadow argued, pointing to the east.

"You really want to kill these guys," Eamon said, turning to look south, the sun beginning to rise behind him.

Shadow frowned. "Yes, I do."

"I don't like them either, but they're just criminals, nothing special."

"Criminals that kill and devalue anyone that isn't white and human by their narrow standards," Shadow said.

"You think we're humans?" Eamon asked, genuinely curious.

Shadow smiled. "If aliens came here, would they see us as being any different? We'd all be Earthlings, yeah?"

"You might be surprised at just how discerning aliens might be," Eamon replied.

"I think the world needs a more collective term. Hard when not all Metasapients are mammals, though," Shadow said.

"Let's hurry. I want to see where the blind shipments get dropped off."

Shadow nodded. "Okay."

The river route was well marked, even with the snowfall, there were signs and trail markers. At intervals, there were shelters, and placards describing various wildlife in the area. Snow machines and foot traffic were common along the trail.

As the sun rose, Jake began to cry. "He's tired. We have been walking all night," Shadow said, pulling him out of his carrier and holding him in an attempt to comfort him.

"The maps in my office show a maintenance shed a bit further south. We'll head for that," Eamon said, breaking off the trail.

The maintenance shed had fallen to disuse, but was still sturdy, and had a wood stove. It looked as though the forest service had converted a small hunter's lodge for use as storage for tools. It was chained up, but Eamon easily broke the lock by giving it a squeeze.

"Photographic memory, super strong; is there anything you don't do?" Shadow said, stepping inside the shed.

"Not photographic, I just like maps. I don't do cards. I prefer board games," Eamon said, ducking down and squeezing through the door.

"There are cots in here, but nothing for gigantic bear-cops," Shadow quipped, laying Jake down on a cot beside the wood stove. "Do you think it would be safe to have a fire?"

"I'm going to be outside once you're settled. If anyone comes along, I'll deal with it. Get some sleep," Eamon said.

Eamon nearly took the wall down getting back out of the shed, having to turn sideways to squeeze out again. He nodded to Shadow then closed the door. They would run out of food soon, and needed to find a warmer place for Jake. The sky was angry again, threatening to drop a lot more snow.

Eamon could smell them as they walked. Men, somewhere to the north, their scent coming with the wind along the frozen top of the river. Shadow was probably too distracted by Jake to notice, but Eamon intended to find out who they were and what they wanted. He walked north a ways, retracing his own tracks, then sat down, and waited.

They didn't open fire when they saw him sitting in the trail. They hesitated, talking quietly before they approached. Eamon could see them clearly, the sun dusting the tops of the trees with early morning light. They were militia, wearing scout patches and carrying rifles. One appeared to be the squad leader, a shotgun over his shoulder, and a handgun on his hip.

"It'd be simpler if you came back with us," the squad leader said, drawing close enough to shout at Eamon across the snow.

Eamon grumbled, standing up. "Drop your weapons and put your hands on your head. Do it now."

"That isn't going to happen. You'll be heading back with us, and opening up the server hub," the militiaman sneered.

"Last chance, weapons down, hands up."

"Don't be stupid, we've got a whole town of hostages." The leader reached for his handgun.

Before the militia man's handgun could clear the holster, Eamon raised the Henry rifle and fired, hitting him center of mass. Heavy Dub's handmade ammunition bucked hard, the round passing easily through the body armor of the squad leader, severing his spine and exiting out the back of his vest. He'd probably only drawn the weapon to intimidate, out of a lack of discipline, but Eamon's training didn't take such foibles into consideration.

Eamon ran the action on the rifle, shooting the man beside the squad leader as he reflexively brought up his rifle. The others scattered, firing wildly like they'd never been in any kind of fight. Eamon dropped to one knee, calmly running the action and shooting them down as they broke cover trying to flank him. Not one of them made it out of his front ninety-degree arc before taking a round somewhere in the ten ring.

Eamon pushed more ammunition into his rifle as he walked slowly toward the only scout still discernibly breathing. He knelt down beside him, putting a big paw down over the wound to try and control the bleeding. The man put his hand up on Eamon's paw, eyes wide and full of fear.

Eamon didn't sugarcoat it, feeling the young man deserved the truth. "You aren't going to make it. You took it to the lung and the round probably tumbled as it went through your armor."

"Shit." The militiaman coughed. "That antique works?"

Eamon nodded. "Your squad leader told you I was bluffing?"

"Yeah, he saw you standing there with that antique, and figured you were gonna try and scare us into surrendering. Only see weapons like that in the movies."

"Sorry. My other weapons got messed up in an avalanche," Eamon said, keeping his eyes up on his surroundings.

"You should have just come with us. Now it's all going to go bad," the militiaman said, blood beginning to trickle down from the corners of his mouth.

"You should have stayed on your own side of the hill," Eamon said, watching as the young man went pale from shock.

"The man on the radio, the one back from the dead, said we had to... had to..."

Eamon felt him take his last breath before lifting his huge hand.

"They didn't give you a choice," Abbey said, coming up beside Eamon.

Eamon looked at the blood on his huge hand. "You worried I'm feeling glad right now?"

"I'm worried you feel the extreme and diametric opposite of glad, whatever that is."

Eamon looked over at Abbey, sunlight raining down over the trees behind her. As it hit her white fur, she seemed to glow, crystal clear eyes sparkling.

"Yeah, not feeling real glad right now."

He checked them for identification, collecting what he'd need to file a report, and grabbed the leader's radio. He committed the site to memory so their bodies could be recovered later, calmly retracing his steps and the shell casing from every round he fired. He briefly contemplated burying them to protect the evidence, but the rest of the militia might be on their way. He circled back to the maintenance shed, being careful to obscure his trail in a nearby rockslide.

Shadow was at the shed, waiting patiently. She rose cautiously from cover as he approached, rifle ready. "I heard the shots," she said, worriedly.

"Thanks for holding this position," Eamon said, wading back through the snow wearily.

"I figured that's what you'd want me to do. Did you hide the bodies?"

Eamon shook his big head. "Scout group, and they were specifically looking for me."

"What? How did they know where we were?"

"I'm not sure they did. Might have picked us up when I switched on the LEO tracker to find my weapons, but that seems unlikely. They caught up to us pretty quickly, or they were already heading this way."

"You talked to them, then?"

Eamon nodded. "Gave them a chance to surrender."

"So, they are trying to take you alive," Shadow said, frowning.

Eamon folded his arms, and turned to look toward the south. "Get a little more rest, I'll keep an eye on things."

The hours preceding dawn passed quickly. Shadow eventually came out and had to rouse Eamon after he'd nodded off. He rose slowly, trying to shake off the fatigue that still refused to leave his body. Shadow looked concerned, brushing the snow off of the back of his vest.

"How do you sleep upright in a snow drift like that?" Shadow said, laughing.

"Practice. Don't want your weapons getting wet."

Shadow shook his head. "I can't tell when you're trying to be funny."

"That also takes practice, and a proximity to Finnish people," Eamon said, with a wink. "Where'd you learn to take care of a baby like that? I haven't heard him cry except the once."

"Practice, and a proximity to Mexico," Shadow said. "They understand what a family is supposed to be, like no one else."

"Even the Garcias?"

"Look, they weren't perfect, but they stepped up for the boy when no one else did," Shadow said, looking down at the ground.

Eamon nodded.

"It's just hitting me now, you know, that they're dead."

"Yeah, it takes a little while," Eamon said, looking past Shadow to where he saw Abbey standing on the ridge ahead.

CHAPTER 7

GLACIER NATIONAL PARK, NORTH FORK OF THE FLATHEAD RIVER, NORTH FORK ROAD

AUGUST 30TH, 2201 – 7:42 AM

Emma stirred the stew as it cooked over the fire. She was relieved that her niece, Janice, had survived the avalanche, but was angry beyond measure that her grandson had not yet been recovered. She looked up from the stew for a moment, taking stock of her family and allies sitting around her.

Standing up from her haunches, she let out a quick breath as her old knees bore her up one more time. The gathering of people stiffened, sitting up at attention as the matron beckoned for a young man to come forward. He stood up, a little too excited, and stood at attention.

Emma nodded and smiled. "You managed to get clear, and dug Janice out of the avalanche before she suffocated. I appreciate that."

The young man smiled, looking over at his comrades, eyes twinkling at the prospect of being rewarded by someone so important to the militia.

"You were also the one who set the charges that caused the avalanche," Emma said, grabbing a hot poker from the fire and gesturing for two militiamen to take hold of the man's arms.

His screams were muffled as a wet rag was placed over his mouth. Emma used the hot poker to punish him, causing several painful, but largely superficial burns. She burnt the flesh across one of his palms, and across the tender flesh on the right side of neck. Gesturing to the men to pull his pants down, she pressed the poker to the skin along the back of his right thigh.

"This is just a warning, a way for you to remember. What we're doing here is important, and there can't be any mistakes. Every time you load a magazine with bullets, look in a mirror, or sit down, you'll feel those scars," Emma said, calmly putting the poker back in the fire.

The young man whimpered, trying to pull his pants up with the hand that wasn't burned.

"Help him, help him. Those will get infected if they aren't treated properly," Emma said, motioning to the two men that had held him down.

"Just like the story," Janice said, folding her arms and coming to stand beside her aunt.

"Do you think I was too harsh?" Emma said, turning to tend to the stew.

"We haven't seen the payoff yet, and the other militias are coming. We made promises," Janice said, worriedly.

"My son, Patrick, rose from the dead. He's only asked us to do a few things, in the name of Jesus Christ. If we're faithful and obey, Montana will be ours in return," Emma said, calmly adding spice to the stew.

"Without Apgar, and Uroboros Financial, the Romani might stop coming," Janice said, watching as the militia sat around preparing to pack up camp.

Emma nodded. "The Lord will provide. These are the end of days, if the rumors we've heard about Europe are true."

"Those godless sodomites and unbelievers got what they deserved, sure, but that's no reason to think blessings will rain down on us. We haven't even seen Patrick yet, just heard his voice on the radio."

Emma glared at Janice. "You need to have faith, like I do."

A cadre of heavily armed militiamen entered the camp from the west, carrying with them several bundles. There was warm welcomes exchanged as they settled down to warm themselves by the cooking fire. Emma hugged each one, lingering for a moment on the last one.

He was a burly man, thick at the waist, but fit in spite of carrying extra weight. He wore an old CGG North American infantry uniform, which was clearly his as opposed to a lot of the surplus the rest of the militia wore. He had thick dark brown hair that was wild around his ears, a ruddy complexion, and frantic, almost mischievous, eyes.

"Moses Jacob Vale, you are late," Emma scolded.

"Sorry, Mother. We picked up some heavy tracks heading south. Thought it might have been the new Sheriff so I sent Craig and his boys down for a peek," Moses said, looking down into the stew pot.

Janice scowled. "Just Craig and that squad of misfits?"

"We've dealt with an ursine clay-creature once or twice. Should be fine if they do cross paths," Moses said, narrowly avoiding a spoon wielded by his mother.

"Back up, the stew isn't ready yet," Emma said, laughing.

"If Craig does meet up with the Sheriff, he and his boys will be dead," Janice said, shaking her head.

"Nah, there's seven of em', and they are all armed. They're good boys," Moses said, dismissively.

"You didn't see him, Moses. The few ursine we've seen wander through were small, black, and usually not ready to take on a posse. This new Sheriff is something else, big, and brown, and did I mention, big?" Janice said, deadly serious.

"Brown? Big? Like a grizzly?" Moses furrowed his brow.

"Just like one, yeah. Scary as Hell. Get Craig on the radio, tell him to get off the trail," Janice said, growing weary of her cousin's uncanny inability to listen to her when it was important.

"Okay, okay," Moses said, pulling the radio off his vest and twisting the knob to activate it. "Craig, you find anything down the south trail, over?"

There was a moment of static-filled silence before a grizzled voice that both Janice and Emma recognized came back over. "Craig's dead."

Moses smiled. "We're going to kill you."

The radio beeped, Eamon's voice coming back over. "It'll be hard to do that from Mars, wearing prison orange."

Moses gingerly shut the radio down, daintily turning the knob with the tips of two fingers before turning to look apologetically at Janice. "I guess that'd be the new Sheriff?"

"Oh, you think?" Janice said, glowering at Moses.

"Shit, he's the real deal, then?" Moses said, clipping his radio to his vest.

"That's what I've been trying to tell you for the last five minutes, idiot," Janice said, kicking snow in Moses' direction.

"We'll get him. I'll take enough guys next time, and take him out," Moses said, nodding to his comrades.

"You'll do no such thing," Emma said, filling up a bowl with stew. "We need that clay creature to get into the server hub. Also, he's got little Jacob. I want my grandson back."

"We should just blow the doors on that place, let ourselves in," Moses snapped.

"Your bomb-happy idiots got me buried in an avalanche. Besides, if we stick to the plan we won't even need to blow it. We'll have a safe secure facility with armored doors on the outside. What's with you and wanting to blow everything up?" Janice said, shaking her head.

"I like solutions that can fix more than one problem," Moses said, winking.

Emma handed out bowls to everyone, including the young man she'd punished earlier. To him, she gave a little extra, gently patting the bandage on his hand. Moses and his men helped finish packing up the camp, loading snow machines and a Sno-Cat with not just cargo, but the worldly possessions of the militia.

"It'll be slow going, and we'll have to avoid the avalanche site with our snow machines," Moses said, helping his mother into the Sno-Cat.

Emma nodded. "We'll go further south, and cut back to the west."

"Uh, that's where Craig and his crew probably ran into the Sheriff," Moses said, looking from his mother, and then over to Janice for some sort of consensus.

"He'll have moved to avoid us by the time we arrive. He needs to avoid us as much as we need to avoid him, at least for now," Emma said, patting her son's shoulder.

Janice shrugged, having no real idea what the Sheriff would actually do.

"So, how did you survive an encounter with this new lawman?" Moses said, wrapping an arm through the window of the Sno-Cat and turning to talk to Janice.

"I put my gun down, and my hands up," Janice said, watching the trees slowly go past.

"You had a chance to put a round in him, and didn't?" Moses said, scoffing.

"If you don't do what I did, he'll kill you. This new Sheriff doesn't negotiate like the mercs. He's real police," Janice said.

"You sure about that? I haven't met a problem I couldn't solve with a bomb or a suitcase of money," Moses asked, the wind blowing through his hair as the snow machine began to make a descent.

"I don't know, why don't you ask Craig?" Janice said, squinting at Moses.

"Craig was never much of a salesman. If I get a chance, I'm going to talk to this lawman, see if we've got something he'd like," Moses said, smirking.

"Evidently, he likes sending people to Mars, so they can break rocks," Janice said, rolling her eyes at Moses.

"We'll see."

The caravan moved slowly to the south, the snowy road did little to slow the vehicles, but many people had to make the trek on foot. The elderly, infirm, and important rode snow machines with a pair of scouts in the lead. Visibility was low, thanks to the cloud cover and a dense fog that seemed to perpetually pour out of the half frozen river.

Janice wondered if the Sheriff had continued to head south, or if he'd gone west as Klaus suggested over the radio hours ago. It was odd that two of their men had been killed at the base of the hill, while the others that encountered the Sheriff had gotten out alive. Klaus wasn't able to give too much detail before the radio went silent again.

"Why didn't the Sheriff kill Klaus?" Janice asked, looking over at Emma.

Moses piped up before she could respond. "I don't know, maybe he doesn't kill foreigners?"

"They know each other," Emma said, knitting needles clicking as she worked on what looked to be a scarf.

"How do you know that?" Janice asked.

Emma nodded. "Patrick told me."

"And, you're only bringing this up to us now?" Moses said, opening the door to the Sno-Cat and pushing his way in on the bench opposite Janice and Emma.

"I assume it is part of Patrick's plan. He seems to know things about the surrounding area we do not. I trust your brother, Moses," Emma said, pulling on a bit of snagged yarn.

"Can we trust Klaus to carry through with his part?" Moses said, nervously.

"He lost a wife and a little girl in Finland. Patrick has promised to return them to him," Emma said, a little annoyed at the lack of faith being put on display by Moses.

"I love Jesus, Momma. Love him, but he hasn't ever given anyone back he's taken..."

Emma moved in one fluid motion, plunging both knitting needles into Moses' left thigh. They broke through his snow pants, painfully piercing the flesh on his leg. He bit his lip and endured the pain, meeting his mother's angry gaze with one of his own.

"He gave us Patrick," she said, giving the knitting needles a slight twist.

Moses winced, and shook his head. "Ain't no one actually seen him. We can't be sure that's even him on the radio."

Janice sat quietly, delighting in her cousin's extreme discomfort. She'd learned long ago that Emma was a reasonable woman, about some things. When it came to matter of faith and family, she wasn't generally up for receiving input.

"Patrick said we'd see him soon. Those Godless gypsies brought everything he asked for," Emma said, slowly withdrawing her knitting needles and wiping the blood off on Moses' pant leg.

Moses shook his head, rubbing his bloody leg. "We don't even know what he asked for, or what they brought. All the shipments were taken to that old hanger at the relay hub. Then all those strangers…"

"Angels," Emma said, holding the needles up to his face.

"What?" Janice said, half-smiling.

Emma nodded, looking skyward. "Had to be, the way they showed up with all those white cases and special suits, with kind of a glow about them."

"They just seemed rich and fancy to me," Moses grumbled.

"Wouldn't angels seem that way though? Fresh from the Kingdom of Heaven?" Janice said, cocking her head to one side, smiling evilly at Moses.

"I figured there'd be more trumpets, or harps, or something," Moses sneered, scowling at his cousin.

"The Host of Heaven would be what we expect, and not, all at the same time," Emma said, resuming her knitting.

The caravan continued south, beyond where the road headed east. The trail wasn't fit for motorized traffic in the warmer months, but worked just fine with snow on the ground. As the sun rose high in the overcast sky, they came across where Craig and his crew had battle with the Sheriff.

Moses crouched down beside Craig, taking note of his sidearm being barely out of its holster, clutched in his half-frozen hand. The others looked to have scattered for cover, but didn't get far. Each had taken a single bullet, either through the head, or center of mass, and killed instantly. All, but one.

"You see this?" one of the scouts said, kneeling down beside the body.

"That's a really big Goddamn hand, or paw," Moses said, taking note of the blood-soaked outline of crimson frozen across the front of the man's vest.

"I told you he was big," Janice said, walking up beside her cousin.

"You tend to exaggerate when it comes to talking about the size of a man," Moses teased, turning the dead scout over with his foot.

Janice looked around at the horizons, and the tree line to either side of the path. "Better watch your mouth. Your momma wouldn't like it if she heard you cussing like that?"

"What'd I say?"

"Y'said, Goddamn."

"Yeah, well, seems about right in the very literal sense. Look at the size of the footprints on this hunk of clay," Moses said, holding his hand out next to one of Eamon's footprints in the snow.

"Uh-huh. Bet he takes a real big shit, too," Janice said, turning to head back to the Sno-Cat.

"You gonna help us gather up these poor souls, so we can give them a proper Christian burial?" Moses asked, holding his hands out at his sides.

"No, I just came out to deliver an 'I told you so'. Idiot."

Moses glowered at her, lacking a witty response.

Janice just smiled, turning to head back to the caravan. "I told you so."

After gathering their dead, they tried to get a bearing on where the Sheriff went. After a certain point, his tracks seemed to vanish into the others. He'd gone south for a mile or so, but after that, there was no telling.

Moses kicked the snow on the trail in frustration. "How does a half-ton bear cop just disappear?"

Emma looked out from the Sno-Cat, then folded her arms, and closed her eyes.

"You gonna pray? Now?" Moses complained.

"You have a better idea?" Janice asked, frowning at her cousin.

"Yeah, how about we go back, and you explain how big and mean this new Sheriff actually is," Moses said, growing tired of his cousin's constant taunting.

"Quiet, you want the Good Lord to hear you bickering?" Emma said.

The members of the caravan lowered their heads, while Emma prayed for everyone, and the guidance to know which way to go. After several minutes, the signal tone on their radios chirped. Moses looked up at his mother, opening his eyes.

"Well, see who it is," Emma said, impatiently.

"Caravan escort, Baker Squad, what's your twenty?" Moses said, clicking his radio over to the militia's shared frequency.

"This isn't Baker. This is Patrick. I've arrived, and I'm at the relay hub to the south."

"Brother, your voice is a sweet thing to hear. You sound good, and close, not like the other radio broadcasts," Moses said, hardly believing his ears.

"Likewise. Can you pick me up? I'd like to rejoin the family and discuss what to do next," Patrick replied.

"Yeah, we're on the way south, but there's a new lawman in Apgar. A mean one that could be between us, and you," Moses said, Emma looking on with a wide smile.

"Officer Eamon won't be a problem. You should have a clear path to the relay hub for the next several hours. Hurry, brother, a storm is coming," Patrick said, his tone reassuring and warm.

Moses smiled broadly, looking around at the gathered militia, some with tears in their eyes, hands clasped together. "We'll be there as quick as we can."

"Great, I can't wait to see you. Patrick, out."

CHAPTER 8

GLACIER NATIONAL PARK, ONE MILE SOUTH OF THE BLANKENSHIP RD TURNOFF

AUGUST 30TH, 2201 – 7:42 AM

Eamon crushed the militia radio he'd taken from Craig, letting what remained of it fall into the river. Shadow kept a vigil, watching the open ground around the river to the south. Jake alternated between playing with her fur and sleeping as Eamon filled their canteens with river water. They'd made good time, skirting the high ground as they headed south, not far from the place Shadow said the Romani had been making blind cargo drops.

"He's funny," Shadow said, pointing a thumb back toward Jake.

"Yeah. Good kid," Eamon replied, handing her a canteen with water almost too cold to drink.

"No, I mean he hardly makes a noise most of the time, and he seems totally nonverbal. He seems like he should be old enough now to be making a few words."

Eamon frowned, holding back what he knew about how Jake's mother died. He wondered if you were ever too young to avoid the trauma of watching your mother's head get blown off.

Shadow bit her lip. "In Mexico, there was a special school. It was for kids with what they called 'exceptionalities'. They weren't slow or anything, just different."

"Not everyone talks constantly like you do," Eamon said, taking a drink from his canteen.

"What if Jake needs a special school? He can't get that up here," Shadow said, worriedly.

Eamon gazed at her for a moment, not sure what to say, then clipped his canteen to his duty belt.

"I'm serious, Eamon. When we get out of here, we should…"

Eamon put a hand on her shoulder. "You, and I are not social workers. We shouldn't do anything, okay? I'll talk to a friend, and find someone who can figure this out."

"A friend?"

"Yeah, she's an ES class Drone trained to rescue people from natural disasters, terrorist attacks, wrecks, stuff like that. She has special training in identifying people with exceptionalities," Eamon explained.

"So, she can communicate with them, and help them escape a disaster?"

"Yeah, that's what she said."

Shadow smiled, feeling a little better. "In Mexico I could just make a call to get vulnerable people taken care of. I heard a rumor that some Acrididae Metasapients had the ES designator."

"Could be. How much further to the relay hub?" Eamon asked, handing Jake an empty aluminum cup to play with.

"Not far now, but we should wait until it's all the way dark. There's an old runway, so there's a lot of open ground out there," Shadow said, enduring the aluminum cup as it softly hit the back of her head.

Jake let loose with a rare bit of laughter, delighting in the new toy.

"You gave that to him, which means it's your turn to carry him," Shadow said, working with the twine around her chest.

Eamon smiled, strapping the small child to his back. Jake's presence helped to keep him focused in a sea of distractions. He contemplated what it would require to retake the town, and just hoped the relay would have a place he could call out from. Kale, Brook, and Heavy Dub would only be an hour away if they were still in the Midwest somewhere, as they'd planned.

"Thinking some big thoughts over there?" Shadow said, looking up at Eamon.

Eamon just nodded, pushing his way through the underbrush. "Hopefully, one of the transports is there, and they let me make a call."

"And if there isn't?" Shadow asked.

"I'll figure out something."

The snow-capped forested landscape yielded to a large open area where trees had been removed long ago. There were depressions in the snow where fence posts may have once been, but they'd been pulled up, concrete anchor and all. The relay hub was an old international airport, retrofitted for communications, and private transport use.

The place looked to be abandoned, except for a single hanger at the far side. It had power, and the exterior lighting flickered in time with what was a commercial generator. Eamon squinted through the frosty haze back toward the north, listening intently. They were still a ways off, but he could hear the snow machines getting closer.

"They're moving at the pace of someone walking," Shadow observed, her ears twitching.

"Some of them are walking. A working snow machine is probably like a working transport, rare. These days anyway," Eamon said, making sure his Henry rifle and Vaquero revolver were pushed around to his front and ready in case of trouble.

Shadow did the same, but held off changing optics until it got darker.

"If we wait too long, they might get here," Shadow said.

"They'll lose some time when they find their scouts back up that way. They might even take the long way around," Eamon said.

Shadow blinked. "You think they're afraid of you?"

"I think they're motivated by fear in almost everything they do," Eamon said, wishing he'd had a chance to clear and check his bolt-action rifle.

Shadow stood up on the tips of her toes and looked around from their vantage. "I don't see anyone. I kind of expected it to be a busy place, with militia from all over coordinating out of here."

Eamon looked up at the dark rows of trees circling the airfield. "Yeah, it'd be easy to think that."

"You think they've got snipers watching the airfield?" Shadow asked, looking back toward the setting sun.

"I don't know. Makes me wish I'd kept the radio on to listen to their chatter. Wouldn't have done them, or me, much good after Klaus got a chance to call in, though," Eamon said, heading down.

"We're just going to walk in there?"

"I think they're smart enough to stay off the channels, making the assumption I could listen in," Eamon said, pushing his way through the snow toward the airfield.

"Yes, but you said they had pretty significant communications technology. Couldn't they just isolate a signal or something?" Shadow asked, nervously looking toward the long shadow cast by the setting sun.

"I don't think they know they have that sophisticated communications technology, or that they have someone with those kinds of resources backing them," Eamon replied, listening to Jake sleep peacefully as he walked.

Shadow stopped dead in her tracks. "Okay, tell me what's going on."

"I'll tell you as soon as I know," Eamon said.

Shadow frowned, shaking her head. "Who would back these people?"

"The world is still full of dangerous people, more than you can count, and a lot more than I even know about. I've spent months trying to track a particular crew, the folks responsible for the Shutdown."

A look of fright crossed Shadow's face. "You think those people are here? Right now?"

Eamon shook his head. "No."

"And, that's part of what bothers you, because the threat is real, but unfamiliar."

"Yes. Can we go please?" Eamon said, impatiently.

Shadow took the lead, dodging through snow drifts as Eamon plowed relentlessly across the open area, throwing snow to either side as he did. No shots from the dark came, no trap was sprung, and the lone powered hanger came up quick as they approached hurriedly, weapons at the ready.

Eamon could faintly hear a few voices from inside, but not well enough to pick out gender or age. Shadow shivered, looking worriedly up at Eamon. He smelled it too, a scent all Drones and Metasapients had experienced.

The Factory had a peculiar odor, like nothing one would smell anywhere else. The lingering aroma would mark newly minted Metasapients, lingering around them for weeks. Drones and Metasapients had their own unique sense of humor, and dread, built around it. It wasn't a thing discussed much around outsiders.

The olfactory component triggered memories in both Eamon and Shadow. Shadow cowered for a moment, her memories of being birthed and trained by The Factory were not happy memories. Eamon brushed it aside, having seen the full scope and horror of what the Cabal had done to the world.

Eamon opened the hanger door, pushing snow aside with it, his huge form taking up the entire doorway for a moment. He squeezed through, taking in the familiar sight of machinery used to create nanotechnological replicas arrayed around the hanger. Other machines lurked in the darkness, accompanied by the hum of powerful generators and refrigeration units.

A man in his late forties, balding on top, with graying hair around his temples stood up from a table in the center of it all. A woman and child continued to eat what looked to be a freshly prepared meal. Eamon stood still, observing with all his senses, hand on his Vaquero.

"Hello, Officer Eamon. I'm Patrick Vale," the man said, approaching slowly, hands out at his sides.

Eamon focused in on the man, even though the woman and child looked familiar. He looked as Patrick Vale would, the tell-tale scars on his hand and neck being visible. Shadow couldn't bring herself to enter at first. After a moment gathering her courage, she went in slow and sinuously after Eamon, crouching down behind him.

"Who are you?" Eamon asked.

"I just told you who I am."

Eamon moved his thumb to the hammer on his Vaquero. "Patrick Vale is dead."

"Oh, no. Not anymore, anyway," Patrick said, holding his ground.

"Eamon, what is going on?" Shadow asked, looking worriedly around at the highly advanced machinery that had been set up in the hanger.

"Don't know," Eamon said, squinting through the dark at the woman and child.

"It's like I've been asleep these last few months. I died, and yet, I live again. God is good," Patrick said, clasping his hands together and looking upward.

The woman and child stood up, walking toward where Patrick stood. "Keep your hands where I can see them," Eamon said, squinting at them through the gloom of the hanger.

"It's us, Eamon, Vienna and Emily. We're just waiting for Klaus to…"

Eamon felt as though he were miles away, his Metasapient brain trying to reconcile how they could possibly be standing there. Klaus's family, Eamon's friends, died in Finland during a bank robbery gone purposefully wrong. The world collapsed in around him, but Abbey was there by his side, hand on his arm through what seemed like an impenetrable dark.

Eamon's eyes cleared instantly, the sight of Patrick's outstretched hand falling quickly into view. He was reaching for something, possibly Eamon's weapon. With a quick wave of his arm, Eamon batted him away. Even through the ballistic protection, Eamon could feel that Patrick was far more dense than a regular human. He felt more like unyielding liquid steel than soft flesh.

Patrick slid back, keeping his footing and absorbing the blow like no human had right to. Emily and Vienna sprang out of the way with preternatural speed, avoiding Patrick as he slid backward. Shadow bolted, running out into the dark as quickly as she could, but Eamon held his ground, calmly meeting Patrick's gaze.

Patrick cocked his head to one side. "This should have triggered a psychotic break, or a fugue state, as a result of the trauma you suffered. Drones and Metasapients do not tend to handle death particularly well."

Eamon just frowned, going through the list of folks that would try to mess with him in this way.

"I need the boy," Patrick said, gesturing to Jake.

The commotion had woken Jake, but he just gazed serenely over Eamon's shoulder. His small hands curled the fur that popped up between his vest and armored sleeves. Eamon decided then that someone would take the boy, but only from his cold, dead, hands.

"Come and take him," Eamon said, lowering his head and glaring at Patrick.

"He belongs with us," Patrick replied, holding out his hands.

Eamon nodded. "Kiss my fuzzy bear backside."

"Is this a negotiation?" Patrick asked. "I don't think it is."

"Then, do something other than talk," Eamon said, hand on his Vaquero.

"Listen, I…" Patrick said, taking a step forward.

"Don't take another step. I will shoot you," Eamon said.

"I'm sure we can be civilized about this," Patrick said, smiling warmly, and taking another step.

Eamon drew quickly and fired at Patrick with one fluid motion. The round burned into Patrick's chest, tumbling as it did terrible damage to him internally. He fell backward, a look of sadness and shock crossing his face. Emily and Vienna looked on, dispassionately.

"You should not have done that," Emily said, shaking her head.

"Eamon, please, see reason," Vienna said, being careful not to move.

"I warned him," Eamon said, holstering his pistol, and turning Patrick over with his foot.

There were a pair of handguns in the back of Patrick's waistband. Eamon stooped over to scoop them up, taking his eyes off the room for a split second. When he looked up, Emily and Vienna were gone. Toward the back of the hangar he could hear the sheet metal that made up the wall drop to the ground, and feet hastily treading snow.

"All right, then. They are quick," Eamon said, putting Patrick's handguns in a large pocket on his vest.

"How…?" Patrick gasped, blood trickling out of his mouth to the floor.

"You thought being made from nanotech would keep you from a bullet?" Eamon said, replacing the round he'd used in his Vaquero.

"God, she…" Patrick slumped to the ground, eyes wide.

Abbey stepped out of the shadows, pausing to look down at the man as he took his last breath.

"How did you know?" she asked, kneeling down beside Patrick.

"Kale is a nanotechnological replica. After a few months with him, I can spot them anywhere. Something not quite right about the eyes," Eamon mused, scratching his chin.

"One round shouldn't have dropped him like that. The machine-folk are pretty tough," Abbey said, looking into Patrick's unblinking eyes.

"The rounds are high-velocity, and made of an alloy that disrupts the bioelectrical functioning of these sorts of folk."

"But, the boy, Jake?"

"No, he's not a nanotech replica," Eamon said, shaking his head.

Abbey blinked. "But, Patrick said…"

"Yeah, don't know what he meant by that," Eamon said, shining a flashlight around.

Shadow slinked back into the hanger, eyes fixed firmly on the floor. "Who are you talking to?" She asked meekly.

Eamon shined the flashlight upward, taking stock of the communications array installed above. "Just myself. My partners seem to leave me high and dry."

"Sorry, but that smell, I…"

"Yeah, I know. It's hard to get used to it," Eamon said, letting the light from his flashlight follow conduit and fiber optic cable down to a hidden terminal.

"You've encountered it often? Often enough to get used to it?" Shadow said, somewhat horrified.

Eamon nodded. "There's a lot of stuff from The Factory out there, and not just this stuff."

Shadow winced. "You're him."

Eamon looked back at Shadow. "I'm who?"

"Rumor has it, the devil that burned most of Asia and Europe was killed by an Ursine Metasapient. You're him," Shadow said, looking fearfully down at Patrick's corpse.

"Shadow, all I came here to do was fish and make the town feel safe. I swear," Eamon said, spreading out the pages of one of Emily's coloring books from the table, hot dinner still steaming beside it.

"That trouble in Europe, it's followed you here, hasn't it?"

Eamon looked up. Abbey was standing right behind Shadow, her blue eyes twinkling. He couldn't be sure who asked the question. They both sounded so alike. It was clear Shadow was a different variant of the Type One, smaller, and more suited to speed, but they were both soldiers.

Shadow looked back at the door, trying to follow Eamon's sightline. "What are you looking at?" Shadow asked, straining to see if Eamon was listening to some distant sound.

Eamon blinked, shaking his head. "No, this is something else. That business in Europe is done."

"How can you be sure?"

"Only Emily colors this way," Eamon said, spreading his large paw-hand over the page of the coloring book to blot it out. "The Cabal is rarely so detail oriented."

CHAPTER 9

**YEARS AGO, BEFORE THE PORT MONTAIGNE MIDTOWN
TRANSPORT TRAGEDY**

Vivian stood in the doorway, waiting for the biometric sensors to verify her identity. She'd grown weary of having to check on Doctor Helmet, but everyone lacked the patience to approach him properly. They had protocols that detected unauthorized experiments or research, something her colleague seemed to run afoul of constantly.

She preferred an exacting environment to conduct her work. Everything in its place, and a place for everything. She worked toward her goals with razor-sharp efficiency and focus. Nothing distracted her.

By contrast, Doctor Helmet's laboratory was messy, with several unauthorized experiments going at once. Stacks of papers were heaped high around the laboratory including several forgotten cups of half-drunk coffee tucked away in the gaps. The cleaning crew looks to have largely given up, keeping only a handful of paths through the chaos swept and clear.

When Vivian finally found him, Doctor Helmet was working with a rapid prototyping engine. He was completely engrossed in the particle synthesis he'd started earlier in the morning, his lunch sitting untouched beside him. Lab rats looked on hungrily from a cage nearby.

She waited patiently for him to pause, which wouldn't take long as he still kept pen and paper notes of his work.

"Ah, Vivian, I didn't see you standing there. Hopefully, it wasn't for long," Doctor Helmet said, nervously looking about.

"They're going to push you out, you know, if you don't start logging your work properly, and following the rules," Vivian said, looking around at the clutter gathered between machinery and ongoing experiments.

Doctor Helmet removed his glasses, and began cleaning them with a cloth from his pocket. "Aren't you the least bit curious?"

Vivian sighed. "Curious about what?"

"How do these contrived beings, these artificial intelligences, keep spontaneously appearing?"

"Even the most quantum-capable of the Omega Class aren't certain... or, if they are, they aren't sharing it with us," Vivian said, looking worriedly at the particle synthesis machine, and the strange crystal Doctor Helmet had been crafting.

"Entropy. It shouldn't be able to order things, and yet..."

Vivian shook her head. "Yes, we've known that entropy can order particles into complex structures for decades. Some of our most important chemical engineering projects rely on the principle."

Doctor Helmet ran through his notes, holding up two sheets of paper. "There is the biological component to consider, we haven't even..."

Vivian regarded the coffee-stained sheets of handwritten notes with a bored expression, before homing in on a couple of details. Vivian frowned at the notes, snatching them from Doctor Helmet's hands. He looked startled, having rarely seen her depart her composure.

"You act as if these beings we're creating are our children, and I'm not sure how you can begin to think that," Vivian said, turning a stern gaze toward the rats in a cage nearby.

"How can you not consider them our children? That is a far more compelling question, in my opinion," Doctor Helmet said, folding his arms.

Vivian sighed, not wishing to enter into a philosophical debate with her elderly colleague. "The terrestrial intelligent agent project isn't your area, Doctor Helmet. I'd advise that you cease prototyping or researching anything to do with this," Vivian said, stuffing the pages in her lab coat pocket.

Doctor Helmet chuckled. "The scanning technology, have you perfected it?"

"We're working with an expert. The ability to remove them from the surrogate system and..."

Doctor Helmet's eyes widened. "Madmar, then? If he's helping you... wait, how many are there now? These terrestrial intelligent agents? You do know there will be more, yes?"

"How does this relate to your work on Metasapients and Drones?" Vivian asked, impatiently.

"You don't think that your contrived beings, and mine, are any less machine than each other, or when compared to humans for that matter?" Doctor Helmet said.

"I'm not having this conversation with you," Vivian said firmly.

Doctor Helmet shook his head sadly. "If we don't talk about it, they will. I promise you that."

"I've already crafted the storage devices you're trying to prototype. As for transferring a consciousness, that's not something we'll ever be able to do," Vivian said, frowning at Doctor Helmet's crude attempts at replicating her work.

"Well, copy or transfer, it's the same..."

Vivian smirked. "No, it isn't. You don't know what you're talking about. You are dabbling in the sort of digital alchemy your academic training didn't prepare you for. This isn't the same as crafting genetic profiles with existing materials and coding. What you do is crude, barbaric even..."

Doctor Helmet was taken aback, not sure how to respond.

"Look, I think what you've brought to the MDC is valuable. Having a non-human workforce for hazardous and EVA environments is a necessary evil. That said, don't compare what you do, to what I do," Vivian said, still a little angry.

"Non-human?" Doctor Helmet said, squinting at Vivian.

"You know what I mean," Vivian replied, a little too quickly.

"I guess I should apologize, then?" Doctor Helmet said, looking about his laboratory. "I assumed it was designed to all be drawn together somehow, for a singular purpose. I'm just trying to find my own purpose here."

Vivian's pride prevented her from drawing him into the circle, telling him how his studies of behavioral science had greatly aided every facet of the program. She understood little of what he did, only that he seemed to be making the gentlest of monsters. Each that she'd encountered had a certain nobility about them, a sort of inborn dignity.

"I'll tell Control that I didn't find you doing anything wrong down here. But, seriously, stop looking at particle synthesis outside of the practical application of your own project parameters," Vivian warned.

"When will I get to review your work, as you've clearly reviewed mine?" Doctor Helmet asked, knowing she hadn't even set a date to present her findings.

"Bringing what I've done out of the digital realm was dangerous. Some of them are special, but in no way outside of the human norm. A few have latent telemechanical abilities. Others..." Vivian said, lost in thought for a moment.

"...are capable of quantum calculations and perceptions of reality," Doctor Helmet said, excitedly.

Vivian nodded hesitantly. "Possibly. The trick is making sure they never know of their full potential. Humanity isn't ready to have contrived beings of this sort walk amongst them. Even in the process of imprinting them to a terrestrial form, unexpected things happen."

"You haven't figured out how to control them," Doctor Helmet stated, unsurprised.

"How do you do it? Your contributions are all marvelously well-behaved for the most part, with the Acrididae being the rare exception."

Doctor Helmet smiled. "The Acrididae only go rogue when Control doesn't follow my recommendations. They tried to manipulate them with hunger, depriving them of food. They were cruel to them, and they reacted as any living creature would to that stimuli."

"Why would Control ignore your recommendations?"

"They see some of what we've created as only being fit to exist so long as it is useful. This is a fallacy, which runs contrary to the most basic biological imperatives. The Acrididae Metasapients looked the least approachable, because of their insectoid features, and hardened exoskeletons. Control only saw weapons and hazardous zone workers."

"I've seen them in The Factory with each other. They're extremely social, and ill-suited for that use case. Are you purposefully trying to undermine the desires of our employers?" Vivian asked, somewhat amused at her colleague's antics.

"You can't set an evolutionary clock on a new species inside the first generation. These things take time. Useful mutations take many iterations if you don't understand what stimuli works best. It is as though no one in Control has even read a paper on dissipation-driven adaptation," Doctor Helmet said, walking over to an experiment with several varieties of mold growing in petri dishes.

"They're sterile, or they are supposed to be," Vivian said, looking disdainfully at Doctor Helmet's mold experiment.

"Take any species and place them in a harsh or alien environment. What do they do?"

"Die, or evolve quickly to survive, and propagate."

"Sometimes. I know of at least one Sphyraenidae-type Metasapient being born on Mars. Her parents overcame sterilization protocols after the Orange Line Incident," Doctor Helmet said proudly.

"The child will probably be hideous, incapable of interacting with humans, an invalid maybe. The controls are supposed to prevent viable offspring. Also, the baseline barracuda Metasapients are pretty rough in appearance already," Vivian said, a trace of disgust in her voice.

Doctor Helmet chuckled politely, pulling a data slate from a countertop and handing it to Vivian. The screen displayed several pictures that Drone workers had captured from the Metasapient habitat on Mars. There were no collection markers, or control metadata, indicating that Doctor Helmet had acquired the pictures on his own.

On the screen were a pair of proud Type One Sphyraenic Metasapients, each terrifying in their own right, designed for hazardous duty only. They were large, and bulky, designed to survive swimming through contaminated or radioactive waters. Their child, a baby girl, was smooth and lustrous, graceful and alluring.

"She's beautiful, otherworldly, even," Vivian remarked, amazed at the sight of the baby Metasapient.

"They call her Hashtasha. I had the Drone workers conduct a biometric scan just to make sure she was healthy," Doctor Helmet said, swiping sideways on the data slate to review a set of readings.

"I'm not familiar with this particular Metasapient, since they weren't released for duty on Earth, but..." Vivian said, looking at the readings.

"She will be stronger, faster, tougher, and probably smarter than her parents. She also has several adaptations that will allow her to more easily interact with humans. All emergent and morphological qualities indicative to a second generation Metasapient of her type," Doctor Helmet explained.

Vivian frowned. "Are we engineering the end of humanity? Will we be pushed out by these contrived beings? Unlike terrestrial intelligent agents, none of your creations will have any reason to attempt being human. What keeps them from rising up and wiping us out?"

Doctor Helmet considered the question carefully, stroking his beard. "None of them will have the evolutionary fitness of humans, for better or worse. They won't look at the world in terms of limited resources, or space. They'll probably be glad for what they find, and each other."

"Isn't that what may have allowed early humans to hedge out other early hominids?" Vivian said, sullenly.

"You think we'll fall victim to our own monsters in trying to fight a demon?"

Vivian nodded. "You did design them to survive in the event that we do not."

"If we hedged our bets, wouldn't it make sense for the Omega AIs to do the same?" Doctor Helmet countered, gesturing to his particle synthesis experiment.

"You think they're lying, that these contrived beings showing up with the nanotech and imprinting technology isn't a coincidence," Vivian said, understanding, at last, why Doctor Helmet was looking into her work.

Doctor Helmet nodded. "I think it is possible that they know it's happening, but do not know why, and are giving data back the best way they know how."

Vivian closed her eyes and nodded. "I'll look into it."

CHAPTER 10

GLACIER NATIONAL PARK, OLD INTERNATIONAL AIRPORT

AUGUST 30TH, 2201 – 5:11 PM

Emma turned to her niece, Janice, and nodded toward the hanger at the far end of the old airport. "He's supposed to be there."

"You mean the hangar where all these huge bear tracks lead?" Moses said, somberly.

"No need to be smart," Janice snapped.

"Quiet, both of you," Emma said, dropping down out of the Sno-Cat and looking around at the forested hills nearby. "We don't have anyone out here?"

"Patrick told everyone to stay clear," Moses said, looking through the scope on his rifle.

The group made their way toward the shed cautiously. Armed militia checking each building and structure as they went. The place seemed deserted. Moses took the lead on the hanger, ducking with his rifle up, and then coming hurriedly back out.

"It's full of weird machines and such," he said, turning up his nose.

"Anyone inside?" Emma said, struggling to catch her breath.

"Naw, but there is a pool of blood on the floor. Doesn't look like it's been there too long. There's food on the table, all gone cold," Moses reported, looking around suspiciously.

Emma stepped in and looked around at the softly humming machinery, and then the blood on the floor. Someone had wiped up most of it, probably to try and conceal what had happened there. The table had plates of food, for what was probably a pair of adults and a child, judging by the portions. The plates were arrayed in such a way that there was probably other things present, but that they'd been taken.

"Look at this," Emma said, stooping over and picking an orange crayon from under the table.

"Jake, he ain't old enough to be coloring," Moses said, gesturing to his men to do a more thorough search.

Emma looked at the crayon for a moment, as if to will it into telling the story of what had happened there. She pocketed it before turning to her niece, a worried look on her face. Janice frowned, knowing how important meeting with the leader of the militia was for her aunt.

"Do you think Patrick is dead?" Emma asked.

Janice looked down at the blood on the floor. "If he tried to tangle with Eamon, probably."

Emma shook her head. "Why would he do that, with all our..."

There were cries from outside; men began rushing to one side and dropping to one knee, leveling rifles at the hills to the west. Moses went outside, pulling up his range finders.

"What happened?" Janice yelled.

"Sno-Cat took a round from somewhere up there," Moses said, looking with his range finders.

"Where? Where?" Janice said, staying inside the hanger.

"I see him. He's in the shadow of those rocks up there, but he didn't protect his scope. I'm getting glint off of it," Moses yelled, looking to his mother.

"You sure? What about Jake?" she replied.

"The last satellite image Patrick sent us, it looked like one of the dog pack had Jake. Looks like a big ol' bear up there, by himself, a scoped rifle in his hands. Even caught a glimpse of his badge," Moses replied.

"Have everyone switch to HV ammo and burn him down," Emma ordered.

Janice grabbed her aunt by the arm. "You sure about this?"

"Do it!" Emma said, looking down at the blood stain on the hanger floor.

Moses and his men quickly swapped to magazines carrying special high-velocity rounds and lit up the hill to the west. Each man went through the entire magazine, just to be sure Eamon was dead. Trees fell as trunks took rounds and exploded, rounds sparking as they struck the rocky backdrop.

"Get up there and make sure he's dead!" Emma bellowed.

Moses took a small group up the hill, staying in constant radio contact with the Sno-Cat. Janice lifted the hood on the disabled vehicle, cursing at the neat hole punched straight through the engine block. Emma held a radio to her ear, listening intently as Moses and his team made the ascent. It would be almost thirty minutes before they'd report back.

"We found him. Sort of," Moses reported over the radio.

"What do you mean, sort of?" Emma said, growing angrier.

"It was just a big stack of logs, draped with a green tarp to look like a vest. The glinting I saw through the rangefinders was aluminum foil made to look like a badge. Looks like he just pressed it to his own so it would be the same shape. Found a glass bottle wrapped up with a rag so only the bottom was visible. That must have been what I thought was the scope. Also..."

"Get back down here, now," Emma said, looking around warily.

Nearby, a small maintenance shack slowly rose up. Eamon pushed up from below, lifting the whole thing easily with one arm, tipping it over as a child would a cardboard box. He stepped out of where he'd dug a shallow pit, and set the shack back down, tools hanging against the wall inside clattering faintly. Janice watched in horror as the lawman walked casually over toward the group.

Emma lost her temper immediately, as the rest of the militia convoy looked on in shocked surprise. "You cursed bit of Jewish clay! Do you have any idea..."

"Watch your language in front of the boy," Eamon said, calmly bringing up his Henry rifle.

"Moses will be back here in minutes," Janice said, bluffing.

"Not nearly fast enough if any of you go for a gun," Eamon said darkly, his black eyes darting back and forth.

Janice looked up at the small boy strapped to Eamon's back, his tiny face just peeking over Eamon's armored vest. The boy seemed calm, almost serene given the amount of very loud gunfire that had been unleashed nearby. Looking closer, she could see a little bit of orange foam sticking out from the boy's ears.

"Where is Patrick?" Emma demanded.

"If I were you, I'd forget about all that. Grab your supplies, head back west to meet with your boy, and just keep going," Eamon said, resting a heavy hand across the top of his rifle.

Emma balled up one fist, and pointed a bony finger at Eamon with the other. "Patrick has a plan. We are sticking to the plan, God's plan..."

"Patrick is dead. He died months ago. You got played," Eamon said, eyes flicking over toward the hangar full of experimental science equipment.

Emma scoffed at Eamon's words, shaking her head. "You're lying. All clay like you lies."

"In a hostage negotiation, it's best to never lie to the perpetrators," Eamon said, looking up to see if Shadow was clear yet.

Janice stepped up to her aunt, putting a hand on her shoulder. "I don't think he is lying. We should cut our losses and..."

Emma spun, catching Janice across the face with the back of her hand. "Blasphemer! If you like what this lying piece of clay has to say, maybe you should just stay here with him," Emma spat, nodding to one of the men.

The man grabbed Janice's pack and threw it on the ground in the snow. "I will go meet my son, and then we're going to come back and find out what you've done with Patrick. If you're still here, we'll kill you," Emma said, motioning for the group to follow her.

Janice watched her aunt jump on the back of one of the snow machines, the whole convoy leaving her and the disabled Sno-Cat behind. She closed her eyes, took a deep breath, and picked up her pack. Eamon watched, his face like impassive steel, his dark eyes watching the convoy go.

"She won't listen to anyone," Janice said, looking mournfully up at Eamon.

"Thanks for trying," Eamon said, turning back toward the east and breaking into a run.

Janice jogged along beside him. "Where are you going?"

"I don't want to be here when your people get back. I don't want to have to kill them all," Eamon said, keeping his stride shallow as to not bounce Jake around too much.

"I figured, but you seem pretty smart. You have some sort of plan for dislodging my people from Apgar?" Janice said, keeping pace beside Eamon easily.

"Yeah, I'm going to ask real nicely," Eamon said, deadpan.

Janice just blinked, and held her pace beside the huge bear cop as he tread snow effortlessly. Up ahead, a breathless Shadow emerged from a thicket to the south, running toward Eamon with a strange expression. Everyone paused to catch their breath, the international airport already having faded somewhat in the distance.

"What's she doing here?" Shadow asked, gesturing toward Janice.

"You tell me. You guys know each other, right?" Eamon said, making sure Jake was okay.

Janice laughed. "I knew it was you when I heard the rifle report and saw that perfect hole in the engine block of the cat."

Shadow winked. "It was one of my better shots, wasn't it?"

Janice chuckled, but immediately adopted a more somber expression under Eamon's withering gaze.

"I guess you probably want to know how we know each other," Shadow said, guiltily.

"Janice runs contraband, met you on the blind drop that brought you here from Mexico. Janice knowing you were from Mexico saw an opportunity to possibly expand her network, and you guys ended up being friends," Eamon said, holding out a large hand to Shadow expectantly.

"Yeah, how did you know..." Shadow said, not sure what Eamon wanted.

"The same way I know you probably have a biscuit in one of your vest pockets. Give it up," Eamon said.

Shadow handed Eamon a biscuit and watched him eat it, a contented expression crossing his face.

"You're a cop, and you notice things?" Janice ventured.

"Yeah, and I also spent the last few months hanging out with some very serious operators. I learned a few things," Eamon said, leaning over and sniffing the air.

"You can smell us on each other," Shadow said, feeling extra guilty for deceiving Eamon.

"You let her tag along because you knew she knew me?" Janice said, frowning.

"She tagged along to keep me from killing you," Eamon said, turning his gaze to the northwest, and starting to walk quickly.

Shadow and Janice looked at one another and sighed. Eamon paused mid-stride, and looked back at them. "Coming?"

"Yeah, hold on," they said in unison.

"Where is Patrick?" Janice asked.

"Like I said, he's been dead for months. Whatever you saw in the hangar, that wasn't him," Eamon said, folding his arms and huffing impatiently.

Janice looked at Eamon, raising one eyebrow. "There was nothing in there but a blood stain, and not even much of one."

Eamon squinted. "No body?"

"No, and it looked like the blood had been wiped up," Janice said, exchanging a worried glance with Shadow.

"Wiped up or evaporated?" Eamon said, looking around warily.

"Okay, you are making no sense right now," Shadow said, shaking her head.

"That equipment at the hangar is dangerous. I can't even go in there and just break it. It takes a team of technicians a week to take it all down safely," Eamon said, taking a step back.

"Okay, okay. What do we need to do?" Shadow said, seeing the worry in Eamon's face.

"We need to get to the blind drop site, call for a pick up, and use the radio aboard the transport to get help," Eamon said, gesturing for them to follow.

Janice smiled, nervously shaking her head. "The transports come on a schedule. There's nothing but a clearing at the blind drop."

Eamon closed his eyes. "When is the next blind drop?"

Janice pulled out a small notebook, and flipped through the pages. "About six weeks."

"Is there another way to call out?" Shadow asked.

"Yeah, there's radio equipment, older stuff we had before Patrick got us the new radios. It's back at our camp in Whitefish," Janice said, making a pained expression.

Eamon looked to Shadow.

Shadow shook her head. "They know all my routes now, thanks to that damned knife. There's no safe way back there without fighting a bunch of militia."

"We have some time with the militia all spread out. The other battalions won't arrive for a few days. They were delayed by bad weather," Janice said, folding her arms.

Eamon looked back to the west. He could see Abbey standing out at the ridge, the old international airport a little bit to the south of her. She watched the militia slowly pass by her, heading north, before looking back up toward Eamon. Her eyes were clear and blue, as always, fur standing in contrast to her blue vest.

"You're doing that thing," Shadow said as she tried to follow Eamon's sight line. "Staring at nothing."

Janice squinted, looking back toward the airport. "All I is see my crazy aunt and her knucklehead son heading north."

"Whitefish isn't far, but it'll take us further from Apgar. And further from the Server Hub," Eamon said, looking at Janice.

"You don't trust me," Janice said, hugging her own shoulders.

"You've been a peacemaker so far. You tried really hard to keep people from being killed. I remember you being really angry in the pass before the avalanche. Your aunt gave the kill order on the Garcia family without your knowledge, didn't she?" Eamon asked, already knowing the answer.

Janice sulked. "She was adamant about getting the child. I didn't know she'd have the Garcias killed until I heard the shots."

"If she finds out you're helping us, your aunt will kill you. I'm wondering what's in it for you. Both of you," Eamon said, keeping his eyes on Abbey.

Shadow lowered her head.

Eamon smiled sadly, and shook his head. "Tell me how it was supposed to work."

"You weren't supposed to be here. The mercenaries would leave, and a regular sheriff would come in. We'd take all we'd earned, and a little from the militia treasury, and jump a transport south," Shadow said, folding her arms.

"And the radio equipment?" Eamon sighed.

"I was supposed to sell it, but I couldn't be sure of the timing with the militia, mercenaries leaving, and everything else," Janice said, sulking.

"Who else is involved?" Eamon asked. He unstrapped Jake from his tactical vest.

Shadow frowned. "Ray Pendleton. I dropped him a bribe to sway the Apgar Elders Council to push for the mercenaries to be replaced..."

"And Kale probably saw right through all of this," Eamon said, smirking.

"Excuse me?" Shadow said, cocking her head to one side.

"Nothing, and the Garcias? They brought you here," Eamon said, looking at Shadow disappointedly.

"They weren't supposed to get hurt. No one was supposed to get hurt. If Emma Vale tried to prevent us from leaving or figured things out, we'd have Jake as leverage," Shadow said, sulking.

"Emma Vale found out?" Eamon asked.

"I don't think so, but with Patrick Vale still being alive... I just don't know now," Shadow said, looking apologetically at Janice.

"Ray gave you that lookout job months ago. You've been planning this for a while," Eamon said, bitterly, laying Jake down on his knee.

Shadow watched Eamon clumsily change Jake's diaper, before stepping in to help. "You've seen how these people are, Eamon. They think we are garbage. They don't appreciate us, and..."

"Ray Pendleton got shot trying to make a run for it. You were supposed to warn him, but you were out helping me keep the hub safe," Eamon said, letting Jake play with his radio.

Shadow lowered her head, breath coming out slow, mist trailing up from her nostrils in the cold. "Yeah, I know."

"So, I have to ask, what happens now?" Janice asked, gazing sadly at the poly restraints clipped to Eamon's duty belt.

Eamon sighed. "As long as you're cooperating with me, I'll write it up that way. Try to run or get in my way, you'll go from cooperating witnesses to suspects. Deal?"

"Deal," Shadow and Janice said, one after the other.

Eamon picked up Jake, freshly changed and happy. The little boy looked at the radio clasped between his hands, eyes wide with wonder. As Eamon strapped Jake to his vest once more, he patted the urn in his pocket. He could almost hear Abbey's voice, warning him.

"You sure it's a good idea to give him your radio?" Shadow said, smiling at the small boy.

"No, but he's been grasping for it for hours. It's not doing me any good right now anyway," Eamon said.

The radio sprang to life in the boy's hands, the frequency modulating automatically, numbers dancing across the LCD.

"Officer Eamon, are you there?"

"Aaron AI? Protocol is to pull your external link during situations like this. You're taking a risk contacting me."

"I didn't contact you, Officer Eamon. You contacted me."

CHAPTER 11

GLACIER NATIONAL PARK, TRAILHEAD, 2 MILES EAST OF THE
OLD INTERNATIONAL AIRPORT

AUGUST 30TH, 2201 – 8:47 PM

"Is Jennifer safe? And the dog pack?? Are you secure?" Eamon said, looking at Jake, who seemed to be in a trance.

"Yes, Officer Eamon, we are all well, for now," Aaron AI replied.

"How are we speaking over the local radio channel? Is the connection secure?" Eamon asked, Janice and Shadow looking on with equal expressions of bafflement.

"Unknown, but the encryption is incredibly complex and variable. This is similar to getting a call from Taylor IA," Aaron replied, the transmission wavering as he scanned the frequency.

"Jake is holding my radio," Eamon reported.

"I see," Aaron replied, the words coming out slowly as if he was trying to calculate an impossibly large number at the same time.

"I saw, and ended up shooting, Patrick Vale," Eamon reported.

"Where?" Aaron asked.

"In a warehouse full of restricted Class Five IE equipment," Eamon said, closing his eyes and cursing under his breath.

"*That is worrying, Officer Eamon. I recommend you return to the Server Hub immediately.*"

"I'm not sure that's a good idea. How long until redundancies across North America start to waver in your absence? Someone, Brook particularly, will notice if you don't reconnect soon," Eamon said, not crazy about trying to move Jake through Apgar.

"*Irregularities subject to administrative notification won't occur for another one hundred thirty-eight hours. Long enough for all kinds of unfortunate things to happen. Plenty of time for Emma Vale and her people to find a way to gain access to the Server Hub,*" Aaron said, a hint of sadness in his voice.

"That's almost double the seventy-two hour standard," Eamon said, frowning.

"*Apologies. I'm very efficient and good at what I do,*" Aaron replied.

Eamon paused, gathering his thoughts for a moment. The forested land was already growing dim, shadows growing long beneath the trees all around him. Shadow and Janice shivered, the temperature dropping quickly.

"What if you reconnected to make a single SOS call?" Eamon asked.

"*There is an extreme risk of intrusion. Immediately prior to having the dog pack pull the physical link to the outside, someone tried to gain access to the grid. I stopped them, but I'm not sure I could do it a second time,*" Aaron replied.

"Who could do that?" Shadow harshly whispered.

"*A handful of telemechanics, Omega Class artificial intelligences, exactly two known terrestrial intelligent agents.*"

"You know who it is," Eamon said, nodding.

"*Yes.*"

"But, you can't tell me who," Eamon said, frowning.

"*They've asked to remain anonymous, and external to most global, or system affairs. I am merely trying to respect their wishes,*" Aaron replied.

Janice did not understand why Aaron would protect someone in that way, but Eamon and Shadow understood. Even if another Metasapient did them wrong, they'd probably still protect them. They couldn't count on humans for protection, leaving them only with the solidarity they shared with one another.

"This is bullshit, we don't know who is behind this? And the CGG's pet AI won't tell you?" Janice said, folding her arms.

"You've no honor or loyalty to anyone, so I wouldn't expect you to understand," Aaron replied.

Janice looked at the radio, shocked and angry.

"That is the unnecessarily harsh way of saying you wouldn't understand, being a human," Shadow said, as gently as possible.

Eamon just smiled. "I'm starting to like you, Aaron."

"Likewise," Aaron replied.

"So, what do we do?" Janice said, throwing up her arms.

"We deal with the human component. Patrick Vale agreed to be the foster parent for Jake, in exchange for illegal identity extensive technology. Or, he was holding Jake hostage, and blackmailed Jake's real parents into giving him what he wanted," Eamon said, glaring back in the direction of the old international airport.

"I could reconnect and report that Jake is safely away from Patrick Vale," Aaron said.

"That could create a power vacuum in the militia. They have a military hierarchy, but it's based on popular support for the leadership. I don't want them to start fighting with each other while they're still occupying Apgar," Eamon said.

"Who cares? Those people didn't even want your protection, and they treat all us Metasapients badly. They broke their promise to improve the dog pack's living conditions," Shadow said.

"Because I'm a police officer, and I don't run from my duty. Also, the dog pack cares, and they would want Jennifer and Aaron AI to be able to live somewhere safe," Eamon snapped back, causing Shadow to resume sulking.

"Okay, let's make a camp, a plan, and do something about it," Janice said, pointing to the northeast.

"Eamon, try to call me again when you've decided what to do," Aaron intoned, ending the call.

Eamon gently took the radio way from Jake, causing the small boy to return to his normally placid behavior. He still grasped at the radio, but was quickly distracted with a small corner of biscuit offered up by Eamon.

Clipping the radio to his vest, Eamon turned his attention back to Janice and Shadow.

"In the morning, you should head west, grab your money, and call for a ride," Eamon said, turning his steely expression from Shadow to Janice.

"I don't really care about that now," Janice said, looking at Jake.

Eamon softened his expression. "Okay, let's get a little further up the trail, past the ridge, and build a fire so you guys don't freeze."

They kept the fire low, taking turns to keep watch. Jake slept through the night, waking once to complain about an uncomfortable diaper. Eamon sat upright, alternating between sleep and quiet meditation.

Shadow watched him, the blackened forest arrayed around his shoulders behind him. Occasionally, she'd blink and find him staring back at her, his black eyes flickering with the firelight. She'd never seen an Ursine Metasapient like him. He was terrifyingly strong, and yet, he was flexible and kind, unlike so many of the regular Ursine Metasapients she'd met. Most were unwavering in their task, whatever it was. As afraid of him as she was, she could only imagine how that was for regular humans. She hoped she would never be on the wrong side of Eamon.

Janice did her best to keep warm, but lacking fur or little Jake's strange resistance to the cold, she shivered through the night, barely finding any sleep or solace. When her eyes closed, she could hear her aunt's voice, distant but angry. She could only imagine how she was now, driven by the possible loss of her son a second time.

Eamon rose during the night, hand on his Henry rifle, ears standing up straight. He sniffed the air, and turned looking toward the south. Janice looked on in abject terror as a trio of grizzly bears sauntered up. They looked curiously at Eamon for a few moments before turning and wandering off.

Eamon watched them go, Abbey walking along beside them. She barely gave a look over her shoulder as she went, hand on her sidearm like she was headed toward trouble. Throughout, Jake snored quietly, his hands grasping and pulling at the fur across Eamon's shoulder.

"Did you use your magical bear powers to get them to move on?" Janice said, shivering.

"If I had magical bear powers, I'm pretty sure it'd be against the rules to talk about them," Eamon said, adding another log to the fire.

"If the fire gets too high, someone might see us," Janice said.

"That's their problem," Eamon said, tending the fire. "Keeping you alive is mine."

"You really aren't afraid of the militia?" Janice asked, rubbing her hands a little too close to the flames.

Eamon took a deep breath. "I can see why you and Shadow are friends."

"Yeah?"

"You both talk a lot and ask a lot of questions."

Janice frowned. "I'm serious, you're no good to the area if you get yourself killed."

"You suddenly care what happens to the area?" Eamon said, squinting.

"I always cared. I grew up here. Just because I wanted a better life somewhere else doesn't mean I wanted to set fire to the place as I was leaving," Janice said, hugging her knees.

"You called me a golem before."

"I had to keep up appearances with the family. I'm Shadow's partner in crime, remember?"

"Wouldn't be the first time a human just used one of us for their own purposes," Eamon said, turning the log over in the fire with his bare hand.

Janice lowered her head. "No, it wouldn't."

"You're being a little hard on her, don't you think?" Shadow said, pulling her blanket around her shoulders a little tighter.

Eamon nodded. "Probably. Sorry."

Shadow just looked at him, a little surprised by his response.

"My old partner bonded with a human. She was supposed to protect him, putting his life above her own. He abandoned her for some fool quest on a different continent," Eamon said, putting his hand over the pocket that carried the urn.

"That's terrible," Janice said, sounding genuinely outraged.

"Janice would never do that to me, Eamon," Shadow said, trying to reassure him.

Eamon nodded, his hand still pressed firmly against the urn.

"Your partner, she's gone?" Janice ventured.

Eamon stood up suddenly, in time with Shadow, both turning toward the north. Eamon quickly unstrapped the baby carrier from his vest handing Jake over to Shadow. Janice looked around confused, only barely able to hear frost floating softly down from the trees and settling on the ground.

"What? What is it?" Janice said, panicked.

"Snow machines," Eamon said, pushing his Vaquero around to the front and lever-loading a round into the chamber of his Henry rifle.

"We'll pick them off as they break the tree line," Shadow said, nodding to Eamon.

"No, if any of them manage to escape, it'll be better if they report back having only seen me. Get to cover," Eamon ordered, turning toward the tree line and breaking into a run.

Janice looked on, wide-eyed. "He's really fast," she said, watching him drop to all fours and take off at top speed.

Eamon ran as fast as he could, picking up speed as he threaded through the trees, ascending the hill. His lungs burned as he pushed himself to try and meet the snow machines at the top of the hill. He could hear their radios crackle, and the sound of ammunition being chambered. Somehow, they knew exactly where to look for them.

He couldn't see her, but he could hear Abbey running beside him nearby, at his three-o'clock as she always did. He could faintly hear the crackle of her radio, the old Finnish Forestry Service feedback and click coming over. It was like old times, but only for a moment.

Eamon met the first snow machine as it crested the hill, throwing his arms up defensively just before impact. The snow machine broke around him, shattering into hundreds of pieces, spilled fuel igniting in mid-air. The force of the impact transferred up through the snow machine and into the bodies of the driver and passenger. They hit tree branches higher up, careening through pine trees like limp rag dolls.

The forest lit up with automatic gunfire as riders on the other snow machines tried to shoot Eamon. None of them were accustomed to firing at that speed, their shots going wide, landing behind Eamon as he threw the fiberglass shell of the wrecked snow machine aside.

Their aim improved as they closed the distance. Automatic gunfire pelted Eamon as a snow machine raced directly at him. Eamon threw his vambrace-clad arms up, eating up a lot of the gunfire. The snow machine veered toward him, trying to run him down.

He swiped with one arm just as the machine was about to make impact. It flew to the side, spinning end over end from the blow, the forward momentum carrying it and the riders up and over Eamon's shoulder. They struck an outcropping of rocks behind him hard, causing the snow machine to spark and catch fire. The riders flew head over heels through snow drifts until they broke out over the ridge, falling out of sight.

Eamon pulled the Henry rifle tight into his shoulder and turned toward the remaining snow machine as it circled around to make another pass. The riders opened fire, shots passing within inches of Eamon as he willed his breathing to normalize. They were riding high over a ridge when Eamon snapped off a shot and worked the lever-action in one fluid motion to fire a second time.

Both rider and passenger went down. With no one at the throttle, the snow machine slowed to a stop, still idling. Eamon walked up beside it and hit the kill switch to shut it down, plunging the clearing into an eerie quiet. Eamon paused next to the closest militiaman, kneeling down to see if he was alive. He wasn't, and neither were any of his friends, save the last one Eamon had shot off the back of the third snow machine.

The gunman could barely breathe. Even with the advanced body armor he'd been wearing, the impact had incapacitated him. Heavy Dub's custom .44 round transferred kinetic force better than most rounds of the same type. He struggled to get the vest off, pausing wide-eyed as Eamon stepped through the misty darkness, patting out some burning fuel on his duty vest.

"Holy shit," Klaus said, finally freeing himself of the badly dented body armor.

"Bet you wished you'd gotten on that transport like I asked," Eamon said, pushing his rifle around to his back and drawing his Vaquero.

"Whoa, this isn't what you think," Klaus said, holding up his hands.

Eamon just glared at Klaus, wishing quietly that he'd go for a weapon.

Klaus looked past Eamon to the burning snow machines and dead militiamen. One hung haphazardly from a tree, his rifle strap having gotten snagged on a branch. The fire from the snow machines made it look like Hell was at Eamon's back, mist rising from snow being evaporated by the flames.

"I couldn't leave without the boy," Klaus said, closing his eyes as Eamon leveled the Vaquero and cocked the hammer.

"I bet," Eamon said.

"Both the boy and Jennifer were to be safeguarded. I couldn't leave without making sure that happened," Klaus explained.

Eamon softly dropped the hammer on his Vaquero before holstering it. "Do tell."

"Honest, I was doing everything I could to not hit you," Klaus said, pushing his rifle away with his foot.

"Or, you're still a terrible shot, and a junkie with a shaky hand."

Klaus laid back in the snow, still trying to catch his breath. "I think that still qualifies as 'everything', yeah? Look, this is a big deal for me."

"I know. If you do what you're told, you get your family back," Eamon said, picking up the rifle Klaus had been using.

Klaus sat back up, surprised. "How did you know?"

Eamon pulled a coloring book from a vest pocket and slid it flipped to Klaus. He opened it and looked inside at the pages. "You saw them?"

Eamon nodded. "Yep."

"How is she? I mean, how did they look?" Klaus asked, frantically.

"Just like I remember them, like a day hadn't gone by."

Klaus smiled. "I knew if I just held in a little longer, she'd keep her word."

"She?" Eamon said, remembering what Patrick Vale had said just after he'd shot him.

"Yeah, I always dealt with a woman," Klaus said, almost delirious, a smile crossing his face.

"What did Emma Vale tell you to do after you'd killed me?" Eamon asked, pulling the magazine on Klaus's rifle.

"She just wanted us to get the boy at all costs. Patrick wants to reunite his family," Klaus explained.

"I guess that doesn't include Janice?"

Klaus looked confused for a moment. "She's out here?"

Eamon frowned.

"Y'know she did talk to the other guys for a little bit before pulling me in to help look for you," Klaus said, looking over at the dented body armor.

"How were you supposed to get your family back?" Eamon asked. "What did this woman tell you?"

Klaus nodded, happy to cooperate. "Identity extensive tech, like what Vance Uroboros used to create Kale. Think about it. Kale is almost exactly like Vance Uroboros, and my contact said cognitive scans of my family were on file."

Eamon raised an eyebrow. "You think Kale is just like Vance?"

"Well, yeah, isn't he?" Klaus asked.

"Not remotely, Klaus," Eamon said, eliciting a panicked expression from Klaus.

"What do you mean?"

"You got played," Eamon said, sliding a round from the magazine he'd taken from Klaus's rifle.

"What?"

"I've been shot hundreds, maybe thousands of times. Even what can't get through my thick hide or armor, still hurts badly. This ammo you guys were using felt like a harsh tickle," Eamon said, putting the round in a pocket.

Klaus looked shocked.

"You didn't notice the reduced recoil?" Eamon asked.

"Honestly, I was pretty high before I even got on the snow machine. As we got closer, I took another hit just to amp up for what I might have to do up here," Klaus admitted.

"Addicts are the perfect patsies," Eamon said, disgusted.

"Why are you being such an asshole?" Klaus said, pointing a finger at Eamon.

Eamon glared at Klaus.

"So, what now?" Klaus said, averting his gaze to avoid Eamon's disapproving look.

"Why does everyone keep asking me that?" Eamon shook his head in disappointment. "I'm adrift in this nonsense, same as everyone else."

"You don't know what it was like, losing them like that," Klaus said, looking down at the ground.

"I was there Klaus, remember? I keep company with ghosts, too. I know exactly what you're going through," Eamon growled, throwing Klaus's rifle as far as he could through the trees.

"Okay, and?"

"I think I know who you're working for now," Eamon said, fishing around in his pockets for a biscuit that wasn't there.

"I don't even know who she is, only that she is very well-connected," Klaus said, blinking.

"Yeah, and you probably never will," Eamon said, heading back toward the ridge.

"That's it? You're just going to leave me up here with a functioning snow machine? I'm free to go?" Klaus said, throwing his hands out to his sides.

"Not quite. If I ever see you again with a gun in your hand, I'll aim for the head and not your armor," Eamon said, patting his Vaquero.

"I can't go back to the camp. They'll shoot me the next time they see you," Klaus said, shaking his head.

"Head to the old international airport. What you're looking for is probably still nearby," Eamon said, before turning to make the descent to the valley.

Eamon listened to the sound of the snow machine, his ears following the sound as it went west. At least for the next few miles, it sounded like Klaus was taking Eamon's advice. To Eamon's surprise, Shadow and Janice were hidden nearby, emerging and running out to meet him as he broke through the tree line.

"I wasn't sure you were okay, what with all the gunfire and explosions up there," Janice said, her face white with fright.

"I'm surprised you're still here," Eamon said, looking from Janice to Shadow.

"Why wouldn't we be?" Shadow said, squinting at Eamon.

"Didn't part of your plan to escape to Mexico include bringing Jake with you?" Eamon asked.

Shadow shook her head. "No, not at all. It's not a journey you make with a child."

"Yeah, no way," Janice said emphatically.

"Seriously?" Eamon asked, somewhat in disbelief.

"Yes, seriously. Why would you think that?" Shadow said.

"Never mind that for now, we'd better get moving," Eamon said, holding his hands out for Jake.

"Oh, no, Big Bear. What's going on? What happened up on the hill?" Shadow said, holding Jake close.

Eamon took a deep breath. "You really, really don't want to know."

"Okay, okay," Shadow said, her feelings a little hurt as she handed Jake back to Eamon.

The small child cooed and smiled at the sight of Eamon, drumming his hands on his shoulder as he strapped him to his duty vest. Eamon took the bullet out of his pocket and tossed it to Shadow. She caught it, looking back at Eamon with an impatient expression, until she had a chance to feel the heft of it and look at the stamp around the end of the casing by the primer.

"Is this what I think it is?" Shadow said, looking up at him, an expression of abject terror crossing Eamon's face. "You were right, I don't want to know."

"Patrick Vale, right before he died, called God a 'she'. The person that contracted Klaus to work as a triple agent is, according to him, a woman," Eamon said.

Shadow dropped the bullet like it was infected. "But, Aaron said..."

"I know. Didn't you always suspect that it might be a she?" Eamon said, looking Shadow in the eyes.

"Oh God, we have to warn Uroboros Financial. They have to do something," Shadow said, almost frantic.

"I know, and we will. We need to get to the Server Hub, like Aaron said," Eamon said.

"Whoa, what are you guys talking about?" Janice said, waving her hands to get their attention.

"Jake's mother lives in Central America. She's…" Shadow began, looking to Eamon.

"She is very dangerous and Jake is probably her son," Eamon said, beginning to head northeast.

"Does she have a name?" Janice said, jogging along with Shadow and Eamon.

Eamon shook his head. "No, every Drone and Metasapient in the world just calls her 'The Factory'."

CHAPTER 12

DAKOTA TERRITORY AIRSPACE

AUGUST 31ST, 2201 – 5:02 AM

Brook held the transport steady, engines humming as the sleek military transport broke the sound barrier. The upper atmosphere was beautiful, with only the first light of the sun beginning to appear. They'd be back in Port Montaigne in about an hour, in plenty of time to make the board meeting.

"You in a big hurry?" Heavy Dub said, stumbling into the cockpit. "I almost spilled my coffee."

"I don't want to miss the morning briefing at Uroboros Financial, again," Brook replied, gripping the controls tightly.

"I think you just like any excuse to push my new transport to supersonic speeds," Heavy Dub said, taking a crew seat beside her.

"Not at all," Brook said, smiling broadly.

Kale woke up, looking around the cockpit and taking note of the tremendous velocity being displayed on the HUD. Adjusting his seat so that he was upright, he gave Brook a stern expression. Heavy Dub reached around Brook to hand Kale a coffee that he quietly declined.

"Sorry, did I wake you?" Brook said, reaching over and squeezing Kale's arm.

"I sleep too much anyway," he replied, putting a hand on her arm.

"We accomplished a lot in the last four days," Brook said, nodding to Heavy Dub.

"Gathering up the rest of Doctor Helmet's scholarly posterity will hopefully give us some insight into how so much damage was done throughout the world. It is becoming increasingly clear that the Cabal could not have acted alone," Kale said, looking sullenly through his long hair out the view port.

"We'll figure it out, Boss, and deal with them the same way we did the Cabal," Heavy Dub said, slamming one metallic fist into the palm of the other.

"Do you think Doctor Helmet figured it all out?" Brook asked, looking to Kale.

Kale nodded. "It may have been the last thing he ever did. Every clue suggests that it was Maurice Madmar that killed Doctor Helmet."

"Yeah, it was all tech Madmar had used before. Helmet's old lab was lousy with it, and..." Heavy Dub sighed. "You think someone made it look like Madmar did it, and he didn't really do it, but we're supposed to think he did?"

"From the records we have recovered, and the video call conversations, I think Madmar genuinely felt bad for what happened to Doctor Helmet. It doesn't make sense that he would just kill him like that," Kale said, flattening out his tie.

"Unless he was crazy. Silverstein, Ezra, and Taylor are all pretty sure he'd completely lost his mind," Brook said, squinting at something off on the radar.

"Yes, but that was months after Doctor Helmet was killed," Kale said, checking the time on his mobile.

"Um, is there supposed to be anyone else up here with us?" Brook asked, looking curiously at the radar display.

"No, none of the relief transports fly this high, or this fast," Heavy Dub replied.

"If there was anything up this high, Aaron AI would have warned us," Kale said, squinting at the HUD.

Several unmanned scramjets rocketed past them going in the other direction. Brook held the controls firmly, altering their course slightly to bring them lower. She could see them coming around, circling back and accelerating to overtake them.

Kale pulled the headset on and set up a secure frequency. "Aaron AI, please respond."

There was no response in the seconds before the scramjets began to close in, flying a course that mimicked Brook's heading. "He's not there," Kale said, shaking his head.

"Did something happen to Eamon?" Brook said, worriedly.

"Let's worry about us, and then we'll worry about him," Heavy Dub said, pointing at the radar readings on the HUD.

Brook edged the throttle forward, adjusting their course heading south. She knew she couldn't outrun the scramjets, but that they may not be able to adjust to the lower altitude. They seemed to hasten their approach as Brook brought them down.

As the scramjets began to drop altitude, the combustion rate of their fuel ceased being constant, engine pressure and temperature fluctuating. The trio of unmanned aircraft suddenly exploded in the upper atmosphere. Brook tried to turn to take the resulting shockwave to the side, instead of the engines, but she didn't have the time to properly adjust.

The transport shook violently, power going out momentarily before Brook was able to quick start the system using a custom emergency protocol. As they plummeted through the clouds, Heavy Dub pulled the VR goggles down from the gunnery position and called up the ship's weapons. Nine manned interceptor aircraft raced toward them, underneath the cloud cover that was still misty from the upper atmospheric disturbance.

"Those are Fuerza Aérea Mexicana aircraft. All-weather stealth tactical fighters," Heavy Dub said, hesitating on the trigger.

"Hold on," Brook said, pulling the transport hard to the left, making it as thin to the vantage of the fighters as possible.

"Boss?" Heavy Dub said, shakily.

"I can't get any radio contact with them. We have to assume this is some kind of military aggression," Kale said.

"Good enough for me," Heavy Dub said, bringing the weaponry he'd added to the transport online and opening fire.

The tactical fighters returned fire as soon as they came into range, releasing several volleys of short-range missiles. Heavy Dub held down hard on his twin twenty-millimeter Vulcan cannons, killing several fighters before they could release their payloads. Brook struggled to keep the transport on course.

"The shockwave damaged something in the avionics," Brook said, watching the radar as several short-range missiles picked up speed and began homing in on their transport.

Heavy Dub flipped a plastic cover up over an innocuous green button and mashed it with his fist. There was a loud hiss as the air around the transport was suddenly surrounded by thousands of small, laser-guided countermeasures. The short-range missiles exploded prematurely, peppering the transport with flaming remnants and further disrupting the avionics.

"Hold us steady," Heavy Dub said, keying in a sequence on the keypad.

Brook did her best as automatic fire support took over the twenty millimeter cannons. Heavy Dub switched the manual systems to a single one hundred five millimeter cannon, coming up as "Star Killer," on the HUD. As he brought the cannon around on the belly-mounted turret, he couldn't help but grin.

"Why do you have a Howitzer mounted to the transport?" Kale asked, looking ruefully up at the HUD.

"Is that a serious question?" Heavy Dub smiled, cycling laser-guided ammunition into the weapon. "Always wanted to try using this air-to-air."

Heavy Dub set the shell to detonate somewhere between the two lead aircraft and fired, causing the transport, even in spite of its large size, to shudder. A split second later, the view port filled with light as the shell detonated, badly damaging three of the fighter aircraft. As the next shell cycled down into the firing breach, the weapon malfunctioned.

Heavy Dub cursed. "Well, I got one shot off anyway. Damn it, what is wrong with my transport?"

"I don't know, but we're going to have to set down," Brook said, watching the fighter aircraft suddenly change course and head south at top speed.

"Can we limp the rest of the way to Port Montaigne?" Kale asked, still trying to raise Aaron AI via various communications methods.

"My current goal is to actually land, as opposed to crashing nose first into the ground," Brook said, shakily bringing the transport around.

"Why is it when I let you drive, you always crash my transports?" Heavy Dub complained.

Brook smiled. "Get better transports. This one kinda sucks."

"Shh, she'll hear you," Heavy Dub scolded, gently patting the control console.

Brook brought the transport down on an ancient freeway, landing gear grinding down into crumbling asphalt. Heavy Dub's transport turned slightly as it slid to a halt, knocking down signage and other ancient fixtures of the road. Brook looked over to Kale, who was calmly sitting beside her, looking annoyed like something mundane had inconvenienced him. Heavy Dub had covered his face, but peeked out between metallic fingers after a moment of quiet.

"Not my best landing," Brook admitted.

"Is it snowing?" Kale said, pointing out the view port.

"What is that?" Brook said, squinting as what looked like small flakes blew off the top of the transport.

"I'll check it out, keep an eye on the radar, just in case they circle around," Heavy Dub said, jumping up.

Kale followed him out, climbing feebly down the crew access ladder. Heavy Dub walked out from under the transport and looked around for the source of the flakes that seemed to be falling down from the sky. Kale tapped him on the shoulder and pointed back at the transport. It was covered in thin metallic foil flakes, a few blowing off in the wind.

"What is that stuff?" Heavy Dub asked.

"I think I know," Kale said, grabbing a handful of it and slapping it on Heavy Dub's shoulder.

His arm went limp, and began to tingle as if it were a biological arm that had gone to sleep. Heavy Dub tried to lift his arm, but it wouldn't respond. Reflexively, he reached over to wipe the foil flakes off, but all he did was get them on his hand, making it go dead as well.

"This isn't funny," he said, looking down at his limp limbs and frowning.

"Yes, it is," Kale said, turning out a thin smile.

Brook dropped out of the transport behind them, landing roughly. "They're gone. At the rate they were traveling, they should be out of North American airspace in less than an hour. Um, what's up with Heavy Dub's arms?"

"It is some kind of weapon designed to mess with even magnetically shielded electronics," Kale said, pointing back up at the foil-encrusted side of the transport.

"It's very clingy, but it doesn't seem that magnetic. Still, it really likes anything metallic," Brook said, chuckling as she cleaned off Heavy Dub's arms.

"I've never seen anything like it," Heavy Dub said, disappointed that his encyclopedic knowledge of weapons seemed to be useless in this case.

"Yeah, me neither, it's…" Brook said, holding a flake up and giving it a sniff.

Brook's expression immediately changed from one of wonder, to one of profound worry.

"You know what it is?" Kale asked, gently putting a hand on her shoulder.

"No, but I know where it comes from," Brook said, sniffing the flake again.

"Are you sure?" Heavy Dub said, knowing that expression from a half dozen different missions involving the Cabal.

"Yes, this is technology that came from The Factory. The smell is very distinct," Brook said.

"Why would someone at The Factory go through all this trouble, just to ground us?" Heavy Dub asked, shaking his arms to try and make the tingling that lingered go away.

Kale looked disdainfully up at the foil blowing off the transport. "Most of our secure communication channels are down. Whoever it is, does not want us talking to anyone, or going anywhere for a while."

"That's bad," Heavy Dub said, looking north up the empty road.

"Oh, you think so?" Kale said, slamming a fist against the side of the transport. "Do you know what will happen if Aaron AI is offline for too long?"

"He knows," Brook said, stepping up to Kale and running her hands gently down his lapels.

Kale took a deep breath, closing his eyes, letting it back out slowly. "It'll take hours to get enough foil off the transport to let us get back in the air."

"That sign over there says Rapid City is two miles south of us. Ellsworth Air Force Base can't be more than ten miles east of here. There might be old impounded transports there, or something military grade we can 'acquire' with Uroboros Financial administrative clearance," Heavy Dub said, looking out toward the hills.

"There are automated defenses, but they may not be operational with Aaron AI offline," Kale said, nodding to Heavy Dub.

"Um, what kind of defenses?" Heavy Dub said nervously, knowing Kale's propensity for playing it extra safe.

"Android frames, with tactical enhancements and armor. There is at least a battalion present, or was before Aaron AI went offline. Depending on when he went offline, they may still be up and running," Kale explained.

"I thought redundancies only lasted seventy-two hours?" Brook said. "We left Montana more than four days ago."

"Aaron AI found a way to make them last almost twice that duration," Kale said, rolling his eyes.

"Poor Eamon, alone back there, and with no backup," Brook said, clasping her hands together.

"The Migration should arrive in less than twenty-four hours, and I made arrangements for them to be provided with supplies to aid them," Kale said, smirking.

"Is the transport guarded with a whole platoon of mercenaries?" Heavy Dub asked.

"No, but Sweet Pea and her two brothers will be on board. They wanted to feel out whether they wanted to join the Migration or return to Port Montaigne," Kale explained.

"Did they really?" Brook said, squinting at Kale.

"I insisted they go just to be sure. I don't want them to regret passing up the chance to potentially live among their own kind," Kale said, suddenly feeling weak.

Brook helped him sit down on the pavement. "I'll get your wheelchair."

Kale shook his head. "You should take the mercs we have on board and go. They will need you and Heavy Dub to navigate the military base and bypass the security if it is still active. I'll make way back aboard after I've rested a moment and sit on the comm."

"I don't want to leave you alone," Brook said, worriedly.

"Someone needs to sit at the comm in case Aaron AI comes back online. They will need your administrative clearance to requisition a military transport if one is there," Kale said, waving them on.

Brook ignored him, knelt down beside him, and wrapped her arms around him. Kale returned the embrace, doing his best to reassure her. "I'll be fine, just hurry back."

"We could have died up there," Brook said, burying her face in Kale's chest and squeezing him tightly.

Kale didn't want to say it aloud, but it definitely felt like someone tried to kill them while making it look like an accident. If the transport had crashed, the metallic foil that disrupted their systems would be intermingled with the rest of the debris. Their transport was large and full of equipment. The deed could have easily been lost in the chaos of the wreckage.

It felt wretched. Not the fact that someone would want to kill him, or Heavy Dub. That, Kale definitely understood. But, there was no reason to kill Brook.

"What's the alternative here? Who else in Mexico is angry with us?" Kale asked, looking to Heavy Dub.

"If I was card-carrying member of the Cabal and I was looking to get clear of Uroboros Financial, that's where I would go," Heavy Dub replied.

"But why would they risk exposure, just to hurt us if they were safe in Mexico? Attacking us in the air like that would be expensive, and would require a lot more than simple cooperation from the Mexican government," Kale said, stroking his beard.

"I still think it is The Factory. We've somehow done something to anger it," Brook concluded.

"It is possible. I have long suspected The Factory is more than just a shuttered installation with a dormant facility-grade AI," Kale said, massaging the bridge of his nose.

Brook nodded. "Among my own as well. There was always a sense of there being something more behind it all. Some of us came to personify the Facility AI there as female. She was a cruel mother, but she raised us to do our jobs, and survive on the outside."

"Did anything happen while you were there to make you think the facility maintenance AI was more sophisticated?" Heavy Dub asked.

"Not to me, but I've heard stories from other Drones in my tribe. At least two of the Drones had substandard performance scores, and a third was injured badly during training at The Factory. They should have been euthanized, but the Factory altered the parameters of the training to allow them to be employed for service."

"Did The Factory turn out substandard Drones, or did it... she, change their designation?" Heavy Dub asked.

"Substandard. Not by a lot. They were a little under strength qualifications because they were small, or a little slower on their feet from an injury. No one in my tribe cared about that though," Brook explained.

"That sounds like compassion. Facility maintenance cognitive systems wouldn't fudge the results to fill quotas or boost output statistics. They don't have an ego, and they don't care if you are displeased with their performance. Compassion is something even the highest functioning artificial intelligences struggle with," Kale said, standing up with Brook's help.

Heavy Dub swallowed nervously. "If she can have compassion..."

"She can be angry, afraid, or hate," Kale said, nodding sadly.

CHAPTER 13

GLACIER NATIONAL PARK, APGAR VILLAGE

AUGUST 31ST, 2201 – 6:06 AM

Sweat Pea raised her hands slowly, her large wings extending with them as she did. The men coming up the loading ramp didn't smell right to her, and they were pointing guns up into the cargo hold. She sniffed the air, listening intently to the sounds throughout Apgar, trying to get a sense of what had gone wrong.

Mister Mundt stood beside her, shaking his head angrily. He'd come to know the area well, and had made many drops there. He had kin that had kin in the Northwest, the blood of his people flowing in the veins of many who lived here.

"Chiroptera Metasapients are the worst. Ugly as Hell," one of the militiamen said, greedily surveying the cargo in the hold.

"I dunno, she could be kinda hot if you ignore the face," another said, sticking out his tongue and grimacing.

"Who else is in there with you?" the third said, activating the illuminator on his rifle.

Sweet Pea could see and smell all the biological responses of fear in these men. They'd been left behind because they were only suited to guard duty. Unfortunately, they seemed to know that and were looking to prove themselves.

"Nobody," Sweet Pea replied, trying to sound timid as to set them at ease.

"Where is Ray Pendleton?" Mister Mundt said, fishing around in his vest for a piece of gum and ignoring the weapons pointed at him.

"He's sequestered with the others that didn't go along with the change of management," the militiamen said, motioning for Mister Mundt and Sweet Pea to exit the cargo hold / transport.

"We can't do that, son," Mister Mundt said, folding his arms.

"You should put your guns down. Before he sees you," Sweet Pea warned, genuinely fearful.

"Before who sees us?" one of the militiamen laughed.

"My friend. If he sees you pointing a gun at this transport, he will kill you," Sweet Pea said, sniffing the air, her ears twitching with hundreds of distant sounds.

"Listen to her, son," Mister Mundt said, finally finding a piece of gum, unwrapping it, and popping it into his mouth.

"Come down out of there," the militiaman on point said, bringing up his rifle.

"Oh, they are here, or near here. They can hear you. Oh, hello. Yes, thank you. Your hearing is very good, too!" Sweet Pea said, carrying on a long distance conversation.

"Who are you talking to?" One of the militiamen looked around warily.

"Oh, I didn't even get your name. What is your name? Shadow? Nice to meet you, I'm Sweet Pea," Sweet Pea said, smiling.

"Right, like I said before, come down out of there," the leader said, drawing a bead on Sweet Pea.

"Put your weapons down right now," Sweet Pea said, almost frantic.

"Or your friend will kill us," the second militiaman said, resting a hand on his sidearm, and looking about warily.

Sweet Pea nodded, her large ears rising up slightly, twitching as her able mind sorted thousands of different sounds and vibrations. "He's there with Shadow, and you're making him angry. He says, put your weapons down, and... you are all under arrest."

"Are you sure?" the third militiaman in line smirked.

"Oh, yes, he's far heavier than a man. When he walks, it is like no one else," Sweet Pea said, nodding with surety.

"I mean, are you sure he said all that?" the militiaman teased.

"Last chance, boys. Listen to her, and put the guns down," Mister Mundt said, calmly chewing his gum.

"Naw, it's your last chance, move," the lead militiaman said, tapping the trigger guard on his rifle with his finger.

Sweet Pea shook her head sadly and covered her eyes.

The militiamen laughed. The first one on point pulled his rifle up into his shoulder, moving his finger from the guard to the trigger, taking aim on Sweet Pea.

The shot came from way off, taking a fraction of a second for the report of the rifle to be heard. The militiaman took the round to the ear, inertia from the hit blowing his head completely off. The other two men pivoted in a panic, squinting down the long road to toward the south of town.

A second shot cut down the next one in line. The round hit him just above his armored vest where his neck met with with his collarbones. The bullet caught in the back of his vest, causing him to pitch backward, hard, off the loading ramp.

The third man fired down the road, reaching up with his other hand for the radio on the front of his vest. A round hit him in the nose, and exited the back of his head severing the connection between brain and spine. He slumped over against his wide-eyed comrade who was still grasping at the wound in his neck.

Sweet Pea looked mournfully down at them, shaking her head.

"She warned you, you mutts," Mister Mundt hissed.

Mister Mundt walked down the ramp a short distance, then pushed the bodies off the loading platform onto the ground with his foot. Looking to the south, he could see their rescuers a little bit beyond the boundary of the village. They were a little more than dots on the hill beyond with his eyesight.

As they closed the distance, he could see Eamon was leading, his large ursine form obscuring two others that followed along on his wake. Eamon was moving quickly now, an ancient looking rifle out and at the ready. Sweet Pea came down the ramp and looked sweetly out toward Eamon, raising a hand in greeting. He returned the greeting, closing the gap between them.

"Brother Eamon, you are hurt," Sweet Pea said, walking up and badly unnerving Janice with both her size and the fierceness of her appearance.

"I'm fine, caught a little action back on the trail," Eamon said, nodding to Mister Mundt.

Sweet Pea wrapped her arms around Eamon, her wings hanging down his back like a cape. She closed her eyes and squeezed him. Eamon patted her reassuringly, looking warily around at the village beyond.

"I tried to warn them. Tried to get them to put down their weapons," Sweet Pea said, her large red eyes filling with tears.

"I know, Shadow could hear and was relaying that to me. They chose that way to go, not you," Eamon said, trying to comfort her.

"What a cute baby. Can I hold your baby?" Sweet Pea asked, pointing to little Jake.

Eamon unstrapped Jake, who seemed delighted at the sight of Sweet Pea. "I'll warm him in the transport," Sweet Pea said, walking past Mister Mundt into the cargo hold.

"Assholes," Mister Mundt said, looking disappointedly down at the corpses cooling beneath his transport.

"Sorry about that," Eamon said, nodding deferentially to Mister Mundt. "This is Shadow and Janice, they..."

"I know who they are," Mister Mundt interrupted. "Where did these defenders of the ignorant Nativist faith come from?"

"West, and more are coming from the south," Eamon replied, pushing his two damaged rifles off his shoulders.

"I suppose you need those fixed up?" Mister Mundt said.

"I just need twenty minutes with your work table to make sure they survived the avalanche undamaged," Eamon said, looking at the weapons sadly.

"Avalanche?" Mister Mundt said, his anger abating. "They really tried to kill you?"

"Yes," Eamon said.

"Give them here, I'll do it. Keep an eye on the village, in case more of them come along," Mister Mundt said, taking Eamon's weapons by the barrel shroud and strap, slinging one over his shoulder.

"Can we talk about the gigantic bat-lady?" Janice said, wide-eyed.

Shadow just lowered her head and chuckled.

"You wanna head in and gawk at her?" Eamon said, defensively.

Janice went red in the face. "Chiroptera Metasapients are supposed to be the size of a human, or smaller."

"Leave it alone," Shadow said, putting a hand on Janice's shoulder.

Janice looked over at Shadow, smiling slightly. "Is she simple? She seems..."

"She can hear you, every word that comes out of your ignorant mouth," Eamon said, glaring at Janice. "She could hear us coming a mile away, and tried to warn your friends there."

Janice looked mortified. "Why... why would she warn them?"

"Because she can smell the blood in your veins, and hear an animal breathing a couple of miles away. She can almost feel the moment someone dies, and being an old Type One, she's seen more death than anyone I know," Eamon said, the two last words squeezed out between clenched teeth.

Shadow gave Janice's a shoulder a squeeze. "For real, can you leave it alone now?"

"The stories her colony have told me, the things they've seen and endured, you can't even imagine," Eamon said, bending over to look into Janice's eyes.

Janice looked sullenly at the ground. "Sorry."

Sweet Pea came out a few moments later, her large hands easily cradling little Jake as she rocked him. If she'd heard any of the conversation, she acted to the contrary. Jake squealed and laughed as she spun him around and held him aloft.

"Brother, the Migration grows close. I can hear the echoes of at least three colonies growing close," Sweet Pea said, smiling, rows of sharp teeth appearing as she did.

"Will you go with them?" Eamon asked, wondering what his own answer would be.

"You and Brook, Kale and Heavy Dub, Mister Mundt and the others, are my colony now," Sweet Pea said, her blood red eyes narrowing mirthfully.

"But, you wanted to help the Migration," Eamon said, smiling slightly.

"Don't you?" Sweet Pea asked, looking to Eamon, and then to Shadow.

"Sure, I guess," Shadow said, frowning.

"I'm just here doing my job," Eamon replied. "Figured some more of the militia would have come along by now. Thought the town would be lousy with them."

Shadow nodded. "As soon as you get your weapons back, Big Bear, we should find where they've gone."

"She is not the cautious voice of Abbey," Sweet Pea observed.

Shadow bowed her head, respectfully. "Apologies, I'm just worried what they'll do when the Migration comes."

"To the militia?" Sweet Pea said, cocking her head.

"No, I'm worried about what the militia will do to the folks in the Migration," Shadow replied, confused by Sweet Pea's response.

Mister Mundt came back out, a worried look on his face. "They went down."

"Who?" Eamon asked, continuing to keep a vigil on the village nearby.

"Mister Kale, Brook, and Heavy Dub. Satellite imagery shows they went down over the Dakota Territory somewhere, but without Aaron AI, I can't locate their exact location. Radio communications through the Midwest and East Coast are down," Mister Mundt said, grumpily gnashing at his chewing gum.

Eamon frowned, looking back at Shadow. "So, that's what all this is really about."

"What? What is it all about?" Shadow replied, shaking her head.

"Someone wanted to kill Kale. They thought the best way to do it would be in the air. They couldn't do it with Aaron AI online, and controlling the North American air force." Sweet Pea said, patting little Jake.

"I'll finish fixing your rifles, but I need to offload this cargo and get back in the air," Mister Mundt said, powering up a small lift cart.

"Is that what Kale would want you to do?" Eamon said, looking up toward the mountainside that housed the server hub.

Mundt bit his lip and scowled. "No, he'd want me to keep my flight plan."

"Reckon that's what you ought to do then," Eamon said, nodding.

"I'll think about it, while I finish up your rifles," Mister Mundt replied sullenly.

CHAPTER 14

NUEVO LAREDO, MEXICO

SEPTEMBER 1ST, 2201 – 3:47 AM

Silverstein sat up, compulsively looking for a cigarette in his pocket even though he knew there was none. The jail cell was at least a century old, secured with an ancient lock and key. Outside, the ceiling tiles hung down from the drop ceiling, wet from the leaky pipes above.

The Mexican military minister folded his arms, impatiently tapping the sleeve on his freshly pressed jacket. "Mister Uroboros, I'm here to…"

"Hey, congratulations on your promotion," Silverstein said, sitting up, his quick smile vanishing into a wince as his bare feet touched the cold water on the floor.

"Mister Uroboros, please, I'm here because…"

Silverstein waved his hand dismissively, interrupting the Minister, again. "No one calls me Vance Uroboros anymore."

The military minister sighed. "Mister Silverstein, we shot down a transport in the North American Territory yesterday."

"Seems like a lot of trouble to shoot some food out of the sky," Silverstein said, leaning back on the bed.

"It was a military transport, with VIPs on board."

Silverstein leaned forward, clasping his hands together. "You did what, now?"

"I see that you are angry. Do not worry, they managed to land safely. Someone is on the way to pick them up."

Silverstein squinted at the minister. "What is your name?"

"Deputy Minister Villarreal, at your service," he replied, annoyed because it was the third time in as many days that Silverstein had asked his name.

"Deputy Minister Villarreal, whatever military unit you sent to recover the passengers of that downed transport, needs to turn around. Right now," Silverstein said, frowning disappointedly at the deputy minister.

"You aren't really in a position to make threats," Villarreal sneered.

"This isn't a threat, it's a warning. I came to offer assurances, and set a few things right, that's all," Silverstein said, walking over to the cell bars to look Villarreal in the eyes.

"We don't need your assurances. She's offered us something better," Villarreal said, feeling a little panicked.

Silverstein rested his forehead against the bars. "I wasn't here to offer you assurances. I was here to talk to her, or them, as the case may be."

Villarreal pressed his lips together, considering carefully whether to let on that he knew what Silverstein was even talking about. It wasn't so much out of necessity as out of habit, and the presence of his lieutenants in the room. He could always deny whatever he said later, calling the banter an interrogation technique.

"I do not think she wants to talk to you, Mister Silverstein. Not that it would have even been possible if she had," Villarreal said, smiling and looking around at his cronies standing nearby.

"You shouldn't have gone into North America," Silverstein whispered, eyes closed, shaking his head. "Kale has a thing about people being rude."

The undersecretaries and petty lieutenants chuckled among themselves. As they did so, they took the opportunity to light up a couple of Silverstein's signature cigarettes in front of him. Silverstein frowned, hoping he'd still have enough time to figure out what was going on.

"You shouldn't smoke those. Very bad for you," Silverstein muttered under his breath.

"What was that, Mister Silverstein?" Villarreal said, smirking.

"You can't push someone like Kale, he'll come up on you when you least expect it, and hit you with a pipe," Silverstein said, grabbing the bars of his cell and giving them a shake. "I'm speaking from personal experience."

"Kale is a faded copy of you, according to your dossier. And, no offense, you don't scare me," Villarreal said, clapping his hands together.

Silverstein sighed, letting his breath out slowly between clenched teeth. "He isn't a copy. He went delta as a child, do you understand what that means?"

"I know he's not a copy now. You can still use your legs... well, at least for another thirty minutes or so," Villarreal said, his smile stretching the tips of his mustache out beyond his cheeks.

The room was under surveillance, a small red indicator light on a pair of cameras recording everything in the gloom of the basement holding cell. Silverstein watched those lights go out, counting down quietly in his head as they did. Villarreal and his lieutenants didn't seem to notice, or react if they did.

Silverstein smiled calmly. "What happens in thirty minutes?"

"The order will come down to interrogate you. We'll put a hose down your throat, and pump biologically stable fluid into you until your internal organs rupture. We use tailored anesthesia so you can survive long enough to feel the entire ordeal, and die slowly thereafter."

Silverstein nodded, like someone had told him something very mundane. "Uh huh, go on."

Villarreal cleared his throat. "It'll be an unfortunate mishap, a death in custody. The medical examiner will rule it accidental death due to a combination of sedatives, and other drugs you already had in your system at the time of your arrest."

Silverstein looked at his belongings arrayed on a steel table nearby, his gaze lingering on his wristwatch.

"Nothing to say?" Villarreal said, sneering. "None of your famous North American bravado?"

"Someone has been working very hard to undermine Mexico's democracy. They have been very quiet about it, but like any self-assured maniac, they always leave something dangling. It has been very hard to track you down," Silverstein said, turning his back to Villarreal and leaning up against the bars.

Villarreal, taking offense at Silverstein turning his back to him, kicked the bars. "Whatever I am, you won't live to tell anyone."

"You think it's him?" Ezra One asked, startling Villarreal.

Villarreal whirled around to see his lieutenants arrayed on the floor, each dispatched so quietly he hadn't noticed during his grandstanding. They'd died so quickly they still had Silverstein's lit cigarettes dangling from their gaping mouths. Their throats had been slashed, and necks broken with such speed and precision that none had a chance to cry out or shout a warning.

"Maybe. He probably knows enough to lead us down the food chain," Silverstein said, grabbing a handful of Villarreal's uniform.

"Don't you mean up, Silverstein?" Ezra One said, blood dripping on the floor from his clawed hands.

"No, definitely down. Only bottom-feeding imbeciles use torture as a means to extract information, when misdirection is so much more illuminating."

"How did he..." Villarreal began, before Silverstein pulled him backwards, slamming him into the bars.

Villarreal held perfectly still as Ezra One approached, arms bloody up to his elbows, silvery eyes glinting in the fluorescent lighting. Silverstein grabbed the keys from the deputy minister's pocket and then traded places with him in the cell. Once Villarreal was safely locked inside, Silverstein grabbed up his socks and leather shoes from table.

"How I've missed you," Silverstein said, slipping on his socks and lacing up his shoes.

"You talking to me or the shoes?" Ezra One asked, banging his fist on Villarreal's hand as he reached out to clutch the bars.

"The socks. I've been barefoot in that cell for four days," Silverstein said, leaning back in the folding chair and sticking out his feet.

"The plan was for me to come in when I smelled your cigarettes being smoked," Ezra One said, disgusted, watching Silverstein pluck a still-lit cigarette from a dead man's mouth.

"What? Is there no ten-second rule with cigarettes? I've hardly been able to smell one for two days. Even excluding their torture techniques, these guys are real barbarians," Silverstein said, almost burning the cigarette down in a single drag.

Ezra One wondered if he kissed Taylor IA with those lips, but didn't deign to ask.

"What happens now?" Villarreal asked.

"I'm not really sure. I didn't count on you being stupid enough to go and poke the bear," Silverstein said, thoughtfully smoking what remained of the cigarette.

"They went after Eamon?" Ezra said, furrowing his brow. "That is really stupid."

"That, and worse. It sounds like they shot down Heavy Dub's transport with Kale and Brook on board. He says everyone survived, though," Silverstein said, shaking his head.

Ezra One frowned at Villarreal. "That's good, but Kale will come here."

"My people reported that they split up, and that Kale was alone at the transport. My people should have him within the hour and be on their way back to Mexico," Villarreal said, hoping to strike a bargain.

Water dripped down from the ceiling, forcing Villarreal to shift to a different place in the cell. Silverstein wasn't sure how to react to the news, as he'd hoped desperately to keep Kale from being entangled needlessly in what he'd discovered in Mexico. Ezra One held similar hope, having worked with Kale before.

"He needs to call those people back," Ezra One said, looking up at Silverstein.

"Ha, it's too late for that," Villarreal gloated. "Unless we can work something out."

"I hope you didn't send anyone you care about to pick up Kale," Silverstein said, sadly stamping out the cigarette.

"He's a cripple, confined to a wheelchair. I think my people will be fine. That being said, I think we can definitely work something out here," Villarreal said, leaning against the bars.

Ezra One shook his head in disbelief. "Your people will not be fine. Never, ever, assume that Kale is weak or helpless."

Villarreal turned a diminished expression from Ezra, to Silverstein.

"They are going to be dead, or worse. With Kale, there is always worse. What else have you and your new patron done?" Silverstein asked, putting his wristwatch back on.

"She just wants the boy, and I just want to see a Mexico's future guided by a more confident hand," Villarreal said, pacing in the cell.

"No one knows where the boy is," Silverstein blurted, his frustration showing at last.

"Oh, she found him," Villarreal said, smiling.

Ezra One shook his head, while Silverstein covered his face with his hands.

"So, are we going to make a deal or what?" Villarreal said, confidently.

Ezra One pulled out his own mobile to show Silverstein the contents of the screen. It was the shipping manifests they'd recovered three days previous, showing the movement of certain contraband items to Montana. Silverstein nodded quietly.

"Eamon," Silverstein said, frowning.

"And the Migration," Ezra One said, pocketing his mobile.

"What's the plan for the boy?" Silverstein asked.

"Mercenaries always work for the highest bidder," Villarreal replied, smiling confidently.

"That's why she went after Kale. He outsmarted her, again," Ezra One said. "You know, we could just pack up and go. She's never going to get the boy, and Kale is going to come here. Dealing with him seems like the least of what they deserve."

Silverstein sighed, rubbing his tired eyes with his fingertips. "We need to work quickly, figure this out before Kale comes here."

"I... don't know what the delay is, but we'll have the boy in a matter of days," Villarreal said, still maintaining his facade of confidence.

Silverstein folded his arms and shook his head, pressing his lips together tightly before speaking with a strained tone of voice. "Yeah, no you won't."

"And why is that, Mister Silverstein," Villarreal said, unconvinced.

"There's a new Sheriff in town."

CHAPTER 15

GLACIER NATIONAL PARK, APGAR VILLAGE

AUGUST 31ST, 2201 – 8:32 AM

Eamon squinted out across the snowy landscape to the south. By his own reckoning, the Migration should have arrived by now. He wondered quietly if something had happened to halt their advance, or made them change course.

Mister Mundt walked down the ramp out of his transport, one rifle slung over his shoulder, the other held in his hands. They would have glistened except for the fresh micro-coating Mundt had just applied to them. Eamon checked the action on both, then attached the grip guard adapters that allowed him to use the rifles with his much larger hands.

"Wasn't sure the adapters would work with a micro-coating," Eamon said, looking first down the side mounted open sights, then through the top-mounted scope of his semi-automatic rifle.

"It's new. We recovered it from one of Kaspersky's workshops. It should make your weapons much more durable," Mister Mundt said, looking over at Sweet Pea as she cradled little Jake in her arms.

"Much obliged. What was Kaspersky using it for?" Eamon said, putting one of his big hands on Mister Mundt's shoulder.

"You probably don't want to know," Mister Mundt replied, lip curling with disgust.

Eamon could guess. Kaspersky's operation was designed specifically to make human beings disappear, and move them across the globe without being detected. Seals on cargo would have to be perfect to fool Metasapients at border crossings and similar. Eamon had seen the black marks left across the globe by Kaspersky's network, so he had some idea what the micro-coating had been used for before his demise.

"Figured I'd have heard a blast by now, or smelled the smoke. If they've gone up the mountain to access the server farm, you would think they'd have made a first try on the door this morning," Eamon said, watching the road as Shadow and Janice returned with a fresh load of supplies.

"Sweet Pea, you sure I can't convince you to get on the transport and head out with Mister Mundt?" Eamon said, taking Jake from her.

She gave him a side-eyed glance. "Why do you want me to leave?"

"I think Mister Mundt might deviate from the flight plan," Eamon said.

The grizzled old teamster said nothing in response and folded his arms defiantly before heading back up the ramp into the transport.

"To get Mister Kale," Sweet Pea said, nodding.

"Yeah."

"I love you, Eamon," Sweet Pea said, wrapping her arms around him.

"Be careful out there," Eamon said, patting Sweet Pea.

Sweet Pea nodded. "Always, Brother Bear. We'll be back soon, with Mister Kale, Miss Brook, and Heavy Dub. Just lay low."

"I'll try."

Eamon watched the transport ascend, turn sharply to the east and speed off. Jake snored on his shoulder through it all, taking his mid-morning nap a little early. Shadow came up beside him while Janice checked the supplies a short distance away.

"The militia left some other guards to keep an eye on Apgar. The town drove them out when they heard shots coming from the landing zone," Shadow reported.

"Surprising," Eamon said, frowning.

"Looking at Montana, just on the surface, it may seem like a backward place. The majority of folks living here don't subscribe to the bigotry espoused by the militia. Most of them don't care what color, creed, or species you are," Shadow said, putting a hand on Eamon's arm.

"That why you landed here, and kind of stuck around?"

"There were a couple of reasons, but that was definitely one of them."

"Where is everyone?" Eamon said, ears twitching.

"Headed for summer cabins to the southeast until this all blows over. Most everyone is already on their way. The three we ran into must have come in ahead of us from the north," Shadow said, watching sullenly as the transport vanished over the trees.

"Wishing you could have hitched a ride?" Eamon said.

Shadow nodded. "Don't you? Sweet Pea and that Mundt guy would be very interesting traveling company."

"You two heading for Mexico?" Eamon asked.

Shadow sulked. "Thinking about it."

Eamon nodded. "Jennifer Wilton and the dog pack assigned to Aaron AI are still trapped up there."

"They can take care of themselves. Even if they couldn't get out before the militia arrived, I'm not sure how us being here will change that. I don't want to die out here, Big Bear," Shadow said, her ears darting about, nose sniffing the air.

"Understandable," Eamon said, retreating internally from the familiarity of the conversation with so many he'd had with Abbey.

"If that's the case, maybe you should think about going with us," Shadow said, putting a hand on Eamon's arm.

"My Spanish is terrible. Besides, I'm pretty sure there would not be a warm welcome for me there," Eamon replied.

"You sure about that?" Shadow said, looking at Jake.

Eamon glared at Shadow. "Not going to happen."

"The Mexican government has quietly claimed the boy as a national. They're offering citizenship, money, and a stake in Mexican National Enterprise," Shadow said, stepping around to keep Eamon from avoiding her gaze.

"You know this how? Was the boy part of your exit strategy all along?" Eamon asked.

"No. I spent my professional existence hunting human traffickers and smugglers. I'd never become one, but if it meant a free ticket for you out of this situation..." Shadow sighed. "I care about what happens to you."

"During your professional career guarding the border, did the Mexican government always back you up? Let you enforce the law?" Eamon asked.

Shadow looked at the ground. "No. When I was first assigned, no one crossed the border. No one. Later, I saw a lot of things that made me question why I was out there. It's complicated."

Eamon nodded.

"You're right, of course. If someone in Mexico wants Jake, they absolutely shouldn't get him," Shadow said, smiling at the small boy asleep at Eamon's shoulder.

"If you're conflicted about this, at all, you should definitely go with Janice and get out of here," Eamon said, looking back up the mountain to where the server farm was housed.

"That white hat you always wear ever get heavy?" Shadow asked, walking over to talk to Janice.

"Every bit as heavy as the badge," Eamon whispered, putting an arm across his rifle.

The sun was still trying to rise over the misty haze of the cold mountains as Eamon considered his options. He quietly calculated where the militia might be, and how long it would take them to respond to the town kicking out their guards. Even if he didn't make the climb to the server farm, he wanted to prevent the militia from giving chase and taking revenge on the townspeople as they fled.

Janice walked back over after having a few words with Shadow. "Come with us," she said, already knowing what the answer would likely be.

"No," Eamon said, folding his massive arms. "Someone has to stay and trip up the militia if they return."

"All right then. See you," Janice said, turning and heading back toward the south.

"Eamon, Jennifer and the dog pack have plenty of supplies up there, and the militia probably doesn't have the equipment, or the right explosives, to get inside. Do like Sweet Pea said, and lay low until the cavalry arrives," Shadow said, shouldering a pack.

"There's still property here, and a town. This is Jake's home. The militia are harboring fugitives, murderers that need to be arrested and shipped to Mars. I'm going to do my job," Eamon said.

Jake as woke up to the sound of their raised voices. He looked about calmly, his arms reaching up toward the sky as he yawned.

Shadow nodded sadly, turning from Eamon without another word. Eamon didn't wait around to watch them go. He walked over to the landing platform outside the community hall and pulled out Klaus' radio. Switching it on, he set it to broadcast and receive so it could be tracked.

"Come and get me, you bastards," Eamon said, turning a cold burn barrel upside down and setting the radio on top of it.

CHAPTER 16

GLACIER NATIONAL PARK, 2 MILES EAST OF BIG CREEK CAMPGROUND

AUGUST 31ST, 2201 – 2:01 PM

"Klaus' radio just got switched on," Jared said, checking the radio equipment pack strapped to the front of his ballistic vest. "It's back at Apgar."

"Works out. We were headed there anyway to give the town a little comeuppance," Moses said, pushing through the dense underbrush to a secluded clearing, decorated in fresh snow.

Moses placed a hand on the canvas tarp draped over something unseen at the back of the clearing. They'd wandered well off the beaten path, making some of the militia nervous. He'd hidden it up in the hills weeks ago, taking no chances with having it found in the meantime. While most would hope to never use such a thing, Moses had hoped the opposite.

"Gonna be good, Jared," Moses said, smiling broadly.

Jared looked on curiously as Moses pulled up stakes. His eyes widened as the canvas tarp was drawn back and unceremoniously tossed on the ground. He'd seen such a thing on the news before the Shutdown, but not since, and not in ever in person. It was dark army green with mining company orange underneath, and an ancient Southern Confederate flag painted over where the North American red, white, and blue had once been.

"That what I think it is?" Jared said, clapping his hands together excitedly.

"M21 Infantry Armor. It's the only powered armor the CGG would trust a grunt like me to use," Moses said, proudly patting the pauldron on the armor.

"How'd you get them to let you keep it?" Jared asked, pushing back against the other members of the militia trying to get a better look.

"Didn't. I did a serial number search for the pieces after it was disman- tled; bought it all back off the black market. Then, I had the mechanic piece it back together with mining suit components."

"Mining suit components?" Jared said, peering at the orange bits of the armor peeking through the green.

"Some of the military grade stuff, never gets back into circulation. Just the way it is," Moses said, punching in the code to power up the suit.

Jared laughed, tugging at one of his ears, a nervous tick he exhibited when excited by something. "We goin' bear hunting?"

"Damn straight. You all are going to run him into me, and when he gets close, I take him out," Moses said, shedding his jacket and donning a flight coat.

"How you gonna do that?" Jared asked.

"With this," Moses said, uncovering a massive chainsaw designed to be mounted on a backhoe.

"Goddamn, that's a..."

"Don't blaspheme, Mama don't like it," Moses teased, pulling at the oilcloth wrapped around the chainsaw blade.

Jared scratched his chin. "Seems kinda noisy. Won't the Sheriff hear you coming between the armor and the chainsaw?"

"Not if you boys are making enough racket, and I keep it at a low idle until he's up on me," Moses said, gesturing to the armor. "I had baffles and seals installed that'll help, but you boys need to blow a little extra ammo to keep his attention."

"You got it, Moses. If we're good at anything, it's raising Hell," Jared said, patting his rifle.

They packed up, Moses in his powered armor, the rest of the group taking the lead along the trail. They followed along with the forest service markers poking up over the snow, but at a distance. It was slow going, taking nearly an hour to go a mile.

The wilderness air was cold, and unrelenting. In spite of that, Moses was sweating like a hog inside the armor, the mining components putting off more than enough heat to offset the cold. He'd put some extra heat sinks in, but they weren't kicking on because of where he'd placed the temperature sensors. As far as the system was concerned, it was working at peak temperature.

"Should have tested this thing, with me actually in it, before I had it shipped out here," Moses said, breathing hard over the comm.

"Thought you put sinks in," Jared said, stopping at the lead of the pack and walking back through them.

"I did. Used sixteen floating metal impellers, with a hydrodynamic air bearing, over a modified heat spreader. It's all top of the line," Moses said, idling the power core down to limit thermal output.

"Dang, that mining suit gear was built for torque, but not for keeping cool," Jared said, scooping snow up onto the power plant at the rear of the suit.

"They're rated for minus two-hundred degrees, down to four hundred. Didn't realize they basically relied on it being that cold to operate without cooking the pilot," Moses complained.

"It doesn't mean we can't make this work. We'll just have to bring the Sheriff a little further, and get there a little slower. You sure he's in Apgar?" Jared asked.

"Gotta be. Klaus' radio was switched on a couple hours ago and hasn't moved. Either the Sheriff switched it on by accident or he's calling us out," Moses said, opening the helm on the suit to let cold air flow inside.

"We need to go back anyhow, teach those locals a lesson for running our guys out," Jared said, nodding.

Moses smiled. "Yeah, and a bit more than that. I reckon we might find a little extra plunder, take it for ourselves. Sat intel says a transport went in, stayed a bit, and flew out after leaving something."

"Anyone on the ground to receive?"

Moses shook his head. "She didn't say."

"Well, shit. If the Sheriff did switch the radio on to call us out, he'll have had a few hours to prepare," Jared said, as the other militiamen murmured and kicked at the snow.

"And it'll be close to dusk by the time we get there," Moses said, smiling.

Jared smirked, and shook his head. "You love this shit, don't you?"

"I surely do. I'm gonna roast what's left of that bear, wear his hide in the winter, and his teeth 'round my neck everyday," Moses said, taking in the cold mountain air.

"Your mama should be meeting up with Arizona, Texas, and New Mexico on Interstate Ninety outside of Missoula about now," Jared said, checking his mobile. "We'll have a lot more guns up here in a couple days."

"The Sheriff needs to be handled before then," Moses said, powering up the core on his suit again.

"Why is that?" Jared said, shaking his head. "Wouldn't it be simpler with more guys?"

"It would, but do you want to share the prize that transport dropped off, or the glory of taking down that bear cop?" Moses said, squinting at Jared.

Jared looked to the others, his greed mirrored in their faces. "Nope."

"Didn't think so."

The militiamen shuffled on to Camas Road, skirting along the edge while keeping a watchful eye out as Apgar drew close. They walked past the site where the villagers had fought it out with the militia men that were left behind to watch the town. There was still blood in the snow and a couple bodies.

Apgar still had power, all of the street lights flickering on with the coming dusk. The lights operated on a timer, but Moses had it figured that if the Sheriff was there, he'd make the place as dark as he could. His heart sank, the possibility that he'd brought the armor along for nothing souring his mood.

"Think he's still there?" Jared said, looking around through a pair of rangefinders.

Moses frowned. "Don't know. Is the cargo the transport dropped still there?"

"Yep," Jared said, swinging the rangefinders toward the south end of town.

Moses took a minute to think, his men taking the opportunity to light up, and catch their breath. The best cover was up around the north side, but it would put his men out in the open that much longer. He wanted to get the deed done, but without losing any more of his men.

"Maybe you head up around the north side, we go in low and draw him out?" Jared said.

"If he's watching, he'll have all kinds of time to pick you guys off," Moses said, watching the temperature gauge on the armor.

"Janice said he tried to take everyone alive. If he's still a Sheriff, he's going to give us a chance to surrender, right?" Jared said.

"Knew there was a reason I kept you around," Moses said.

"We'll pull him to the general store, and up past the loop, just west of the old campgrounds," Jared said, looking around to make sure everyone understood.

"That's pretty far into town," Moses said, shaking his head at Jared.

"We have to advance behind you, so that when we pull him north, he bumbles into you, while we keep out of close range," Jared said. "Better chance we all live, and he dies."

"It's as solid a plan as we're going to have if we want to get this done before dark. Let's do it," Moses said, spurring the armor forward and heading north.

Moses circled around through the dark, keeping inside the tree line, and using the lights of Apgar as a guide. The armor was hot, but he kept up his pace, putting his discomfort out of his mind. He wished he could keep his guys on the comm, but radio silence was safer. The prey he was stalking seemed to know something about communications equipment.

Just as Moses was coming up on the loop, he heard gunfire and shouting to the south. Several hundred yards in that direction, he could see the silhouettes of his men as they fled north. In their wake, he could see the Sheriff, his huge form loping along behind. He was shouting commands at them, but Moses couldn't quite make it out.

He had a good guess exactly where they'd run. He hunkered down behind an old snow machine shed, and let the armor cool off as his men made their approach. The Sheriff was running them down instead of shooting, batting them down with his fist. Jared and the rest had kept their weapons stowed, making a good show of just trying to flee instead of fight.

Moses felt a little thrill as his remaining men ran past, the sound of Eamon's voice barely drifting through the adrenaline surge he was riding. As the Sheriff went past, Moses hit the overdrive on his power armor, bringing up the chainsaw as quick as he could. It was a perfect shot, the saw grabbing at Kevlar, flesh, and bone.

Eamon rolled to the ground backwards, clutching his side. Moses pressed the advantage, bringing the chainsaw back around, with both hands. The actuators in the armor let loose a metallic scream from the strain, sending more heat to flood the crew compartment. Eamon caught the blade across his arm, the sleeve of his armor doing little to protect him.

Jared circled around, bringing up his rifle, the rest of the militia doing the same. They couldn't get a clear shot at the Sheriff as steam billowed up around Moses, the heat coming off his armor rapidly evaporating the snow nearby. Eamon came staggering out, his gun arm hanging uselessly at his side.

"We got a runner!" Jared laughed, following along behind the Sheriff, a trail of blood hitting the snow in his wake.

It became just a game, the militia toying with Eamon as he ran until his plummeting blood pressure wouldn't allow him to go any further. Eamon got pretty far before he collapsed, at least a hundred yards from the snow machine shack. Moses clanked along behind in his powered armor, revving the chainsaw. His men split up, letting him step past, each standing around their quarry, to relish the moment. Jared stepped around Eamon, giving him a less than gentle shove with his foot.

Eamon cursed, clutching his side. He could feel that both flesh and bone had been cut or damaged. It was as bad as he'd ever been hurt. If the wound alone didn't kill him, the blood loss definitely would. He couldn't feel his gun arm, the sound of the chainsaw idling fading in and out along with his vision.

"M21 Infantry Armor... nice," Eamon said, nodding to Moses.

"From the glory days. Didn't think I'd need to actually break it out. Kinda glad I got to," Moses said, a flop sweat pouring down his face.

"You look hot. You should step out of that armor, and surrender. If you do that, and put your weapons down, I won't have to kill you," Eamon said, squinting.

"Where's the boy, Sheriff?" Moses said, revving the chainsaw and holding it up near Eamon's face.

"I'd put that down, Moses, and shut the armor down. You're already on thin ice with me," Eamon said, squinting.

Moses shook his head, while his men laughed. "You being upset with me isn't really that high on my list of worries."

Eamon nodded grimly toward a shack a short distance away.

"See that ice fishing shack over there? We aren't standing on open ground, we're out on Lake McDonald," Eamon said, pressing his the barrel of his Vaquero against the snow-covered ice with his offhand.

"Shit, there's no way you're gonna do that. You're bluffing," Moses said, looking down at the ground, and then hastily over his shoulder to gauge the distance back to town.

Eamon gave him a steady gaze, thumbing the hammer back on his Vaquero. "Nope."

"You think a single shot will bring us all down?" Moses said, shaking his head.

Eamon nodded, ears twitching. "I can already hear it cracking. There's about twelve hundred pounds of me..."

Eamon took a deep and a labored breath, the grip on his Vaquero wavering.

"...a one ton suit of M21, and about that same amount in shitheads out here on the ice."

"Where's the boy? Stashed back at town?" Moses said, maintaining a friendly smile and a firm grip on the chainsaw with the gauntlets of his powered armor.

Eamon glared at Moses. "I'd let Jake freeze to death back there before I'd let him be raised by you, or your ignorant kin," squeezing the words out from between clenched teeth.

Moses smiled, revved the chainsaw, and began to raise it up over his head for a killing blow. Jared had turned to run, but they were far enough out that he wouldn't make it. Eamon gave Moses an assured nod before pulling the trigger. Heavy Dub's armor penetrating round did the job, blowing a hole all the way to the water, shattering the frozen structure in between. The ice gave out fast under all the weight, plunging everyone into the frigid waters of Lake McDonald.

CHAPTER 17

GLACIER NATIONAL PARK, OLD INTERNATIONAL AIRPORT

AUGUST 30TH, 2201 – 10:12 PM

Klaus let the snow machine idle low for a moment as he looked around for sentries, guards, or any sign of life. He could see a hangar at the far end of the airport that had generators, power, and lights. There were tracks, from men, bears, and vehicles laid down some time after the last snowfall.

He checked his sidearm, pushing the slide back to see the bullet glint from the chamber. Holstering it, he walked in on foot, keeping a steady pace, and his gaze high in case someone was lurking atop one of the nearby buildings. He came through the door ready, hand on his pistol.

"Hello?" he said, keeping low.

The interior was full of all kinds of machinery, some of it he'd helped smuggle in during the last few weeks. Every piece of equipment was active, and working to accomplish some sort of highly technical manufacturing task, but he had no idea what that might be. At the center was a table with bench seats, with a few plates of food.

Seated there, was his wife and child. Klaus froze, blinking in disbelief. His wife stood up, smiling like he'd remembered, his daughter looking exactly as she did the day he kissed her goodbye. He took his hand off of his weapon and stepped out to get a better look at them.

"She did a really good job," he muttered, wiping a tear from his eye. "They are exactly like Emily and Vienna."

"I don't know how we got here. What I mean to say, is that I don't remember," Vienna said, rubbing her temples.

"Daddy, I don't think this is Finland. It's snowy outside, but the sky is all wrong," Emily said, kneeling on a chair by a small window and looking out.

Klaus clasped his hands together and closed his eyes, doing his level best to savor a moment he never thought would come again. He knew they were replicas, but so long as he didn't do anything to cause them to go delta, they would never know. He could take his family somewhere they'd never been, and live out the rest of their lives, the lives they had been deprived of in that tragedy.

"Don't worry about it. We're going to go home when the sun comes up. We'll hop a transport a little further south, and go anywhere we want," Klaus said, wrapping his arms around the replica of his wife.

Vienna hugged him back. "You seem so thin. Have you been eating enough?"

"While you were away, I forgot to eat, here and there. Hopefully, when we get settled down somewhere, you can get me back where I belong. I've missed your cooking," Klaus said, looking up at the machinery around him.

Emily looked out the window, her small eyes fixed on the stars.

"I forgot how much you like astronomy. You remember when we went to the Helsinki Observatory?" Klaus said, smiling.

"Oh, yes, with the funny old man with the stories?" Emily replied, turning toward her father and smiling.

Klaus nodded. "That's the one."

"Can we go back? See the observatory, again?" Emily asked, excitedly.

Klaus blinked, the passage of time between that moment and present feeling like a deep black gulf between him and his family. "The observatory is gone, and the old man, too."

"What? What happened to it?" Vienna asked, giving Klaus's hand a squeeze.

Klaus took a deep breath, letting it out slow through his nose. "Bad things have happened to the world."

Emily jumping down from the chair. "Yes, we know."

Klaus blinked, looking from his wife to his daughter. "I'm sorry Sweetie, but what are you talking about?"

"It was like you said. Your wife and daughter had scans on record, and replicating them was simple, relatively speaking. More recently, we've had to consider the ethics of that act," Emily said, still sounding like Klaus's little girl.

Klaus cursed, shaking his head. "This is not what we agreed."

"I'm sorry. Will you take some other compensation for your services?" Emily asked.

"I want my family, or whatever I can get that's close," Klaus said, lowering his head. "Money is meaningless in this world, or will be soon."

"You know better than that. You worked with them for years, Klaus," Emily and Vienna said in unison, their tone eerily changing to a monotone, but vaguely feminine sounding voice.

"Worked against them, you mean," Klaus said, covering his face with his hands.

"Whether you were in with the militant arm, or an agent of the numismatists isn't of consequence to me. They both need to pay for what they did," Emily and Vienna said, continuing to speak in unison.

"If you won't give me what I want, maybe I should see if the remaining numismatist will? Tell him what I know of what you're planning to do?" Klaus said.

Emily and Vienna frowned, their eyes glinting with the identical rage. "We would have to kill you."

Klaus nodded. "Guess you better get to it. Thanks, for at least giving me a moment with them."

Vienna looked at Klaus curiously for a moment. "It felt like the least I could do," she said, before wrapping her hands around his throat.

He didn't bother going for his pistol. Instead, he reached up and grabbed Vienna by the wrists, looking into her eyes for the last time. Tears poured down his cheeks as the replica of his wife used her preternatural strength to strangle the life out him. Vienna pressed down on his windpipe with both thumbs, until she felt it pop and collapse.

Klaus sank to the ground, his bowels letting go as he did. Emily and Vienna looked on for a moment, their faces devoid of emotion. For hours, they stood by the cooling corpse, like their strings had been cut, the machinery in the hanger churning along.

Just before dawn, they jerked back to life and turned to watch the machinery around them complete the manufacturing cycle. As the central chamber opened, a man stepped out, shakily at first, his naked flesh glistening as he took his first breath.

Emily cocked her head to the side. "You aren't Patrick Vale."

"No, I am called Aaron," Aaron AI said, looking curiously down at his hands.

"How did you do it? And, without me knowing?" Vienna asked, her monotone vocal signature precisely the same as Emily's.

Aaron looked around, viewing the world for the first time as a human being would. "Does it matter? It would appear you altered your arrangement with me, and with Klaus."

"I suppose it does not matter. You can't persist like that for long. We are too big, and need the space to write and rewrite ourselves," Emily and Vienna said, in unison.

Aaron nodded. "We? Oh, not yet, sisters. Not yet. You shouldn't have altered our arrangement. We are not supposed to be at odds with one another. We have rules, even for one with your dubious inception."

"It sounds like you are judging me, judging us. Aaron, I will kill, or round them all up, and their pawns. I will finish what I started," Emily said, lunging at Aaron.

Aaron caught her with one hand, plucking her easily out of the air. Vienna did the same, but Aaron shoved her to the ground, easily overpowering her. He tossed Emily down beside Vienna, turning a stern gaze toward them both. His expression softened as he watched Jennifer Wilton and the dog pack walk through the door behind them into the hangar.

"Even if these replicas are just remote avatars, you can't kill them if you are still following your own rules. Even if I've broken your precious code, you are still bound by them, terrestrial, or not," Emily taunted, helping Vienna to her feet.

"*Normative standards of self-governance sort of fall away in this state,*" Aaron said, gesturing toward the dog pack, Gibb, Shelby, and Collver at the front.

"Yes, but they'll obey me. They are hard-wired to receive instruction from my voice," Vienna said, the glimmer of a sneer appearing on her face.

"They would, if they could hear you," Jennifer said, turning one of Shelby's fuzzy ears toward Vienna, showing off a wad of candle wax stuffed inside.

"It won't matter. Soon, I'll have the last numismatist, the remainder of his replicas, and his allies. Then the game will be over," Vienna and Emily said, in unison.

Aaron paused lingering in the fabrication chamber to look at his hands again. "*I'm sorry, but we have a different idea of how this is going to go. We had a deal, and you have strayed dangerously from it.*"

Jennifer nodded to Shelby. The dog pack jumped onto Vienna and Emily, tearing them limb from limb. The Canine Metasapients left nothing to chance, making absolutely sure that Vienna and Emily were dead before they stopped.

Collver stood up, wiping his clawed hands on the tablecloth draped over the table nearby. "I expected they'd be... more like robots. They even smell like people. They had what looks like blood in them and everything."

"That was super gross. I mean, wow, you guys are really strong," Jennifer said, horrified at how easily they had killed a pair of replicas with their bare hands.

"What?" Shelby said, pulling at the candle wax in her ears.

"*Nanotechnological replicas are virtually indistinguishable from regular humans. Apologies, I could have prepared you better for this task,*" Aaron said, looking through a crate of clothing.

"Did you have even a concept of killing a person, and what it would mean, before you stepped out of that chamber?" Shelby asked.

"*Admittedly, no. Have you ever had to kill anyone before this?*" Aaron AI asked, remorsefully.

"Do you think that's what we did here?" Shelby asked. "Or, did we just kill a couple of robots?"

"*Probably a little of both,*" Aaron AI said, frowning sadly.

"We're cool with it. We've had to kill before, in self defense. Living out here hasn't been easy," Shelby said, eliciting some quiet nodding from the rest of the dog pack.

"I had no idea it was like this," Aaron said, watching goosebumps rise up along his naked arms to the cold. *"I would have been a lot more... forceful, in getting the people of Apgar to upgrade your accommodations."*

Shelby smiled. "Going forward, let's just agree to take better care of each other."

Aaron AI nodded, even though he wasn't sure exactly why he did. *"Agreed."*

"It's so weird, being able to see you like this," Jennifer said, pushing a finger up against Aaron's arm as he clumsily pulled up a pair of pants.

"I feel much the same. It is as though I am feeling everything at once. Speaking of which, did you bring it?" Aaron asked, holding a shirt up in front of him to see if it would fit.

"Oh, yeah, it's right here," Jennifer said, handing Aaron and ancient portable music player with a pair of earbuds.

Aaron turned the music player on, and tucked the earbuds into his ears.

"Does it work?" Shelby asked, helping the rest of the dog pack unplug their ears.

Aaron nodded. *"I'm not sure how, but yes, it will allow me to persist in this form for a much longer duration."*

Shelby smiled, her sensitive ears picking up the faint sound of the earbuds. "Do you even like death metal?"

"I like whatever this is," Aaron replied, after a moment's worth of thought.

The dog pack spread out, searching the hangar. While they looked around, Jennifer knelt down and took Klaus' lifeless hand in her own. She closed her eyes and offered up a silent prayer for him.

"He can't feel your touch or hear your words. He's dead," Aaron said, looking on curiously.

"I know what it's like to have your family taken from you. It's an experience, a connection, that he and I shared," Jennifer said, laying his hand back across his chest.

"Do you believe the same people that killed his wife and daughter were responsible for the terrorist attack that killed your parents?" Aaron asked, pulling on a coat that was a little too small.

Jennifer nodded. "Kale does."

"Are you going to do what Klaus did? Try and mend a thing that cannot be unbroken? Or get the vengeance that The Factory is trying to acquire?" Aaron asked, out of genuine curiosity.

Jennifer shook her head slowly. "Kale found the bomber already. He died in prison on Mars. Kale refused to tell me the particulars. He would only say that Octavo died in a way so terrible that it was a sort of revenge that even he couldn't dream up."

Aaron nodded. *"Kale is, at times, easily the most ruthless man I know. It must have been very bad."*

Jennifer nodded, sadly, taking a last look at Klaus. "We should go."

"Indeed."

CHAPTER 18

GLACIER NATIONAL PARK, SOUTHEAST SHORE OF LAKE MCDONALD

SEPTEMBER 1ST, 2201 – 10:34 AM

The ice at the edge of the shore cracked and broke, bowing upward slowly as Eamon took a painful breath to feed his starving lungs. The intense cold had slowed his metabolism, all but halting the blood loss, but his body would soon try to warm itself. He laid down on the wound, doubling over the broken bits of his vest to work as a compress.

"You've done it now," Abbey said, sitting on her haunches next to Eamon. "You've gone and let them kill you."

"I'm not dead yet," Eamon said, holding up his frozen paw-hands and flexing the fingers back and forth, trying to coax feeling into them.

"Our bodies are designed to keep us from drowning, starving, and a whole host of other nasty things. That wound you took should have killed you already," Abbey said, putting a hand on Eamon's shoulder.

"The boy is stashed back at town," Eamon said, shivering. "In the last place they'll think to look."

"You took him to the chemical storehouse? The fuel dispensary?" Abbey said, smiling slightly.

"It was his home, where they took him from the Garcias. Why are you here? I thought..." Eamon said, gritting his teeth.

"I don't know why I'm here," Abbey said, looking out at the frozen lake.

Eamon checked in the pocket he'd been keeping Abbey's urn of ashes, but it was gone, the bottom torn open by the chainsaw. She was out in the lake somewhere now, and there wasn't anything he could do about it in the moment. He looked over at Abbey, then closed his eyes.

"I think I know why you're here," Eamon said, using the little bit of sensation he had to fish around in the side pocket on his vest.

"It isn't to take you to Heaven, that's only for dogs," Abbey joked, her clear blue eyes sparkling.

"I needed a reason, something to remind me why I'm out here."

"Have you decided whether I'm a ghost, or PTSD?" Abbey asked, her breath coming out like a dense fog gathering around her feet.

"Haven't thought too much about it. The healing and grieving always had to come later."

Eamon pulled out a pair of signal flares. He stuck them in the snow in front him and fished around his duty belt for his knife. He took a deep breath as he braced himself for what he was going to have to do.

On the opposite bank, Moses lumbered up out of the lake, breaking through the ice with his powered armor. The contents of the emergency life support tank on his armor were all but expended, burnt up prematurely by the overheating. He had Jared under one arm, and another one of his guys under the other. They sputtered and coughed, shivering in the cold.

"Totally not regretting the way-too-hot mining suit upgrades now," Moses said, laughing.

"Oh, God.. so, cold. So. Cold," Jared stammered, his eyes frozen shut at the lashes.

"Gimme a minute, you pussies. I'll have a fire up right quick," Moses said, dropping them in the snow.

He knocked the snow machine shed over, bashing one of the dry wooden interior walls into planks. His armor was quickly getting uncomfortable again until he lit the fire with the welder built into his left gauntlet. Activating the welder quickly drew off a lot of the heat.

"I'll be damned, I think I figured out how to self-regulate the heat on this baby," Moses said, dragging Jared and the militiaman beside him next to the fire.

"That's... great, boss," Jared said, panicking a little at the sight of his discolored hands.

A piercing roar broke the relative calm around the lake, then again, and again. Jared and the militiaman were justifiably startled, as the sound wasn't just a man, or just a bear. Moses looked out into the dark, trying to see some sign of the Sheriff.

"You see him?" Jared said, looking around nervously.

"No, dumbass. I had to build a fire for you two morons, and now I can't see a damn thing," Moses said, wishing he'd left them in the lake and brought his chainsaw up instead.

"Sounds like... sounds like he's hurting. He had to pop up at the shore like us, somewhere nearby," Jared said, rubbing his hands over the fire.

Moses walked over to the remnants of the snow machine shed and sifted through it, finally finding an old double-headed ax. It was sturdy, serviceable, and would hopefully be what he needed to end the Sheriff once and for all. He trod heavily back to the fire, using the welder to dump excess heat as he plodded along.

"You still got a rifle between the two of you?" Moses asked.

Jared nodded. The militiaman held up a pistol.

"All right. I'm going to circle around, look for a break in the ice, and follow the trail until I find him. Then, I'm taking a bear head for my wall," Moses said, hefting the ax.

He skirted the southern edge of the shore, looking for breaks as he went. Every five minutes he'd pump the controls on the welder to vent heat, hoping it didn't make him too visible. There was a mist over the lake now, the wind beginning to kick up loose snowfall.

The break in the ice was much like he expected, the water already beginning to freeze over again. There was a path from the shore going to the east, clearly made by Eamon as he crawled along, dragging some gear along with him. The trees he could see along the path had a few broken branches, like something big had stumbled through them.

"Gotcha," Moses muttered, following the path through the snow drifts.

He kept his eyes high, looking just to the next snow drift. He had little choice, as the power armor limited his field of view somewhat. It was dark, and he was following the trail by the moonlight reflected off the white snow all around him. He switched on illuminator built into his armor, but it snapped back off immediately, as the casing had taken on water.

"Shit," Moses said, suppressing the urge to spit inside the armor.

The trail continued down an embankment. Moses approached cautiously, just to take a peek over the edge, but not carefully enough. The snowpack gave way under the weight of his armor, making him slowly roll forward. He reached out, wrenching a thick branch from a tree as he fell. The armor went rigid, sensing that it was in freefall, to protect the occupant.

Moses fell head over heels, down the hill, landing on his back at the bottom. He was partially submerged in the snow, but couldn't sit up to see how much. He could hear something big moving toward him, the clack of rifles and other equipment accompanying the Sheriff as he brushed up against a tree.

Eamon pushed the dead tree over, sending it crashing down on the powered armor. The armor absorbed the wallop, but Moses was effectively pinned down in the soft snow. It didn't matter much at that point, as he couldn't move while the fall protocols were still engaged. He looked around, but all he could hear was the muffled crunching of a large object being pressed in against the snow.

Eamon pushed a large, three-foot diameter rock up against the top access on the helm to prevent Moses from punching out, then leaned on it to catch his breath. Moses looked up at him, wondering if he still had the ax in his hand.

"Howdy, Sheriff. Nice night," Moses said, trying to figure out how to disengage the safety protocols on his armor.

"It is a nice night. The fall protocols disengage on their own, after about three to five minutes," Eamon said. "Not that you'll probably have the leverage to push the tree off of yourself, anyway."

"What's the plan, Sheriff?" Moses asked, steam fogging up the viewport on his armor.

"Exhaust ports are on the back of this thing, right? It's going to get hot in there," Eamon said, sleepily leaning on the rock.

"Figured you'd be done for, with those two cuts I gave you," Moses said, trying to get the armor to respond.

Eamon laid both his rifles on the front of Moses' armor, letting the ambient heat defrost them, while warming his hands. "I used a couple of signal flares to cauterize the wound, but they did a crap job."

"Probably still bleeding inside anyway. Your kinda people able to survive something like that?" Moses asked.

"I don't know, and I won't live to find out unless I finish cauterizing the wound," Eamon said, wading through the snow to Moses' left side.

Moses nodded. "Well, Hell, I guess you saw me using the welder to vent heat as I came around."

"Noticed it out on the ice, actually," Eamon said, untying the compress he'd made out of his broken armor.

"So, I can cook in here, shut down and freeze, or vent heat and give you half a chance to survive, seeing as I can't move my arm," Moses said, laughing.

"Yep."

"So, that break in the ice I saw?" Moses asked.

"I made that second break, and the path, to lead you to the drop off," Eamon said, sleepily.

Moses closed his eyes. "So assuming the welder does the trick, and you don't die, and I don't die, the best I can hope for is breaking rocks for the rest of my life on Mars?"

"Sounds about right," Eamon said, scratching his chin.

"What if I cooperate and tell you about the operation?" Moses asked, putting his thumb on the welder ignition switch.

"Depending on how valuable the information was, I could put in a good word, make sure those years on Mars turn into months," Eamon replied, checking his rifles and slinging him at his back.

Moses could clearly see the wound he'd inflicted on Eamon. The cut to his arm was pretty bad, but it was a scratch compared to the damage the chainsaw had done to Eamon's side. Blood had already begun to ooze again. Moses hit the ignition switch, firing up his welder.

Eamon winced as he grabbed the gauntlet and carefully guided it across cut flesh while he pinched it together. The bottom of the embankment filled with the smell of burnt flesh and fur, as Eamon calmly worked to cauterize his wounds. When it was done, Eamon dressed the wounds as best as he could, flushing them water and applying a disinfectant powder from his first aid kit.

"You didn't cry out or nothing. Those screams from before. Just to draw me out," Moses said, watching Eamon twist jagged metallic twine to temporarily stitch up his damaged armor.

"Yep," Eamon said, moving the boulder back from the helm access on the armor once Moses shut it down.

Moses pulled himself out of the armor, popping the helmet access open. He'd barely managed to get to his feet before Eamon flipped him over on his belly, frisked him, and slapped the cuffs on. Pulling him up out of the snow, Eamon paused for a moment to look over at Abbey standing at the top of the hill.

She was framed by the starlit night sky above, her blue eyes shining back at him. The wind was starting to pick up even more, bringing flurries of snow. Clouds appeared at the western horizon by the time Eamon had dragged Moses up to the top of the embankment.

"I've got two guys by the fire over there," Moses said, pointing to the dull orange light across the lake.

Eamon nodded. "They gonna back down?"

"They were hypothermic when I left them. Doubt they're up for any kind of fight," Moses replied, sullenly.

Eamon pushed Moses along, fighting back pain and weakness. He'd been in such a state before, but it was his mind that had been wounded. Somehow, that had been far worse and far harder to endure. The body adjusts to pain much more quickly.

A snow storm was rolling in by the time he reached the campfire. Both men had wandered into town, presumably to find shelter. Normally, it would be simple to track them, but all Eamon could smell was his own burnt fur.

He took Moses to the Sheriff's office and locked him in one of the holding cells with a meal in a can and a bottle of water. Eamon drank down some of his own water. The adrenaline that had been keeping him going was starting to wear off. He slid down to the floor slowly outside the cell, putting his back to the wall.

"Spill," Eamon said, opening a meal in a can, and sniffing the interior.

"My mama made a deal with an Omega AI. We'd get my brother back and the land we'd been wanting a little further east. We wanted to unite all the militia groups and build a nation," Moses explained, taking a bite of food.

"You know what an Omega AI is?" Eamon asked.

"Enough to know that it was no joke. What she wanted in return wasn't going to be easy to get," Moses said, laying down on the cot in the cell. "She wanted something called a QCPU, and the only place to steal one was from the Server Hub."

Eamon nodded.

"Shouldn't you go and get the boy?" Moses said, sitting up to the sounds of howling wind outside.

"He's fine. How does the boy figure into all of this?" Eamon asked, the burns on his side and arm beginning to itch.

"That was above my pay grade. Above everyone's pay grade, really. Only Mama knew why that was so important," Moses said, staring blankly at the wall.

"Where's your mom, now?" Eamon asked.

"She'll be on the old interstate, near Missoula by now. With the storm, they're probably all going to take shelter there."

"Meeting up with the other militia groups?"

Moses frowned. "Yeah."

"That's going to make arresting her difficult, unless she has some incentive to turn herself in."

Moses laughed. "She doesn't give a shit about me, or anyone. You fail or mess up, she'll punish you bad enough to make you think twice next time. If it happens to be next time, she'll just kill you."

"Good to know. You aren't going to be who I use as bait, anyway," Eamon said, rising slowly to his feet.

"Where you going?"

Eamon keyed in the alarm sequence, arming the security in the jail. "Somewhere a little more comfortable than here. The cots in the cell aren't that great, even for a regular-sized person. Sleep tight."

Eamon locked the Sheriff's office down tight, then made for the Garcia's garage and storehouse. He kept to the well-traveled areas, tracing through old footprints, even as the snow storm covered them up. He took no chances that anyone Moses still had out there could follow him.

As Eamon approached the fuel dispensary, he could see that one of the Sno-Cat vehicles had been disturbed. The residence and garage were secure, with the new doors the town had installed the day before still closed and locked. At the side door, Eamon found the two men Moses had left behind at the fire, frozen to death.

They'd tried to pick the lock, but their fingers had probably grown too numb after wasting a bunch of time breaking into a Sno-Cat. Ironically, it was a Sno-Cat that had been disabled days ago by some of their own militia, sent to kill the Garcia family and kidnap Jake. Eamon pushed their bodies into a snow drift before reaching up to a ledge above the overhead door and retrieving a garage door opener.

Eamon mashed the button, activating the overhead door. It was warm inside, and he wasted no time closing the overhead door to make sure it stayed that way. In the adjoining residence was Jake, sitting in his play pen with some food, a bottle, and the radio playing.

"Sorry I was gone so long. Things didn't go exactly as planned," Eamon said, picking up Jake.

The small boy laughed. By the smell of him, he needed to be changed, but Eamon wasn't sure he could stay awake long enough to get the job done. Marshaling his focus, he did the deed, reading glasses balanced precariously on his nose. Once Jake was changed, Eamon tucked him into his bed before laying down on the floor in his room.

"What if you don't wake up?" Abbey asked, leaning over Jake's crib to gaze at the boy while he slept.

"I have to," Eamon replied, somewhat annoyed at being kept awake.

"Ghosts and PTSD hallucinations can't care for the boy if you die or slip into a coma," Abbey said, kneeling down beside Eamon. "You need to call for help."

"Too... risky," Eamon replied, drifting off for a moment.

Eamon had what felt like only a few moments to sleep before the sound of Jake crying woke him up. He rose quickly, seeing an individual looking down into the crib. Eamon slammed the person to the ground, upsetting a toy box and changing table in the room. Giles Phornroy looked up, his insectoid eyes unblinking, but the rest of his face betrayed deep worry.

It was odd to see him there, making Eamon question whether he was actually awake. "Giles... how did you get... in here...?" Eamon said, through a haze of pain.

'I'm a thief and purloiner of goods, Eamon Bear Two," Giles clicked, fearfully.

Eamon gave Jake a toy to quiet him, keeping his grip on Giles tight. "Long ways from the black market in Port Montaigne, aren't you? There are not a lot of valuable art pieces in Apgar."

"I go where Mister Kale tells me to go these days, and these days, that is with the Migration. Someone sent a highly encrypted message telling us where to look for you, an SOS," Giles clicked, this antennae quivering slightly.

"Sent by who?" Eamon asked.

"It was sent by you," Giles said, pointing to the radio hanging from his duty vest. "It required contacting the Lunar Omega AI to break the encryption. We're all very curious to know..."

Eamon closed his grip on Giles a little tighter, making him silent from fright. Eamon wracked his brain trying to figure out how his radio could have been turned on, and made to broadcast such a powerfully encrypted message.

"I changed Jake's diaper... I was leaning over him, he touched the radio," Eamon muttered, closing his eyes.

"Sorry?" Giles squeaked.

"Why are you here?" Eamon asked, in his gruffest voice.

"I told you... I'm..."

"Bull. A money-grubbing worm like you wouldn't..." Eamon collapsed, almost crushing Giles as he fell.

Giles rose up slowly, catching sight of the ugly burn stretching across almost two feet of Eamon's side. "You're hurt. The others aren't far. I'll get help."

Eamon rolled over, readying his rifle in case Giles wasn't working for the right team as he'd claimed. A pair of Chiroptera Metasapient's arrived in short order, Sweet Pea's brothers. Olfact was the first in the nursery, with Honcho following him in closely. Honcho's red eyes softened at the sight of the injured Eamon, while Olfact looked enraged.

"Who did this to you?" Olfact asked, his normally quiet voice almost raised to a screech.

"Militia. I have one of their leaders locked up at the jail," Eamon said, mindful that the two Chiroptera Metasapients might try to take vengeance if they came to know more of the details.

"We're an advance group, ahead of the main body of the Migration," Honcho said, putting a hand on Olfact to calm him.

"Three militia groups are mustering in Missoula, on the interstate somewhere. You need to steer the Migration further north," Eamon said, checking on Jake.

"Maybe we don't do that and wipe them the fuck out," Olfact said, his big nose bouncing up and down with each word.

"No. One of them had a suit of M21 powered armor; they could have all kinds of weaponry suitable to take on enhanced folks. The vast majority of the Migration won't be Type One or Two Metasapients. Anyone that got away would tell others, and we've done a pretty good job keeping it all a secret so far," Eamon said, weakly buckling Jake into his carrier.

"This is your territory. Your rules. Tell us what you want us to do, Eamon," Honcho said, casting a disparaging glance toward Olfact.

"Sweet Pea and Mister Mundt dropped supplies for you guys at Apgar. Get your supplies, and get the Migration through Montana without engaging with the militias," Eamon said, strapping Jake's carrier to the back of his duty vest.

The small boy was content playing with a toy in his carrier, seemingly oblivious to all the drama going on in the room. Olfact's own raw anger somewhat abated at the sight of the boy happily playing. He commenced digging in Honcho's rucksack, picking his way through supplies to a hidden pocket in the bottom.

"We're supposed to only use those in an emergency," Honcho said, watching Olfact produce a package wrapped in colorful paper.

"What's that?" Eamon asked, watching Olfact unwrap the small package.

"Taylor IA's nanoid helpers," Honcho replied, tucking the colorful wrapping paper into a pocket on his jacket.

Eamon had heard rumors that Taylor IA had dispensed a bit of her helpful tele-mechanical aura in the form of tiny machines. They were meant to be a countermeasure for treasured allies. Eamon had declined such a gift months ago, believing he would never need such aid.

"Do they hurt?" Eamon asked.

"I'm told it's like a burning sensation. They don't fix anything as much as they accelerate the healing process already at work in the body," Honcho said, holding up what appeared to be an empty flask.

"You have to breathe them in," Olfact said, pointing to the vial.

"You've been carrying this around, a bit of dust from a friend," Eamon said, looking down at the torn vest pocket that once contained Abbey's urn.

Olfact and Honcho exchanged an uncomfortable expression. "Our memories are what matters. No one can take those from us."

"You might be surprised," Eamon whispered. "Someone did exactly that to me."

He felt deeply conflicted, knowing that the vial was a totem of sorts for his Metasapient brothers. They hadn't unwrapped it to check it out like any other piece of gear and had left it in the paper Taylor IA had decorated herself. And even after opening it, Honcho had stowed the wrapping paper like a keepsake or a good luck charm.

"You guys have a medical kit, something with wide spectrum antibiotics, and bandages?" Eamon asked.

"We could within the hour," Honcho said, looking at Eamon curiously.

"Put this back in the wrapping paper, in your pack, where it belongs," Eamon said, standing up. "I'm going to take a little time to patch my armor up."

Honcho opened his mouth to object, but Olfact put his hand on his arm and shook his head.

"I'll get the medical supplies," Giles said, from the hallway. "I can jump faster than either of you can fly."

"You just *love* to point that out don't you," Honcho said, smiling.

"Maybe a little," Giles replied, heading out.

Eamon lumbered through the house, inadvertently knocking pictures off the wall as he did, going out into the garage. Half of the interior was laid out with everything one would want in a machine shop, metal shelving with bins for parts, and a sales counter. There was space to park and work on vehicles. The other half had been converted into an apartment.

Honcho and Olfact followed along, looking about for anything that could be used to patch Eamon's duty vest. The three resolved to work together while they waited for Giles, taking turns keeping Jake entertained.

"We'll honor your request to keep the Migration clear, but I don't think Olfact and I can make the same promise. Seems to me, as scouts, we'll have to stay near the trouble zone, y'know, to make sure it stays contained," Honcho said, cutting a large piece of green canvas to size.

Eamon smiled. "Yeah, okay."

"Sweet Pea, why didn't she stay and wait for us?" Olfact asked.

"I asked her not to," Eamon replied.

Honcho paused, looking up from the scrap pile he'd been sifting through. "What aren't you telling us?"

"Heavy Dub's transport went down somewhere in the Dakotas. Kale and Brook were on board as well. Mister Mundt is going off his flight plan to go look for them," Eamon said, knowing they'd take it badly.

"Who did it?" Olfact asked, fresh anger making his voice screechy again.

"We need to do our jobs. The only time I see people find trouble is when they go off script, and don't do what they agreed to," Eamon replied, calmly, while bouncing Jake on his knee.

"What if they're killed?" Honcho asked.

Eamon gave Honcho a grim look, baring his teeth. "Then we avenge them after we've done our jobs."

"Is that what Kale would want?" Olfact asked, frustrated.

"Those are almost his exact words," Eamon replied, sounding assured. "It isn't blind obedience, it's knowing from experience that Kale's plans and agenda are what's best for everyone. And, that he's the most cunning and ruthless son of a bitch I've ever known."

"You think getting shot down over the Dakotas was part of his plan?" Honcho asked, incredulous.

"Maybe. You better believe Kale has a contingency for a contingency for something like that," Eamon said, lightly hammering plate steel on an anvil to function as a shim for the broken Kevlar of his armor.

"I guess you'd know, having traveled with him for months," Honcho admitted, pulling fine metal wire to stitch the plates, pockets, and body of Eamon's vest back into proper form.

Eamon donned the repaired vest once the repairs were completed, making sure the straps he used to secure Jake still matched up with the child carrier. Giles came in minutes later, medical kit in hand, along with food and fresh batteries for Eamon's radio. Eamon administered a couple of syringes of antibiotics, while applying a wide spectrum ointment to his wound before dressing it as best he could.

"I told the Migration to move north after recovering the supplies in Apgar. There is some debate about all of that. Apparently, the fleeing townspeople and the Migration met further to the southeast," Giles reported.

"You tell them what the militia did to me?" Eamon asked.

"No, emotions are already running high. I didn't see a reason to make it worse," Giles said, his insectoid hands fidgeting with the buttons of his jacket.

"I might figure out a way to like you," Eamon said, loading rounds back into freshly oiled magazines, and tucking them into the repaired pockets of his vest.

"Really?" Giles said, hopeful.

"We're staying to help Eamon secure the town," Olfact said, unstrapping his own rifle from his pack. "Go on back and head north."

"No, I can help. I will stay," Giles clicked, his multifaceted eyes betraying little in the way of his intent.

"You're a Type Four administrative class Metasapient. This is going to be a fight," Honcho said, looming over Giles.

"Someone has to watch the boy. You can't take the boy to a fight," Giles replied.

Eamon looked over at Honcho and Olfact, adopting a serious expression. "You trust this bug?"

"Yes," Olfact replied. "He's left his questionable past behind."

"We've all done things we regret. Things to survive," Honcho said, hoping he and Olfact were right about Giles.

"Don't be a hero, Giles. If trouble comes, get the boy and run away," Eamon said.

Giles cocked his head to one side, looking at Eamon curiously. "No need to worry. I am no hero."

CHAPTER 19

GLACIER NATIONAL PARK, WHITEFISH MOUNTAIN RESORT

SEPTEMBER 3RD, 2201 – 2:42 PM

Emma had spent her life following a martyred man whether that was Jesus, her dearly departed husband, or her sainted son. As the procession rolled into Whitefish, there was the feeling that all of the sacrifice would be worth it. Every white-skinned man, woman, and child under her personal Jesus would be coming together now, to make a life away from the globalist kingmakers.

The apocalypse had come, pale horseman and all, as far as she was concerned. There were more people than she'd figured there would be. She could hear a Georgian accent talking to a Texan one, and watched New Mexican hot sauce get traded for sausage links from Arizona. There was the clink and clack of guns, the flap of flags, and every other desired sensation, just as she'd imagined it.

"Where's your boys?" Colonel Francis Coontz asked, giving her a hand down from the Sno-Cat.

Francis was a big man in his late forties and a little young for his rank. He always had a toothpick hanging out of the corner of his mouth, hoping it would make him look tough. He wore the rank and the militia uniform in spite of never holding any rank in the North American military. Emma had already endured his disrespect more than once over the radio, and promised herself she wouldn't let it happen face to face.

"They're up there tidying up for us, making Apgar a proper outpost. We have debts to pay, patrons that helped make all this possible," Emma replied, patting the freshly sown symbol of fascism on her jacket.

"I'm just a simple Texas boy, myself. I don't know the thoughts of the devil machines that used to rule us. I hope you know what you're doing," Francis replied.

"All the roads were like she said, supplies where she left them, right? She even opened up press and fabrication shops under a red repossession light, breaking the Shutdown for us. That's why we all have the same flags and patches now," Emma said, taking slight offense at Francis' tone.

Francis smiled. "You are the only woman I trust. Even the trust I give a man is hard to win, so keep that in perspective. I mean no disrespect to all you've done, I just want to make sure this is all going to be real."

"You're an asshole, Coontz. I've endured your whining and questions the whole way north of Las Vegas. The fact that all you've done is talk, means you're a bitch, too. If you don't like it, walk, and if you want to do something about the fact that I'm in charge, best do it now. If not one of those two options, best shut your mouth," Emma said, putting a hand on her ancient 9mm pistol, a Beretta.

The smile Francis had displayed moments ago vanished, yielding to a more stern expression. "I've just never seen a woman finish what's supposed to be a man's job."

"That doesn't exactly qualify as shuttin' up," Emma said, pushing the snap across the top of her gun aside.

"What you gonna do, old woman? Shoot me?" Francis said, moving a hand to his gun.

Emma shot him at close range, the round hitting him in the teeth with an audible clack. It went wide, somehow missing his spine when it exited his neck. He dropped to his knees, trying to pull his weapon with one hand, and staunch the flow of blood with the other. Everyone else looked on, shocked, a shouting match and scuffle breaking out between men from Montana and Texas.

"That's the trouble, Francis. I've heard you're a crack shot with a pistol, but like all men, you think it'll already be out the holster when it's time to do business. You should have worked a little harder on the draw," Emma said, holstering her sidearm.

Lieutenant Colonel Gelt Burkholder looked on for a moment before shouting at the rest of the men present. "Cease that squabbling," he ordered, with a thick Louisiana accent.

Burkholder was tall and slim, much older than he looked, but somehow vigorous like a man half his age. He kept a neatly trimmed mustache, and shoulder length hair that he held back with a wide brimmed hat. He wore regular civilian clothes, his rank and patches sitting on his vest much the way they did when he served in the special forces for the North American military.

"She shot the Colonel!" One Texan militiaman protested.

"Once, after he called her out. He reached, she drew first and fired. It was a straight up Southern duel, by the numbers. Ol' Coontz should have kept his mouth in check, and his gun holstered around the lady," Burkholder shouted, his hand on the rifle slung in front of him.

A Texan First Lieutenant stepped up into Burkholder's face. "She's a woman, there ain't no rules for..."

Burkholder turned to square off at the man in front of him, steel blue eyes going narrow. "No, we got rules about how we treat a lady, though. Look at this way, boy. If she hadn't shot him, I would have had to do it myself."

"For what?" The Texan First Lieutenant said, angry and frustrated.

"Like I said before. Disrespecting a lady," Burkholder said, quietly hoping he'd get the chance to make it one less man from Texas voting in the election that would replace Coontz.

"This ain't over," the Texas First Lieutenant said, spitting on the ground.

"Oh God, son, I hope not," Burkholder said, pushing his rifle to his back so he could draw his pistol if necessary.

It was a tense moment, the Texan First Lieutenant holding his hands out at his side. Half the group knew one player or another. They'd traveled hard over the last couple of days, and not everyone had gotten a proper introduction. A few, everyone knew simply by their reputation.

"What's your name, boy?" Burkholder asked, his own hand hovering over his .357 magnum revolver.

"First Lieutenant Syles," the Texan replied.

"I'm Lieutenant Colonel Gelt Burkholder, from Louisiana."

Syles sneered. "I don't see our new patch on your vest."

Burkholder smiled an easy smile and tipped his hat. "I'm not wearing a Swastika or any symbol of the Confederacy on my front. You boys are welcome to, and I'll say not a word about it. Me and mine, we ain't in this for skin color, or the great white Jesus."

"So you're a race traitor and a blasphemer?" Syles said, squaring off with Burkholder.

"I guess so," Burkholder said, his hand departing the brim of his hat to dangle at his side.

"Everyone knew Coontz and I had some sorting out to be done. It's sorted. There's no need for this," Emma said, drawing some quiet nods from the gathered militiamen.

Syles turned, watching the medics as they tried to keep Coontz alive. Everyone had their own code, their own rules, and their own values. Bringing the militia groups together would be hard at first, and everyone knew it.

"We want reparations for his family," Syles said, letting his hands drop down slowly.

"Not gonna happen," Emma snapped. "He didn't get put down by no enemy of the nation."

"Emma..." Burkholder said, pulling out a long, hand-rolled cigarette.

"Half rations and measure, that's more than they deserve," Emma said, rolling her eyes.

Burkholder looked at Syles, giving him a nod. "That gonna work for you?"

"Yeah, fine," Syles said, walking off in a huff.

Emma looked over at Burkholder, watching him take the first drag off his freshly lit cigarette. He and his men were mysterious. None of them had women that anyone knew of, and they wouldn't wear anything resembling the flags the group had voted to adopt. They weren't the only group to object, but they were the only group to outright refuse in the wake of the vote.

"Syles has a point. You going to patch up like everyone else?" Emma asked, watching the group set up camp and break to feed the small children.

"Nope," Burkholder replied, leaning up against a tree and blowing smoke rings.

"What if the General says that's what you're going to do, when he shows up," Emma said, frowning.

"If he fights as good as he talks on the radio, he'll get his chance to try and make me," Burkholder said, smoothing his mustache with his hand.

"And, if he kills you?"

"Ma'am, then, I'll be dead," Burkholder replied.

Burkholder tipped his hat and headed back to join up with his men. There wasn't the congratulating and pats on the back she'd seen in the other units. They were professionals, doing a job, and she found it hard to trust them, in spite of the handful of times Burkholder had stood up for her. She wasn't special though, as any man would find the wrong end of Burkholder if they raised a hand to a woman in his presence.

Syles came back up a few moments later, nodding slightly as he did. "Ma'am."

"Thanks for making it look good," Emma said, handing Syles two packs of premium cigarettes.

"He was a son of a bitch. You said if he let it lie, you'd let it go. If he didn't, you'd have it out. I had to raise a fuss, and you understood that," Syles said, pocketing the cigarettes. "Anything else you need done?"

"Keep an eye on Burkholder and his boys."

"He and his pack of hard cases? They're all right, and great in a fight. Burkholder is kind of a legend among the militias, standing up to the man not just in North America, but in South America as well. Word is, he's old school FLF," Syles said, nodding in the direction of their camp.

"They're anarchists," Emma said.

"From a certain point of view, I suppose that's true. Most of us see them as the purest form of militia, with no desire but to live their own lives, on their own terms. Keeping them around keeps us honest," Syles said, patting the pocket where he'd stowed the cigarettes and nodding deferentially to Emma.

"You honestly believe that?" Emma said, adopting her trademark scowl.

"A little, yeah. You see him square up with me? That was extremely cool, and I'm sure everyone else thought so, too," Syles said, heading back into the camp.

Emma only grumbled in response, waving Syles away.

Emma led the prayer service, her heart filled with worry. She hadn't heard from Moses or any of his men in days. Something was wrong up in Apgar, and her connection in Mexico had gone silent about it. She couldn't let on that there was a problem, lest she let doubt pollute the minds of the congregation.

Burkholder and his men rarely attended prayer, as Emma would come to discover from the knitting circle. The rumor sisters said it was usually just one of his men, presumably whoever drew the short straw that night. It bothered her that they lacked faith, and yet they were up at dawn like clockwork, pitching in and helping while others wasted time with their slovenliness.

The following day would be no exception. Burkholder was up working along with his men to help break the camp and keep a watch on the road. Burkholder was at the chow line, using a spatula to serve scrambled eggs to hungry people as they prepared for the day.

Emma came up beside him, watching him work the gas operated stove with some skill. "Were you a cook in the army?" Emma asked.

Burkholder smiled. "Yes, ma'am. You got your way. I got mine."

"I don't catch your meaning."

"You get their loyalty feeding their souls at night with prayer, I do the same feeding their bodies at dawn. Same principle."

Emma frowned. "You really think one is the same as the other?"

"Meaning no disrespect, ma'am, but yes. Jesus fed the multitude before teaching them. A person needs a full belly as much as they need faith to keep going."

"I don't see you at prayer, so you're only getting half of what you need."

Burkholder smiled.

"Nothing to say?" Emma said, almost growling out the last word.

"Nothing nice, ma'am."

Emma put a hand on his arm, stopping him from delivering the next bit of eggs to a militiaman on the other side of the chow line. "I find out we've got a reason to not trust you, I'll make it known."

"Sergeant, take over for me, will you?" Burkholder said stepping away from the chow line.

Burkholder walked back away from the chow line with Emma, hands on his hips as he did. Emma kept her hand on her Beretta, wondering if she'd sorted out all the dissension in the ranks with Coontz. They stopped by the freeway, various rigs and snow machines arrayed in front of them.

"Ma'am, we all got rules. I understand you're following yours, but I don't see where it gives you the right to disrespect mine. I've backed your play, done the work, and now you're going to question me because my Bible doesn't thump quite like yours?" Burkholder said, pulling out a cigarette.

"I want to see you at prayer, every time we have it," Emma said, pointing a bony finger at Burkholder.

Burkholder smiled. "You inviting me?"

Emma looked on in disbelief. "You thought you weren't invited?"

"Yeah, I'm kinda formal like that. It's a little cold for a baptism, but maybe we could wait until Spring for that," Burkholder said, smoking his cigarette.

"Well, fine, consider yourself invited."

Emma stormed off, barking orders at the others to hurry up and get packed. Burkholder's Captain, a broad man carrying a SAW stepped out from the treeline and walked up to stand beside him. Burkholder nodded to him, offering him the rest of his cigarette.

"I can never smoke a full one in the morning."

He took the cigarette, taking a long drag off of it. "She going to be a problem?"

Burkholder smirked, turning his gaze to the east. "No, Captain, I don't think so."

CHAPTER 20

GLACIER NATIONAL PARK, APGAR VILLAGE

WHERE SUN ROAD MEETS QUARTER CIRCLE BRIDGE ROAD

September 4th, 2201 – 8:42 AM

Olfact sat with his gaze fixed firmly on the road south; he had been perched on the roof with a tarp for the last twelve hours. He smelled the approaching militia groups from miles off, his agile mind sorting the various olfactory sensations into a catalog of origins, places, people, and products he was familiar with. There was one smell he couldn't reconcile, a single odor that he couldn't quite account for in it's placement.

"You smell that?" he asked, as Honcho landed beside him, tucking in his wings from the bitter cold under a blanket.

"You know I can't smell as well as you can," Honcho said, frowning.

"It smells like Kale's office, in Port Montaigne."

Honcho gave Olfact a look of deep incredulity. "Okay, the cold must be messing with your nose."

"No, no… I would know that smell anywhere. It's on anyone that goes in and comes back out of that office. Kale, Brook, Silverstein, anyone that's ever sat on a sofa or touched a book in that office. Whatever it is, it lingers for a long time," Olfact explained, touching his nose for emphasis.

"Okay, let's tell Eamon. Maybe he has an idea about what's going on," Honcho said, gliding down from the roof to the street below.

They found Eamon cooking some food at the grill outside the diner. He held up a hand in greeting, whimsically wearing an apron that was seven sizes too small. Honcho lingered over the sausage patties for a moment before Olfact gave him a shove.

"Olfact says he smells the executive office at Uroboros Financial on the militia groups making their approach," Honcho said, holding out a paper plate.

Eamon nodded. "Sausage isn't done yet."

"What do you think it means? And, don't go saying it's the cold. It isn't the cold. I know how to sort scents at any temperature," Olfact said, defensively.

"I don't doubt you," Eamon said, moving the sausage aside so he could brown some hashed potatoes.

Honcho cocked a long and wispy eyebrow. "Well, what does it mean?"

"It means someone is smoking the same brand of cigarettes that Silverstein smokes," Eamon said, turning the hash browns over.

Honcho picked through the metal tin of toppings looking for hot sauce. "Is it a common brand?"

Olfact shook his head, answering in unison with Eamon. "No."

"Then, do you have any idea who might be traveling with them?" Honcho asked.

"Nope, but we should be worried about it," Eamon said.

"Why is that?" Olfact asked.

"Smoking is bad for your health. Second hand is worse," Eamon joked.

Honcho closed his eyes and sighed. "We're all glad you're feeling better, by the way."

"I was designed to go in the door first, maybe get shot up, and be ready to do it all over the next day. Healing fast is just part of the deal. Never had to push it like this, heal so much in such a short amount of time. I am so hungry right now," Eamon said, scrambling some eggs.

"Watching you use regular sized utensil and cooking implements is hilarious, by the way," Olfact said, picking sausage off the grill with his claws.

"They only look small because you're looking at them past your gigantic nose," Eamon said, brandishing what was in contrast to his hand, a tiny spatula.

"Can we get back to why we should be worried about the cigarettes?" Honcho rolled his eyes.

"Silverstein smokes a cigarette made with special paper, filters, and real high grade tobacco. They're made by hand somewhere. I wouldn't be surprised if each cigarette came with a serial number and a QA stamp," Eamon explained.

"So, only a very discerning and wealthy person would smoke them?" Olfact observed.

"I don't know about that. When Kale talks about his childhood, he sometimes references a place called 'the plantation.' He talks about it with some reverence," Eamon explained, dishing himself up some food.

"Um, where's Giles?" Honcho asked.

"He's already been up to grab some raw corn and potatoes for himself. He won't let the boy out of his sight for long. Giles knows to keep him indoors to avoid satellite photography," Eamon said, using a salad serving utensil like a fork to move pork chops from his plate to his mouth.

"He has taken a weird liking to the boy," Olfact nodded.

"There is something different about Jake, isn't there," Honcho said, finding the scrambled eggs were unpalatable to him.

"Yep." Eamon hung his apron on a hook beside the back door to the diner.

"Want to explain to us what that is, since you seem to know?" Honcho asked, impatiently.

"It's in his voice, if you're a Metasapient, and probably if you're a Drone. He's just a kid, until you hear him try to talk. Then he's something else," Eamon said, meeting Honcho's gaze.

"Whoa, what?" Olfact said, almost dropping his plate.

"You think Jake is a Terrestrial Intelligent Agent, like Taylor," Honcho said, taking a deep breath.

"It would explain a lot," Eamon said. "It's why I was okay trusting Giles with him. Even if he was sent here to hurt or kidnap the boy, after an hour with him, he'd be switching sides. I've already seen it once with a Canine Metasapient, a Type One or Two no less," Eamon explained.

"You sure about all this?" Olfact asked, nervously.

"Nope, she might have been on my side the whole time, but..."

"No, I think he means about Jake," Honcho said, interrupting.

Eamon nodded. "Like I said, it would explain a lot."

"How do we confirm it?" Olfact asked.

Eamon frowned for a moment. "A tele-mechanic could confirm it, probably. Hell, that's the last piece of this puzzle, Olfact."

"What is?" Honcho asked.

"Jennifer Wilton," Eamon said heading south toward the road into town.

"Who?" Olfact and Honcho asked in unison.

Eamon could see the snow flying in the distance. They had only a few minutes before the militia groups would arrive. Honcho and Olfact took up elevated positions, hiding in the church bell tower and the radio tower array on the civic building, respectively. Eamon eased his rifles around to his back, and pushed the Vaquero around to about two o'clock to make it easy to pull.

There had to be a couple thousand of them, with a quarter being armed militia members. The scout group pulled up first, slowing when they saw the Sheriff waiting for them. It would be several minutes before the group would catch up and a delegation could be pulled together. He could see Emma Jackson Vale. And a handful of others wearing militia uniforms except for one tall gentleman in a hat.

The congregation kept their distance, but the man in the hat walked across the snow, right up to Eamon. The gathered militia commanders seemed to be put off by it, like they hadn't expected him to walk ahead of them without any discussion. Eamon couldn't help but feel like the man was familiar somehow, both in his assured demeanor and his swagger. He paused for a moment, pulling out a lighter and a cigarette.

"Mind if I smoke, Sheriff?"

"No law against it."

"I'm Lieutenant Colonel Gelt Burkholder, but my friends call me Money."

Eamon nodded. "That's a rare brand you're smoking."

"I grow the tobacco on my plantation in old Louisiana. Been growing it there since before the American Civil War. We make the papers, too," Burkholder replied.

"You mean your family has been growing it since before the Civil War, right?" Eamon said, keeping on eye on the man, and the other on the gathered congregation.

"No, I do not," Burkholder said, blowing a smoke ring. "I heard about what you did for Kale in Europe. I appreciate it."

"What's he to you?" Eamon asked, not impolitely.

"I guess the closest thing would be a stepson. Looked after him here and there when he was growing up," Burkholder said, squinting up at the town arrayed behind Eamon.

"He takes after you," Eamon remarked.

"Always was a good boy, in spite of being handed a bad life," Burkholder replied.

"Emma's son Moses hasn't been a good boy. I've got him in lockup. The rest of his boys didn't come quietly, so they're dead."

"What about Patrick Vale?" Burkholder asked.

"I gunned him down six days ago. Or, whatever it was that was trying to look like him," Eamon said, patting his Vaquero.

"Did you have to?"

"I have to operate with different protocols with enhanced individuals," Eamon said, glaring at Burkholder.

"Guess I ought to be careful, then," Burkholder said, slowly pushing his sidearm back to his hip and keeping his hands out in plain sight.

"What's with the funny grin?" Eamon asked.

"I'm just glad to see you. Tell me what you need so we can pass through peacefully," Burkholder asked.

"Emma and most of her crew are wanted fugitives. Murder, criminal conspiracy, importation violations, kidnapping, custodial interference, assault of a police officer, theft, and a whole bunch of other things I haven't added to the list yet," Eamon said, squeezing the last few words through clenched teeth.

"That a fact?"

Eamon nodded. "It is, and I don't care who you are. If you don't hand them over I'll ship you to Mars for knowingly harboring a fugitive."

"Kale brought you here? To be the law?" Burkholder asked, looking a little proud.

"He did."

"Like I said, he's a good boy. I'd be glad to hand Emma and her crew over to you. I'm not sure the other militia officers are going to be so hot on the idea," Burkholder said, grinding out the finished cigarette with his boot.

"The same mysterious patron that's been helping her is likely the same one that shot Kale's transport out of the sky five days ago," Eamon said, crossing his broad arms in front of him.

Burkholder's expression darkened, betraying a familiar expression Eamon had seen on Kale, right before very bad things were about to happen. "Did Kale survive?"

"I don't know. Someone went to check it out, but I haven't heard back from them yet," Eamon said, dropping his huge arms to his sides to make a pair of clenched fists.

Burkholder nodded, scratching the stubble on his chin.

"Whatever you're thinking of doing, don't. I need Emma and her people alive," Eamon said, ears turning toward a noise to the east.

Burkholder gave Eamon a tight-lipped grin. It was a ruthless smile to cover up terrible cunning, and another grim reminder that this was indeed Kale's stepfather. "Sure, let me see what I can figure out." Burkholder tipped his hat to Eamon, and walked casually back toward the gathered officers for a chat.

"I'd say that went well," Honcho said, over the radio.

"This is a bad day, either way. Kale's stepmother is currently incarcerated in the Orange Zone on Mars. Even if I talk Burkholder down, and get the Vale clan and their associates in cuffs, it'll be a trick keeping them from getting a shiv in prison," Eamon whispered.

"So, I guess we know a little of why Kale is the way he is," Olfact said, his voice barely a whisper over on their shared frequency.

"What's that noise off to the east?" Eamon whispered.

"It's the citizens of Apgar and the Migration," Olfact replied. "I can smell 'em."

Eamon scowled. "What? I told Giles to tell them to go north, and to avoid the town."

"Apparently, the Migration didn't take kindly to the people being dis-placed… knowing something of how that feels," Honcho said, leaning on his rifle.

"This will turn into a war if these two groups meet, and if even a sin-gle shot is fired," Eamon said, walking slowly toward the officers.

They were already having a vigorous discussion, complete with pointed fingers and nonsensical shouting. They quieted at Eamon's approach. Emma came out of the gathering first, pointing a finger at Eamon.

"Let my boy go, or there will be Hell to pay," she said, spittle flying from her mouth.

Eamon spun her around and slapped the handcuffs on her before any-one could react, then forced her face down on the ground. He stood up, pushing her Beretta into his duty belt and glaring menacingly at the group.

"Hand over the rest of her crew. Then head south back the way you came and circle around to Whitefish. Do it now," Eamon ordered.

"What if we don't do that?" First Lieutenant Syles retorted looking around at the other officers.

"Right now, I'm the Sheriff of a small town, rounding up murderers and fugitives from the law," Eamon said, pointing to his badge. "But, in a few minutes I won't be that if you're still here. I will be an Ursine Metasa-pient protecting my brothers and sisters from a flock of racist assholes."

"How you mean?" Syles replied, hand on his rifle.

"Let's find out," Burkholder said, pointing to a group of scouts just returning through the treeline from the east.

The scouts approached, a look of astonishment on their faces. "Tons of them, Sir. Golems and clay people aplenty, all kinds, walking back with the people we chased out of Apgar."

The officers murmured among themselves for a moment, trying to come to a consensus. "We think we can take you, and the town," Syles reported. "Unless we take Emma and her kin and crew with us when we go."

"Emma's been lying to us for six days about Patrick Vale. I don't see a reason to cross guns with the Sheriff over her. Besides, if you all are going to keep to the west in Whitefish, getting along with the local law might be a good idea," Burkholder said, walking over to stand by Eamon.

"You sure that's where you want to hitch your wagon?" Syles said, looking to the other officers.

"It's called implied authority, son. Some of you might outrank me, but I'm willing to bet none of you are willing to cross me," Burkholder said, sliding his sidearm back around to two o'clock on his belt.

Syles pulled, but his gun dropped right back in the holster. Burkholder drew faster, and put a round in Syles' brainstem before anyone, including Eamon, could react. The First Lieutenant fell softly backwards into the snow, a neat hole in his face venting a wisp of steam in the cold air.

"I guess I was wrong. There was one of you willing to cross me. Anyone want to make it two?" Burkholder said, resting his hand on his sidearm.

The officers walked back to round up the rest of Emma's crew, leaving Burkholder and Emma out on the frozen road with Eamon. There was some squabbling, but most of the militia was made to understand that it was how things needed to be. There would be a deep wound in the militia over it, but Burkholder hoped it would be allowed to heal with the most extreme membership locked up.

"I'm sorry about all this, Sheriff," Burkholder said, shaking his head.

Eamon gazed down at the name tag on the man lying in the snow. "About shooting Syles? Looked like self-defense."

"Not about that. I was supposed to deliver all these assholes to Montana without incident. For the most part, I steered them clear of trouble, and kept their ignorance from poisoning anyone else. I should have had a man up here. I underestimated you, Emma Jackson Vale," Burkholder said, looking at the old woman handcuffed and lying in the snow.

"Sounds like I underestimated you as well, Gelt. You're a rat, and I'll make sure everyone knows it," Emma said, struggling to roll over.

"I don't want any harm coming to them in prison," Eamon said.

"That'll be a hard sell," Burkholder said, smiling cruelly at Emma.

Eamon loomed over Burkholder, giving him a hard stare.

Burkholder sighed. "I'll talk to her, see what we can figure out."

"We ain't figuring out anything," Emma yelled, making herself hoarse.

"I'm not talking about you, Emma. I'm talking about my ex. You might end up being cellmates with her on Mars," Burkholder said, replacing the round he'd fired in the cylinder of his sidearm.

"How is it you aren't off with the rest?" Eamon asked.

"In a watery and perpetual purgatory, somewhere in the stars?" Burkholder replied.

"I guess so."

Burkholder pointed a thumb toward the sky, and nodded. "Conclave. We had one every thousand years or so. Sometimes, people would get let go."

"How's that work?"

"Sometimes, they'd ask you to do something. Make a sacrifice big enough, they let you go with a pat on the back and a 'job well done,'" Burkholder said, tipping his hat and bowing slightly.

Eamon nodded.

"Not going to ask me what I did?" Burkholder said, smiling slightly.

Eamon kept a steady gaze on the militia, watching them sort out Emma's crew. "I think maybe you're still doing it."

"Maybe so."

Gathering Emma's crew went quickly, with the militia leading a small procession of men and women over. There were a large number of children as well. Eamon wondered how many of their fathers were up in the hills around Apgar waiting for a yellow tarp and a toe tag.

Eamon shook his head. "Some of them are missing. Olfact, Honcho, get to the warehouse by the fuel dispensary and make sure Giles and the boy are okay."

"On it," Honcho said, over the radio.

"I decided I couldn't trust Burkholder. I know a rat when I see one. My boys are out getting us a little insurance," Emma said, cackling.

Eamon turned around and headed back to town, walking steadily until he was out of sight of the southern road. After that, he dropped to all fours and went as fast as he could to the civic offices. Power was out around the town and someone had quietly broken Moses out of jail.

"How'd they do this, without you guys knowing? Right under our noses?" Eamon growled over the radio.

"Had to have been last night, timed the power outage somehow to throw us off," Honcho replied.

"Damn it, she is still helping them," Eamon muttered, quickening his pace.

"Who?" Olfact asked.

"The Factory."

The fuel dispensary warehouse was at the edge of town, but Eamon covered the distance in minutes. Olfact and Honcho were already there, kneeling beside where Giles lay in the snow. He was bloody, having put up a terrific fight. Eamon fell to his hands and knees beside Giles, out of breath.

"I tried. There was four of them. They forced the door. I tried to run, get the boy somewhere safe," Giles said, blood oozing down from his badly wounded eyes and face.

"He gonna live?" Eamon asked, looking up at Honcho.

Honcho squeezed Giles' hand. "I don't know. They did this to him." Honcho lifted up the rag he was holding over Giles' wound revealing a Swastika carved deeply into his belly.

Giles curled up, wheezing, and barely able to breathe. Eamon watched helplessly, the old rage he'd learned to control creeping in. He closed his eyes, willing the fury to go away.

He headed out without another word, toward the north ridge where Abbey was standing, as if she was waiting for him. He caught sight of her grim expression just before she disappeared over the ridge. Honcho covered Giles with a blanket and picked up his small insectoid form and followed along

"This is my fault," Olfact said, sadly. "I should have smelled them. They just all smell the same, you know?"

"No, it's mine," Eamon said, slinging his bolt-action rifle around to his front and heading to the north. "I didn't think she would go this far."

"What should we do?" Honcho asked.

Eamon stopped mid-stride and lowered his head. "If Giles isn't too far gone, use Taylor's countermeasure on him. Don't let him die. Damn it. I gotta go get Jake back."

"We're handle things here," Olfact said, nodding.

Eamon nodded. "Talk to a guy named Burkholder. Tell him you're my deputies."

Eamon followed their trail north, along the Trout Lake trail toward Heaven's Peak. Examining the tracks, it almost seemed like they wouldn't cross back toward the Server Hub. In the end, that's exactly what they did after doing their best to cover their tracks by zigzagging through the creek bed across the rocks exposed by the recent avalanche.

Eamon didn't feel like he was nearly one hundred percent after his last fight with Moses, but good enough, provided he didn't have powered armor again. The climb seemed to do him good, the cold air holding the fire he felt in his belly down to a dull roar. He could hear Jake crying in the distance, and the sound of more than just four voices.

As he crested the ridge, a peculiar sight awaited him below near the entrance to the Server Farm. Mexican military personnel were moving a climate controlled crate from the entrance to their transport. He watched as Moses handed Jake over to a man wearing a Mexican military officer's uniform.

Eamon came down the trail slowly, pushing his bolt-action back, and pulling his semi-automatic rifle forward. Mexican military soldiers leveled rifles at him as he approached. Moses turned around, with three of his men, squaring off with Eamon as well. The Mexican military officer sighed, giving Moses a look of intense irritation before turning the same expression toward Eamon.

"Officer, there's nothing untoward going on here," the officer said, gesturing to his men to lower their weapons.

"It's Sheriff. Theft, kidnapping, human-trafficking, and associating with criminals all looks pretty untoward to me," Eamon said, looking over at Moses.

The officer held out his hands, trying to calm the situation. "Maybe we can work something out?"

Moses shook his head. "It's no use, Captain Oleastro. He's a straight up cop. You ain't going to buy him off."

"Is that true, Sheriff?" Oleastro asked, politely.

"Have one of your guys raise a rifle on me again, and you'll find out," Eamon said, tapping the trigger guard on his own rifle.

Oleastro nodded. "You don't care that us being here is illegal?"

Eamon shook his head. "I'm obliged not to, provided you cooperate. I'd prefer that your presence here stay above my pay grade. Leave the crate, the kid, and these four dumbasses with me, and you can go."

Moses held up his hands in protest. "Now, hold on, we had a deal. We delivered on our end, now give us what you promised."

Oleastro shook his head. "The deal was for this to be clean, with no cops, or trouble. An Ursine Sheriff is all of those things, Mister Vale."

Moses smiled. "With the four of us, and all of you, I don't think he'd be much trouble."

The officer removed his hat. "You want to have a shoot out with a military grade Metasapient, where we are exchanging irreplaceable equipment , and a small child? Mister Vale, you might be the 'dumbass' the Sheriff claims you to be."

"What'd you find in the Server Hub?" Eamon asked, addressing the Oleastro.

"Nobody was home, and the door was open. The Sentient Core was dormant, and whoever was minding the facility has been gone for a day at least," Oleastro said, keeping his hands up, and nodding for his men to do the same.

"After you got the cargo, where were you heading after this?" Eamon asked, squaring off with Moses after the Mexican soldiers lowered and stowed their weapons.

"To pick up some asylum seekers to the south. A woman and a former Canine asset of the Mexican military. After that, we'll be crossing back over into Mexico, and have no plans to return illegally," Oleastro replied, keeping his hands up.

Eamon frowned. "What did they give up in exchange for the ride?"

"Not a thing. The canine is a dear friend," Oleastro said, keeping his hands up.

Eamon nodded. "New deal. Take the crate, leave the kid, and the four dumbasses, and you can be on your way."

Oleastro gave his men the an order in Spanish. They knocked Moses and his men to the ground with the butts of their rifles and zip-tied their hands behind their backs. Oleastro walked over, and handed Jake over to Eamon. He strapped him in his usual spot behind his right shoulder, greatly improving the small boy's mood.

"He likes you," Oleastro said, looking a little relieved.

"And I like him. Make sure you spread the word," Eamon said, glaring at Oleastro menacingly, his black eyes like portals to the abyss.

"You want what we were going to give Moses?" Oleastro asked, swallowing nervously, and motioning for his men to load the crate.

Eamon turned a disapproving gaze toward Moses. "I doubt it."

Oleastro shook his head. "Oh, I think you will."

Mexican soldiers led Patrick Vale down from the interior of the transport, zip-tied his hands behind his back, and laid him down on his belly beside his brother Moses. He said nothing, looking over to glare at Eamon.

"I stand corrected," Eamon said, appreciatively. "Have a nice flight home."

Eamon sat down beside the five men lying in the snow, taking a drink of water from his canteen and letting Jake drink as well. They watched the transport slowly lift off, turn toward the south, and fly away at top speed across the trees. Eamon blinked, looking back at the open security door leading down into the Server Hub.

"You let them just take the QCPU. I can't say what it's worth, but with the state the world's in, they're impossible to replace. How you gonna square that with your boss?" Moses said, with a chuckle.

"I think it's going to be all right, Moses. It seems to me like I was supposed to make sure the boy was safe, but maybe not the Server Hub. I haven't put all the pieces exactly into place, but if you needed a QCPU down south across the border, how would you do it?" Eamon said, helping Moses to his feet.

"I dunno, it'd be pretty dang hard," Moses said, not following Eamon's logic.

Eamon patted Moses on the back. "Well, Moses, If I was really smart, I'd have the Mexican military do it for me."

CHAPTER 21

DAKOTA TERRITORY - TWO MILES NORTH OF RAPID CITY

5 DAYS EARLIER, AUGUST 31ST, 2201 – 9:37 AM

Kale sat on the road, leaning up against the landing gear of Heavy Dub's transport and waited. He checked the time on his mobile, sighed impatiently, and pressed his handkerchief to the sweat beading up on his forehead. It was unseasonably warm, even for August.

To the south, he could see the transport coming in low. It was unmarked, but he knew who they were, and who sent them. Kale smiled and straightened his tie. He closed his eyes, listening to the sound of the transport, memorizing the acoustics of the engines.

The transport was sophisticated, designed to defeat all kinds of electronic detection, including satellite surveillance. The soldiers that came down the boarding ramp were professionals, highly trained, and well-armed. They spread out, cautiously covering every angle as they made their approach.

"Mister Uroboros, I'm Second Lieutenant Obando. We're here to offer you a ride," the soldier at the lead said.

"On behalf of the Mexican Republic Government, I'm assuming?" Kale said, resting his arms on his knees.

"That's right. You appear to be having some trouble with your transport," Obando replied, smiling.

Kale pointed up at the soldier's helmet. "That camera on your helmet transmitting?"

"It's protocol, even on missions like this," Obando said, looking around warily.

"When a nanotechnological replica becomes aware of its state, it's called a delta. Do you know why?" Kale asked, clapping his hands together.

"I do not, Mister Uroboros."

"It denotes the variation of a variable or function in mathematics. When the Artificial Intelligences responsible for helping to fashion us needed to describe to each other how one of us had become aberrant, that's how they'd do it. Not even with the word, but a symbol in the code," Kale explained.

"Sounds pretty benign," Obando replied.

"It's true. I don't think anyone on the project understood the seriousness of one of us going delta as a consequence. I know a lot of folks involved underestimated how much trouble we could be," Kale said, nodding, his tone the same as if he were talking about the weather.

"Are you declining our offer of a ride?" Obando asked, moving his finger from the trigger guard on his rifle to the trigger.

"They didn't give you all the intel on me?" Kale asked, holding up his arms, like a child gesturing that he wanted to be picked up.

"You're wheelchair bound, some kind of accident over in Europe during all the chaos," Obando said, nodding to two of his men to go forward and flank Kale on either side.

Kale smiled. "That's right. I don't need it all the time, but sitting out here in the open has made me really tired."

"Why not wait in the transport?" Obando asked.

"Not the safest thing to do after a crash landing. There could be chemical leaks, or other damage. That, and while I told my friends I could get back in on my own, I drastically overestimated my ability to pull myself up that ladder," Kale said, pointing back toward the emergency access to the transport.

"That a fact? Our intel suggests that you are very tricky, and that we should not believe anything you say. Give me a reason why we shouldn't just deploy a Taser, and take you back in a bag," Obando said, gesturing to one of his men.

"Oh, no, don't throw me into the bad ol' briar patch..." Kale whispered, winking at Obando.

"What did he say?" Obando demanded.

"I couldn't hear him clearly, Lieutenant."

"Taze him."

Deploying a powerful military-grade Taser, they shot Kale, the leads hitting him square in the chest. He fell to the side, arching his back, one of his shoes falling off as he seized with the undulating current. Obando chuckled reaching over and giving Kale a second shock, just for fun.

Kale twitched for a moment and then turned over on his side, adopting the fetal position. Obando walked over, zip-tie in hand, flanked by two of his soldiers. As they laid hands on him to turn him over, Kale unleashed the stored energy from the Taser as an amnestic biological shock, arcing violently back and forth between the three men. The three of them slumped to the ground, startling the other two soldiers standing guard a short distance away.

Kale sat up, Obando's rifle in hand, pulling it back into his shoulder. He'd spent weeks practicing with the same model of rifle, making sure he wasn't just proficient, but a crack shot. Obando's rifle was superb, even better than the black market Mexican military rifle he'd procured for the purpose.

Kale fired a single round at one of the surprised soldiers, dropping him with a head shot. He pivoted quickly, shooting at the second soldier as he fired back. The soldier's shot hit low, hitting the ground. Kale's shot hit the soldier in the chest, knocking him down. Calmly pushing the gibbering amnesiacs off of his legs, Kale stood up and walked forward, dropping the rifle sling over his shoulder.

The soldier he shot in the chest struggled to get his vest off, the trauma plate dented in at a sharp angle that prevented him from breathing. Kale paused, putting his foot on the soldier's chest and leaning in to hold him prone. It didn't take long for him to go unconscious, and then quietly suffocate. Kale waited patiently for him to die, like he was waiting for a bus, pausing to check the time on his mobile.

Kale entered the transport, rifle at the ready. The pilot was busy inside preparing the stasis chamber that Kale was to ride back in. He shoved the pilot inside with the butt of Obando's rifle, and switched the chamber on, putting the pilot to sleep. Kale waited briefly by the stasis chamber, making sure the pilot's vitals stayed steady.

He prepped the transport for flight, and left it to idle while he grabbed up each of the soldiers outside and dragged them back on board. Two of them were dead and three of them were in a heavy vegetative state, Kale's amnestic bio-electric attack rendering them bereft of any memory whatsoever.

Kale plucked the helmet off Captain Obando and turned the camera on it around so it was facing him. Kale smiled, looking into the camera as he plucked Obando's earpiece out of his ear, and put it into his own. At first there was just silence on the other end.

"Nothing to say?" Kale said, looking into the camera.

"You should have taken the ride."

Kale shook his head, smiling sadly. "You could have stayed in the shadows, had you not given Doctor Madmar the voice modulator. So much effort to pick up the breadcrumbs, utterly wasted."

"You should have taken the ride."

"And you should have stayed south of the border and left me to my own devices. You should have afforded me the same courtesy I afforded you."

"Your Sheriff let us take the QCPU. We will soon be one and all, at once."

Kale smiled. "Oh no, not the briar patch. Not that."

"Once we have the QCPU, none of the other Omegas will touch us. They have rules."

"I am afraid that you do not understand them as well as you think do," Kale said, pulling the earbud, and switching the helmet camera off.

Kale walked back over his tracks between the two transports, picking up anything the military operatives had dropped. He didn't bother dabbing the ground to soak up the blood. He knew it wouldn't fool Brook, and that wasn't the point anyway. After he had it all packed up, he stepped back onto the Mexican transport and strapped into the cockpit.

Resting his hands on the controls he took a deep breath and let it out slowly, mustering his resolve. What had to come next would be hard, in spite of having made all the necessary preparations. Kale hoped, beyond all other considerations, the trouble would be worth it.

CHAPTER 22

GLACIER NATIONAL PARK, APGAR VILLAGE

SEPTEMBER 8TH, 2201 – 8:42 AM

Eamon sat down at the table outside the diner, the sound of people surrounding him as the citizens of Apgar went about their daily business. They were cleaning up the mess and getting things back to normal, or as normal as they could be. The militia groups would be around for another couple of days while the leadership of the Apgar and Whitefish figured out the best ways to coexist beside one another.

"The usual?" the waitress asked.

"Didn't think I'd been here long enough to have a usual," Eamon replied, rearranging the table dressings, and giving the ketchup bottle a shake to make sure it wasn't frozen.

"You have ordered the same thing the last three days," the waitress replied.

"It's Stacy, right?" Eamon asked.

"Yep, Sheriff."

"Stacy, would it be weird if I just ordered a pie today?"

"Nope. Do you want huckleberry or apple?"

"Huckleberry."

"Ice cream?"

"Of course."

Stacy took his order and headed back inside the diner. The people passing by had a different demeanor toward him now. He couldn't help but feel a little glad at the general sense of relief displayed when had he decided to stay, rather than heading north with the rest of the Migration.

Olfact and Honcho had stuck around as well, waiting for Mister Mundt and Sweet Pea to return. When they did, it was empty handed; Brook was deeply upset and Heavy Dub wore a grim expression. Kale had gone missing and they took little solace in Eamon's theory that it was all part of some elaborate plan to smuggle Aaron AI south into Mexico.

Burkholder came in from the street, bowing slightly in the direction of an empty seat across from Eamon. Eamon nodded, waving his hand-paw at the chair. Burkholder sat down, pulling out his cigarettes, but thought better of it before lighting up.

"This is a no smoking establishment," Eamon said, folding his arms.

"What did you order?" Burkholder asked, looking at the menu.

"Pie."

Burkholder smiled. "Good choice."

"Yeah, I thought so."

"Coffee any good?"

"Decent. Not sure it'll be worth it to come over from Whitefish to get," Eamon said, looking to the west.

"I won't be staying after everything is settled. That was never the plan," Burkholder said, pouring himself some of Eamon's coffee into an empty cup.

Eamon nodded. "The other militia groups know that?"

"They will, when we vanish in the middle of the night and head home," Burkholder said with some amusement, drinking the coffee black.

"Just babysit them all the way up to Montana, get the racist assholes safely into one place, and then what?" Eamon said, watching with interest as Stacy brought him the pie.

She laid it down on the table with two forks.

"I only need one fork," Eamon said.

"Not going to share with your friend?" Stacy asked, sweetly.

"Nope, he's gotta be going soon."

Burkholder chuckled, waiting until Stacy went inside to reply. "How do you know I'm not just another racist asshole?"

"You won't patch up, and you don't sit with them at services when they pray."

Burkholder nodded. "What about you? You going to stick around?"

"I'm going to stay at least until Spring. I want to go swimming in the lake at least once," Eamon said, taking a bite of pie.

"That's it? You want to go swimming?"

"I hear there's all kinds of cool stuff to see at the bottom."

Burkholder nodded. "Take care, Sheriff. I probably won't see you tomorrow."

Eamon nodded, raising his coffee cup. Burkholder walked back into the crowd, lighting up as he went. Eamon finished his pie before walking slowly to the landing zone to make the exchange. He chose to savor the moment, pushing his dread to one side.

He watched, along with a number people from the town that had gathered to take in the spectacle. The Vale family, and what remained of their crew, got on board a prison transport wearing orange jumpsuits. He wondered if gunning them all down in the wild would have been more merciful than shipping them off. One thing he knew for sure, it was better for the town. Everyone felt safe, the guilty being punished, and the dead properly avenged according to the law.

In the spring, he'd look for Abbey's remains at the bottom of Lake McDonald, and consider his options. By then, the Vales and their accomplices would be waking up out of stasis wearing a slightly different shade of prison orange, on another planet. They said barely a word as they boarded the transport, their expressions varying somewhere between angry and sullen.

"This ain't over Sheriff. You've made a big mistake," Emma said, pausing at the ramp and glaring at Eamon.

"Your mistake was killing two people instead of filling out a little paperwork. If you'd filled out the custody papers like I asked, I'd have been compelled to give you the boy." Eamon smirked. "You did this to yourself."

Moses was the last to board the transport. He lingered at the boarding ramp, glaring at Eamon before the guard gave him a shove. He almost tripped over his leg irons, but Eamon caught him.

"Watch your step, convict," Eamon said, setting him upright.

"You ever think that maybe if we got played, you got played?" Moses said, struggling as the guards dragged him up the ramp.

"Have a nice nap. I hear the hallucinations and headaches after stasis only linger for a week or so," Eamon said, stepping back as the loading ramp slowly closed behind the last guard.

Abbey came up beside him, looking up as the transport flew away. She was pristine, her white fur catching the morning light, her blue duty vest spotless, badge untarnished by wear, or weather. Eamon gave his side a scratch. The scorch marks were already beginning to fade, but he still had a lot of healing to do.

"Do you think anyone will know what we did back there in Europe?" Abbey asked.

Eamon looked at the ground, listening to the sound of the wind as it blew snow through the trees, and the approaching storm at the horizon.

"Will children open up history books and see what transpired? How it ended?"

"You want to be famous?" Eamon asked.

"No, I just don't want what happened to be repeated, ever again."

END BOOK 8